TORCHWOOD

EXODUS CODE

D1535552

TORCHWOOD

EXODUS CODE

John
Barrowman

and
Carole E.
Barrowman

BOOKS

1 3 5 7 9 10 8 6 4 2

Published in 2012 by BBC Books, an imprint of Ebury Publishing.
A Random House Group Company

This paperback edition published in 2013

Torchwood is a BBC Worldwide Production for the BBC and Starz Originals.
Executive producers: Russell T Davies, Julie Gardner and Jane Tranter

Original series created by Russell T Davies,
and developed and produced by BBC Cymru Wales.
BBC, 'Torchwood' and the Torchwood logo are trademarks of
the British Broadcasting Corporation and are used under licence.

The Random House Group Limited Reg. No. 954009

Addresses for companies within the Random House Group
can be found at www.randomhouse.co.uk

A CIP catalogue record for this book is available
from the British Library.

ISBN 978 1 846 07908 5

MIX
Paper from
responsible sources
FSC
www.fsc.org
FSC® C016897

The Random House Group Limited supports The Forest Stewardship
Council® (FSC®), the leading international forest-certification
organisation. Our books carrying the FSC label are printed on
FSC®-certified paper. FSC is the only forest-certification scheme
supported by the leading environmental organisations, including
Greenpeace. Our paper procurement policy can be found
at www.randomhouse.co.uk/environment

Editorial director: Albert DePetrillo
Editors: Steve Tribe and James Goss
Cover design: headdesign.co.uk © Woodlands Books Ltd, 2012
Production: Alex Goddard

Printed and bound by CPI Group (UK) Ltd, Croydon, CR0 4YY

To buy books by your favourite authors and register for offers,
visit www.randomhouse.co.uk

For all the Woodies in the world and beyond

'He may be above;
He may be below;
or, perchance, abroad in space.'
Inca prayer

'Time moves in one direction, memory in another.'
William Gibson

Part One

Part One

1

Southern coast of Peru, 1930

A Hawker Hornet banked out over the Pacific, cut a tight circle, and swooped inland over the red cliffs of the southern Peruvian coastline.

'It's about to get rough, my friend,' said the pilot.

His passenger secured his goggles over his eyes then adjusted the straps of his shoulder harness. A dense morning mist wrapped around the top of la Madre Montâna, reducing the pilot's visibility to inches and the temperature in the open cockpit to bloody freezing. The wind gnawed at the passenger's face and neck. Shivering, he slid down in the seat, turning up the collar on his coat, but it wasn't enough to warm him or shrug off the uneasiness that had been swelling in his gut since they'd taken off minutes ago from the airstrip at Castenado. The feeling wasn't dread so much as discomfort, a sharp piercing pain in Captain Jack Harkness's gut.

The Hornet's wooden frame bucked in the air currents of the southern Pacific. Jack's stomach flipped. A sudden drop lifted him off his seat, thumping his head on the cross bar of the wings.

'What is it you want to show me that's worth this?' Jack

yelled over the noise of the propellers.

'I promised you amazing, didn't I?'

Jack grinned at the handsome pilot. 'Renso, we already were.'

Shifting forward, Renso guided the Hornet towards the jagged cliffs that to Jack looked like the gaping maw of a brooding monster. He'd seen far too many of those in his time. Jack sighed, slouching down in the rickety bucket seat.

'Ready?' Renso asked.

'Does it matter if I'm not?'

Renso laughed, flying the Hornet straight into the cloud of mist. Almost immediately the small bi-plane was shrouded in a damp cloak of grey. Jack shivered again and the sensation that earlier he couldn't name uncoiled itself from his stomach, crawled into his chest, up into his throat, settling painfully behind his eyes. Jack put his head down and moaned.

Food poisoning, he thought. Had to be.

'All right back there, amigo?'

Cold sweat was beading on Jack's forehead, and a burning sensation was knotting the muscles at the base of his neck. His eyes were stinging.

'Fine. I'm fine.' But Jack was far from it. In fact, he hadn't been feeling anywhere close to fine since he arrived on the South American coast at Renso's request two days ago.

Seconds later, the plane shot out the other side of the fog into a shocking blue sky. The scene displayed beneath Jack jolted him from his reverie, and he stared down into the basin of the mountain.

'What the hell is that?'

'You mean you don't know?' said Renso. 'I thought if anyone would, it'd be you.'

2

Jack gazed in astonishment at three vast glowing rings of igneous rock pulsing deep inside the bowels of the mountain. He knew there'd been an eruption back in January and, at first, he thought the rings were smouldering magma from that. But the closer the Hornet dipped, the more clearly he could see that each ring was seething, spinning, shifting in and out of the other. He could hear their syncopated rhythm in his head. It sounded as if the mountain had a heartbeat. The effect was mesmerising.

'Can you get me down there?' he asked, forcing his attention from the rings.

'No place to land,' said Renso. 'It'd be a long hike to get up here from the nearest canyon. But I can manage closer.'

Renso pulled back on the stick, the propellers whined, the engines coughed and the Hornet lurched violently. For a beat, Jack thought the plane had died, but then Renso corrected his manoeuvre, punching the Hornet into a vertical climb.

'What're you doing?'

'Trust me, Jack. This will get you closer.'

'Not now, Renso. I don't think I can take any more of your tricks.'

'You love my tricks,' grinned Renso. 'Brace yourself!'

With all the skills of the best WWI dogfighter Renso had once been and the crop-dusting pilot he now was, he flipped the Hornet, cut its engines, and sent them into free fall. The plane spiralled dangerously towards the face of the plateau and the spinning rock.

'Stop showing off. Bring her up, now!'

'Don't be such a backseat flyer, Jack,' laughed Renso, pulling back on the stick. The Hornet nosed up, inches before its wings strafed the pitted plateau.

'Better?'

'Not much,' whispered Jack, his breathing laboured. Every exhalation was squeezing his chest. It was the air, he realised; it was even thinner up this high than he'd reckoned. Dropping his goggles around his neck, Jack wiped his eyes with his coat sleeve. Leaning out of his seat, he peered down inside the basin of the mountain. He pulled a notebook from his coat's inside pocket and began to sketch the rings. As he sketched, each stroke of his pencil set off a chime in his head, like the distant notes of a half-remembered tune. Jack frowned, the drawing dancing before his eyes. The closer he looked, the faster the rings appeared to spin through each other. Cautiously, Jack touched the paper with the point of his pencil, feeling it contort like India rubber, sending the rings dancing from the page into the air before settling down. Jack's vision cleared as he stared at the pattern.

'They look like hieroglyphs,' said Jack, scribbling intently. 'Kind of familiar. My ancient Egyptian isn't so hot these days.'

Renso raised an eyebrow. Like a lot of things Jack said, he didn't know if it was an outrageous lie, or an even more outrageous truth. He glanced down at the pattern smouldering in the landscape beneath them. 'Egyptian? Given the land we're flying over, it's more likely to be Incan.'

'Yeah,' agreed Jack. 'Could be.' As he talked, his hand sketched on, every movement of the pencil playing out more of that tune in his head. Despite the buffeting wind and the jostling of the plane, Jack drew on.

Renso glanced back. Jack's notebook pages were filling with words, geometric shapes, drawings of what looked to Renso like a series of odd lines and circles and lines of musical notes. It looked as if someone else was controlling his hands; they were moving furiously across the pages. Renso knew Jack well enough not to question his capabilities, but still something was not quite right about Jack's demeanour.

When Renso looked into the maw all he could see was an odd smouldering rock formation. No movement. No pulsing and certainly not forming any of the shapes that Jack was sketching. Keeping the Hornet as tight to the basin as he could, he asked, 'Jack, are you sure of what you're seeing?'

'If you're asking do I know what this is and what it means, then no,' said Jack. 'Not yet. I've seen all sorts of things, met all kinds of life. Don't think I've ever met anyone that could carve something like that out of the inside of a mountain, though.'

As he spoke, Jack realised that that was exactly what he was looking at.

'One thing I do know, though – whatever it is, whatever it means, it's been in that mountain for a very a long time.'

'How do you reckon that?' Renso's voice sounded odd to Jack, distant and confused. Jack swallowed, tasting vanilla and cinnamon when he did.

Renso pulled the plane above the basin, trying to present Jack with as many angles as possible.

'The Spanish Conquistadors destroyed most of the temples and the holy sites that were part of this landscape when they came to the Americas. They stripped the surface of these mountains searching for gold and silver centuries

15

ago. See that dark line running through the centre of the plateau?' Jack nudged Renso's shoulder and pointed up ahead. Renso nodded, pulling the Hornet higher, the line Jack was pointing to stretching out more clearly in front of them. 'That's a vein of ore and that's not something you'd normally find at the surface of a mountain. You'd find it under its surface.'

'So these rings have been hidden until now,' said Renso. 'That's what I thought.'

'I really need to get into that basin, to get a closer—' Jack's throat tightened. He choked out 'look.'

'Jack? Are you sure you're all right?' asked Renso, turning the Hornet to approach the basin from yet another angle.

'Fine,' croaked Jack, ignoring the lone voice in his head, his voice he was sure, that kept saying, 'No you're not, Jack. Something really bad is happening to you.'

Jack shook his head to clear the solo voice that in a heartbeat became two voices and then three and before Jack could shut them out, a chorus of voices all sounding like his were taunting him about how bad he was feeling, how awful flying was, how loud his heart was beating, how breathless he felt, and how things were only going to get worse.

Worse, Jack – much, much worse.

Renso seemed to be oblivious to his passenger's growing anguish and panic. Jack forced himself to concentrate on what the pilot was saying.

'All I'm sayin' is that if these rings had been visible for a while, I'd've noticed them sooner because I've been flying this route at least once a month since winter.'

The stabbing pain behind Jack's eyes was worsening as the voices were getting louder, and then they stopped, at least until Renso banked the plane into another turn and came over the basin and the rings from the south. When the

Hornet swooped over the mountain once again, Jack could swear he was hearing music deep inside his head. A thin violin melody. Jack leaned back in his seat, and squeezed his eyes closed. The music was a lament of some kind. It sounded familiar, he was sure of it, but he couldn't place where he'd heard it before. And then the deep chords of the strings dropped behind a voice, a woman's, melodic and rich, cut into the strings, harmonising with the music. The sultry crooning was enthralling.

When Jack glanced at Renso, the man was concentrating, silently, on the Hornet's controls. The music and the woman's voice ascending together in Jack's head, beautiful, heartbreakingly so. Jack's mother's image danced in front of him. Squeezing his eyes closed against her memory, he could feel her pain and her suffering in every bone of his body. When the Hornet swooped across the plateau once again Jack felt enveloped in anguish for everything he'd ever done. Hopelessness squeezed his throat closed. He was choking, his breath labouring again. Then the music in his head swelled to its crescendo, its beauty washing over Jack in ribbons of blue directly above Renso's head.

With all his energy, Jack forced the music and the voices to the back of his consciousness. Sweat dripped down his spine. He put his hand on Renso's shoulder, squeezing, feeling some relief from the contact, the warmth of his friend's body.

'One more turn, Jack?' Renso hoped he'd say no. His friend did not look at all well back there.

'Fine, Renso. Then I think I've seen enough for now.'

Renso took the Hornet up again, the wind whistled through the open cockpit. With his binoculars, Jack scanned the horizon and thought he could see more glyphs, drawings the size of football pitches etched out across the dusty plateaus. One looked like a bird, the other a monkey, a candelabra. Renso turned and the plane came back over the basin and the rings from the north east.

Jack leaned over the side of the plane, staring into a clearing on the plateau below, an oasis on the mountain, a pueblo village circled by huarango tress, their roots like veins pulsing beneath the surface of the soil.

Jack watched as one by one the trees pulled their roots from the ground and began dragging themselves towards the mountain.

3

The Hornet dipped, jolting Jack from his seat. When the plane evened out, Jack looked down at the mountain's meseta. The oasis beneath him was lush and edenic, the trees unmoving.

That was weird.

'Renso, when did you discover this was here?'

'Has to be right after the eruption in January. Right before Lent began,' replied Renso. 'I do an occasional, um, favour, transport work, for the locals,' he grinned back at Jack again. 'Keeps me in pisco and out of trouble. I think I'd've noticed if these rings were inside the mountain before that.'

Jack forced himself to focus on Renso's words – the voices and the music fading, but the pain in his head, the tightening in his chest, they were getting worse. 'The volcanic eruption must have cracked the top off the mountain – I've seen that happen before.'

Leaning back in his seat, Jack squeezed his eyes shut, hoping to push the pain away while Renso forced the Hornet higher, banking into its final turn.

The beauty of the Andes, the southern tip of the Gran Tablazo de Icas, spread beneath them like a canvas, the lush green lowlands, the highland peaks drizzled with snow, the canyons like ribbons winding between them, the plateaus dotted with sagebrush and the pyramids of sand lining the coastline. The landscape reminded Jack of Boeshane, with its giant pyramids of rock and mountainous sand dunes erupting from the ground like golden obelisks.

'Do you feel that?' asked Jack.

'Feel what?'

'The air? Suddenly it feels heavy. Oppressive. Shouldn't be so dense this high... and it tastes like —'

'Tastes?' Renso laughed and wagged his finger. He was really worried now, but replied lightly. 'I suggest no more tequila for you tonight, amigo.'

Jack's heart was racing, a bitter taste filling his mouth. And that smell? Like oil of vitriol... and fear.

His.

'You realise this isn't something we're going to be able to keep to ourselves for much longer,' said Renso, flying the Hornet low enough for Jack to get one more look. 'Soon I'm not going to be the only one who owns a plane in this part of the world.'

'I know,' Jack replied, rubbing his temples. Now he felt really sick. This was definitely much worse than a bad burrito.

'So what are you going to do about it?' Renso asked.

Jack's head weighed a ton on his neck, his eyes wouldn't stop watering, and every nerve in his skin was on fire. Was he dreaming? Even his hair seemed to hurt. 'I'll do... some... some investigating, Renso. I'll return when I know more.'

'I don't know, amigo,' said Renso, glancing at Jack, holding his stare for a beat. 'Perhaps this isn't a place you should ever return to.'

'Why not?'

'You look like shit.'

Jack forced a smile. 'Ah, thanks. It's the altitude or something I ate.'

'Ha, very funny, my friend. When has flying ever bothered you? I'm taking us back to Castenado.'

'Good, but then I want a closer look, Renso. I need to get into that mountain. I need to examine those rings.'

'Not on my watch, Jack.'

'Why not?'

'Cause, my friend, your eyes are bleeding.'

'What?' Jack wiped the back of his hand across his eyes, his tears pink against his pale skin. Before he had time to process what was happening to him, adrenalin shot up his spine, spiked across his limbs, and exploded into his brain. Jack's back arched, his legs stiffened, and his entire body convulsed, rocking the tiny biplane. He couldn't control his limbs, but he was aware of every violent flailing movement. It was as if someone had wired an electric current to his brain and was making his body dance.

'*¿Qué diablos?*' yelled Renso.

Horrified, Jack watched the words spew from Renso's mouth in waves of green and yellow, but the only sound Jack could hear was a woman's shrill pitch. And her voice tasted like ginger.

And then as if a switch was flipped inside Jack's brain, every sound around him became painfully amplified – the howl of the wind, the roar of the propellers, even the scratching of his coat against his neck. And that stench. What was that smell? It was like trench mud and rotting corpses, mountains of them, suffocating him. Jack gagged. He bit down on his tongue. His blood tasted like… like death.

What the hell was happening to him?

Jack lifted his hand to his face, forgetting he was still holding his notebook. It flew from his fingers. Instinctively, Renso reached up to catch it.

'Man, what the hell was that?' Renso yelped, yanking his hand back. The notebook swooped up into the air and out of reach. Renso screamed, and the sound felt like a knife had plunged into Jack's leg. He pressed his hand to his thigh, but there was no wound. Slowly, he pulled himself upright, the convulsions finally abating.

Jack stared in horror at Renso's right hand. His fingers looked as if a hammer was crushing them one by one.

'Oh Jesus, what's happening? Do something, Jack!'

At first Jack was too stunned to move. Renso's hand seemed to have a life of its own, bone and cartilage pushing through Renso's shredding skin.

Renso howled. Jack loosened his harness and at the same time Renso's wrist snapped in half, arterial blood spraying across the cockpit. Jack scrambled from his seat. The Hornet plummeted towards the mountain.

'*¡Madre mía!*' Renso whimpered, his face draining of colour, his head lolling against the Hornet's controls as he fought to keep the plane in the air with his other hand.

'Stay with me, Renso,' Jack yelled, 'Stay with me.'

Jack tore his scarf from his neck, but when he tried to stabilise himself in the cramped space the Hornet bucked and he was thrown back into his seat.

Renso was bleeding out. No doubt in Jack's mind. He was watching his friend bleed to death in front of his eyes. Jack climbed up on his seat, doubled over because of the wing, and hooked his arm over the frame above him. He stretched as far forward as he could in the tilting, tumbling plane, trying desperately to get the scarf around the ragged bloody stump that moments ago had been Renso's hand. The screaming in his head was getting louder, the taste in his mouth sickening.

The Hornet lurched against Jack's shifting weight, his clumsy movements wedging Renso tighter in the tiny cockpit. Renso's head knocked the throttle forward as he fell into unconsciousness. The Hornet pitched into a spiralling dive, once again plunging towards the mountain.

The Hornet tossed Jack into the air like a rag doll. Windmilling frantically, Jack lunged for the first thing he could, his fingers reaching, slipping then grasping the edge of the wheel-base, his legs flying out behind him. The plane shrieked towards the ground, the wind tearing into Jack's flesh as he hung by his fingertips from the Hornet's side.

Jack hooked his arm over the wheelbase and swung his legs, hoping to reach the cockpit. The Hornet flipped, trying to shake him off. Jack's body slammed hard into the side of the plane, knocking the wind from him. Jack gasped and lost his grip.

The screeching violins, the strident voices, the tragic laments of hopelessness fell silent inside Jack's head.

With his coat billowing out behind him like enormous wings, Jack plummeted towards the face of la Madre Montâna, the plane spiralling next to him.

'This,' thought Jack before losing consciousness, 'is really gonna hurt.'

Isela

4

Southern Coast of Peru, Hacienda del Castenado, present day
Isela was preparing to shoot someone. From her position
on the north side of the Hacienda del Castenado's chapel
belfry, the 14-year-old had a clear view of the Pacific to her
left, the high desert tables of the Andes to her right, and the
narrow canyon through la Madre Montâna in front of her.
She was hot and bored and tired of always being the sniper
in the tower.

In the 1640s, a Spanish Viceroy had erected Hacienda
del Castenado to enclose (and strangle) the ancient Inca
village of Isela's ancestors, the Cuari. The terraces of the
hacienda were now a tourist gem carved into the west face
of the mountain. To solidify his power, the Spanish Viceroy,
Alphonsa Castenado the Great (or the Despised depending
on the colour of your skin) had constructed the chapel as
the hacienda's focal point. It stood on the ruins of a native
temple that had lasted for thousands of years until it was
torn down by the Conquistadors.

Centuries later, Isela, a direct descendant of Alphonsa
and his Cuari concubine, lurked here, an automatic rifle
resting at her side.

Isela's mother like most of the population of the

25

surrounding villages was a devoted follower of the region's religious cocktail of Catholic rituals and native rites. She believed that the chapel's position on top of the ancient temple meant the hacienda and all who lived within its pink-washed adobe walls were doubly blessed. As far as Isela was concerned, the place was continually serving a crushing blow to her dreams to say nothing of her spirit, which Isela's mother and her *abuela*, her grandmother, insisted was the reincarnation of a Cuari goddess.

Despite the strange dreams she'd been having all her life, and her uncanny ability to see clearly in the dark, Isela wasn't sure she bought their explanation, but tourists did and so she was forced to dress and act the part during the Cuari Festival of the Goddess every Sunday afternoon at 4 p.m. in the piazza. Not this week. This week the festival would have to find another deity. Isela planned to be long gone by Sunday.

Isela swatted a fly from her face and spat grime onto the cobbled stone of the belfry. She cursed her mother for the hundredth time that morning. If not for her mother, Isela might have had a chance to escape this oppressive existence before today. If not for her mother, Isela might have had a chance to put her talents, and she had plenty beyond her skills with a rifle, to more legitimate uses. If not for her mother, Isela might have killed her stepbrother, Antonio Castenado, years ago.

In the cobbled piazza in front of the chapel, Isela watched the local artisans setting up their stalls round the shaded arched perimeter. Every morning these men and women readied their wares for the influx of tourists arriving from Ica and Lima and regions further north. A river of buses would stream one by one through the narrow canyon, until the hacienda and the outlying area were swarming with people.

Isela watched the men and women uncover their carts

filled with shiny glazed pots, wooden crosses with brown Jesuses etched on them, and bright tapestries stitched with Inca designs, likely made in Mexico, Isela figured.

For a few seconds, Isela kept her eye on a couple of men and two women she'd never seen before who were struggling to steady their carts on the cobbled stones.

Isela picked up her rifle. She sighted at a cart layered with T-shirts stamped with everything from the pop image of Che Guevara to the silhouetted outline of Zorro. Tourists were such dicks, she thought.

Staring at those two men and women for a few beats, she guessed they must have been running the carts for a family member, someone who'd been taken ill perhaps. Then Isela mouthed the sound of a shot, letting her imagination invent the chaos she could cause in the piazza if she fired at them.

All hell would break loose. She couldn't wait.

Despite the early hour, the businesses around the square bustled with life. Each corner housed a bar or a café with barrels of the region's famous pisco brandy sweating on stone slabs outside every establishment. Most of the umbrella tables were already occupied with the wealthy tourists staying at the hacienda's luxury spa hotel, which sat at the opposite side of the colonial piazza.

From her angle, Isela didn't have a clear view of the chapel's steps directly beneath her, but she knew they'd be filling with Indian women wrapped in multicoloured shawls with baskets balanced on their heads. She could, though, see a group of four or five boys beginning a football game on the airstrip, a dusty field with a prefabricated concrete shed built just outside the hacienda's walls. Two mangy llamas were munching sagebrush near the makeshift goal, the boys' kicks erupting in clouds of dirt.

Before she set her gun down, Isela spotted two of the food vendors rolling their steaming carts to either side of the hotel's carved wooden gates.

Where had they come from?

Her father would not be happy with their position directly in front of his expensive but incredibly garish entrance and that made Isela smile. Perhaps the day held more promise than she'd first thought.

Lifting her binoculars, Isela scanned the canyon road running north to the highway and beyond that to Lima. Paradise.

God, she couldn't wait to escape this place. She searched the far horizon, noting the clear line where the brush of the desert became the lush green rows of olive trees. To her left, the ocean swelled in waves of cobalt blue, a fishing trawler bouncing on the horizon.

She squinted against the sun, and then with a raised fist she signalled down to Antonio. Her stepbrother was slouching across a massive white limb of the huarango tree, his cigarette smoke pluming through its broad canopy, his spurred boots cutting into its thick bark.

Inside the walls of the hacienda, the huarango tree dominated the apron of the chapel, its roots creating a fault line that ran unevenly under the entire church, some thought for fifty kilometres beyond the adobe walls.

Isela's *abuela* used to tell her stories about how the tree gave life to the region, its leaves absorbing the fog and the dew from the ocean drawing water to the aquifer beneath them, its yellow bean pods nourishing the landscape and its canopy sheltering the goddess who lived far beneath it deciding the fate of mankind.

According to the story, when the world came to an end the tree would stretch its limbs, crack open the earth, and walk into the mountain.

Glancing over the wall of the belfry, Isela stared at Antonio and the tree. Every story her *abuela* and her mother told about her ancestors involved the tree and the mountain in some way, which was one of the reasons why, her mother explained, the Inca terraced their dwellings into the rock face of la Madre Montâna so as not to disturb the tree's far-reaching roots and yet still be close enough to the mother of all things.

Antonio nudged his cowboy hat off his forehead and stretched across the tree's limb. Four years her senior, Antonio was well practised in the art of machismo, his olive skin, slim muscular frame and the thick blond hair he had inherited from his California surfer mother simply reinforced his beliefs about the world and his place in it, including the notion that running this godforsaken region was a right he had earned, instead of the fact that he was the spoiled bastard son of a spoiled bastard son.

He caught a glimpse of Isela staring down at him from the belfry. He cocked his finger at her. She raised her middle one at him.

¡Que huevón! What a dick.

Reaching into the pocket of her denim shorts, Isela pulled out her grandfather's journal, quickly turning to the pages where she had left off the night before. The journal was wrapped in a tattered square of cloth, its edges folded neatly around the small book. Unwrapping it, she prepared herself for the rush of emotion she felt when she had first flipped through its pages, as if the sensations that her grandfather was experiencing as he wrote in this journal remained trapped in its pages. She hadn't told anyone that she had found it, so she couldn't ask anyone for help deciphering its sketches and notes, only one or two of which she recognised.

The drawings, the equations and the notes made no sense to her, but the letters tucked into the tiny pocket in the back cover were something else entirely. She had glanced at those only once, folding them back in their place, embarrassed and confused by their content, undelivered love letters to a man.

The sounds of the market rose up to Isela in waves of colour, snippets of conversations, snatches of melodies, animal cries, children's shouts, a truck backfiring, all floating in her line of vision in ribbons of blues and yellows. Then a click. Click. Click. A series of chirping sounds from the piazza below.

She tasted sour milk.

Lifting her binoculars again, she turned to face the hotel bordering the opposite side of the square. Its salmon-coloured walls glowed in the morning sun, its white shutters closed against the encroaching heat. The hacienda might no longer be run from Spain, but it was still a colony. Because history has a sense of irony, the land was once again in the hands of a usurper – her father, Asiro Castenado. He was her mother's second husband; the bankruptcy and death of the first had meant the hotel would have to be sold. Isela's father had married her mother just hours before the bank could close a deal with a North American corporation. Isela's mother had welcomed the purchase because it meant she'd never have to leave the mountain. Isela did not want the same fate.

The wooden doors into the hacienda's tropical courtyard were slowly opening, the hotel's armed security guards settling into their positions for the arrival of today's influential mark. The guards were dressed in what her father believed was authentic uniforms of the Spanish Conquistadors.

¡Que huevón!

The sooner she could escape this place the better.

Gaia

5

Southern coast of Peru, 1930
'*El Cóndor! El Cóndor!*' yelled a child, sprinting down the steep canyon path and into the village, sure-footed despite the loose rocks and dust she was kicking up. 'A man with enormous wings has fallen from the heavens.'

The tiny pueblo village sat near the flat top of la Madre Montâna in the Sacred Valley of the Andes, nestled against the cliffs on its highest plateau and one of the holy places in the coastal plains that the Conquistadors had failed to discover when they marched their armies across Peru. During Manco Inca's great final rebellion, the Cuari had carried their belongings and their secrets higher into the mountain to this sacred spot where they had survived, secluded and protected, ever since.

For centuries, the Cuari had little contact with civilisation beyond the immediate valley. On occasion a dogged slave runner, an intrepid missionary, or a curious university scholar had ventured unaware into their village. They tended to leave just as quickly, never quite sure of what they'd seen or done or discovered. The village gradually became a myth, a Peruvian Shangri-La, fragmented stories making their way back along the trail to Cuzco and Pisco and Lima and beyond. Eventually, any remaining curiosity about the hidden secrets of this mysterious place faded in comparison to the all too tangible draw of the stunning cairn temple ruins at Machu Picchu and the discoveries of the nearby Nazca lines. As time passed, the stories about the village and the whereabouts of the Cuari tribe became forgotten.

Now no one spoke of this sacred place, and the Cuari did all that they could to keep it that way. When the time came, the universe would know of their existence.

The Cuari's High Priestess and medicine woman ducked out from her hut. Her skin was as pocked as the side of the mountain, her white hair knotted in a thin braid, her layers of skirts revealing thick calves and bare feet. Most of the village's younger women were crouching over a large fire pit, pounding maize on huge flat stones and rolling tortillas in their nimble fingers. One or two of the women had sleeping babies wrapped tight to their backs. They looked up as the girl skidded, breathless, to a stop in front of the Priestess.

'It's him,' the child exclaimed, bouncing with excitement. 'I saw him. He came down with the flying machine.' The girl pointed to a funnel of thick dark smoke pluming to the heavens from the crashed Hornet.

'Where are your animals?' the High Priestess asked her. Together, they crossed the clearing to a stone temple, a round cairn with a stepped roof reaching a pyramid point, built before the conquest beneath the canopy of two huarango trees. Their monstrous roots ran below the surface of the plateau like giant claws holding the mountain in their grip. The Cuari believed that they did.

'Grazing with Rojas. She is capable.' The girl's voice dropped to a whisper as they got closer to the round stone temple. She hated the goats, and she wasn't that fond of

Rojas either. They both smelled badly, which is why she had wandered off to explore when she heard the mechanical bird flying overhead. Her heart was thumping in her chest. 'We should go quickly. I know where he fell. The mountain didn't take him yet.'

The Priestess frowned at the girl. 'Did you touch him?'

'No!' she said, looking at the ground, scuffing her bare toes into the dirt, ashamed that the Priestess would even think her capable of such dishonour. The girl knew that she was not worthy of looking upon a deity, and so all she had done was to gather up the belongings that had fallen from the sky and scattered across the plateau, avoiding the smouldering flying machine as she did. The giant bird frightened her, the noises of the wood snapping and crackling in the flames like an angry night lion.

'Good,' the Priestess replied, tousling the girl's curly black hair and accepting the belongings that she had wrapped in her striped poncho. Behind the Priestess, the heavy curtain of reeds covering the entrance to the sacred cairn rustled.

The Priestess dropped to her knees. The girl fled.

Two hands wrapped in wide strips of red gauze reached out from behind the screen, palms up. The Priestess hooked the poncho over the gauze, making sure the fabric did not touch any skin. The poncho disappeared inside.

'The time of the prophecies is at hand,' said the High Priestess in the ancient tongue of her ancestors. 'I will prepare myself to enter.'

'I am ready,' said a low, sultry female voice.

The Priestess was the Cuari's *amautas*, the keeper of their historical narrative, the protector of the tales of their ancestors, tales told and retold from the times aeons before El Diablo Pizarro – from the time when the stars had fallen into the mountain and the world was born.

The old matriarch had spoken to traders at the lowland villages, and to the archaeologists who were now digging at a temple ruin on the other side of the mountain. She knew from them that the gods were using men to wage battles in the world beyond their village. But as always the Cuari had been spared the encroaching violence because they had an ancient prophecy to fulfil and the mountain to protect them.

Back inside her hut, the Priestess undressed, letting her skirts fall in a bundle near the door. She stood in an iron tub and bathed, scrubbing her skin until every sharp angle and soft sagging spot was rubbed raw. She let the warm moist air in the hut dry her mottled skin before she unfolded a clean grey tunic and pulled it over her head. At her door, she slipped her feet into leather sandals and stepped outside. A small grouping of villagers, who had gathered in front of her hut when they heard the girl's yelling, backed away quickly to let the Priestess pass.

At the entrance to the temple, she stopped and knelt, making sure her knee did not touch the ground.

'May the gods protect you, Gaia.'

Then she pulled aside the heavy screen and stepped inside the temple of the Star Guide.

The Priestess carefully dropped the curtain behind her, aware of every crackle and rustle as she did so. She remained in a small outer chamber whose walls were draped in red and black embroidered fabrics, waiting until Gaia adjusted to her presence and summoned her forward. When she did, the Priestess lifted the final curtain of heavy draping on another arched entry and stepped through into the main chamber of the temple.

In this chamber the sunlight was muted, its beams filtering through the slits in the stone and diffusing across lush red fabric that dressed the walls and draped the ceiling. The ground was carpeted in alpaca skins, softened and dyed to match the colour of the walls. The colour red tasted like sweet paprika to Gaia and, in her solitude, when she willed it, the colour brought her contentment and a deep sensual pleasure.

A fire was burning in a centre pit, its basin-shaped lid filled with water, a myriad of holes funnelling the smoke up through the opening in the stepped roof. Under the netting, almost every brick was covered with brilliantly coloured glyphs, describing the story of the Cuari and the history of the mountain.

A thick cushioned mat piled with embroidered blankets stood against the far corner while a second mat of yellow reeds had been unrolled next to the fire, a single row of decorated clay pots set at its head. The air in the hut was dense, humid, but cool and scented with eucalyptus and balsam, the only oils for which Gaia's senses had developed a tolerance.

Gaia stood at the other side of the chamber, naked, staring at the Priestess, a look of such agony on her face it brought tears to the old woman's eyes. Gaia's skin was the colour of cinnamon, her eyes shining like black polished stones, her hair cascading over her shoulders like soft velvet. She was tall and slender, her breasts and her hips already full and round, and every few seconds she bobbed up on her toes, inhaling and exhaling in sharp short breaths, the intensity of the Priestess's presence an assault on Gaia's senses no matter how well the old woman had scrubbed.

When the pain eased and Gaia had managed the cacophony of sounds in her head, she waived the Priestess further into the chamber, where she stopped and dipped her hands into a pot warming on the fire. She cleansed her hands one more time, a ritual the Priestess had been carrying out every day for over seventeen seasons, since Gaia had moved from her wet nurse to the temple. After a few more minutes,

Gaia would be able to tolerate the Priestess standing almost at her side.

'You will need to climb the mountain,' the Priestess whispered, her quiet voice filling Gaia's mouth with the taste of lemons. 'In sunlight.'

'I know,' said Gaia. She had never ventured outside in daylight – her body had no capacity to filter the light and the noises of the village. Some day, she had prayed. And some day had come.

'I'm prepared,' she whispered. 'I have been for ever.'

The Priestess nodded, glancing at a garment draped across a mahogany trunk that resembled chainmail in its design and its weave, the kind of protective garment the Conquistadors may have worn beneath their suits of armour. With the help of three Cuari weavers, Gaia had fashioned her suit from the softest cotton, layering the outside with black suede from animal pelts, the stitching glimmering with silver threads.

The priestess picked up the garment and helped Gaia dress, carefully slipping the suit over her head, lifting the young woman's sleek hair over her cowl, fastening the delicate silver claps on the breastplate, lacing the supple leather skins to her feet and legs. When the Priestess finished dressing Gaia, she stepped back.

'You are your night self,' said the Priestess.

And she was. Gaia looked like a sleek black puma.

Isela

6

Southern Coast of Peru, minibus from Lima, present day

Juan Cortez was a man of diverse talents, but only a few passions. Unfortunately, he had fallen victim to one of his passions for the last time. Cards, cockfights, football games, weather patterns, anything where he could wager what little money his talents as a driver earned him, which wasn't much. That was why for the past three months he had been driving the route from Lima to the Hacienda del Castenado four times a day.

Juan owed money to his bookie and that meant he owed money to Asiro Castenado. He had no choice as to how his debts were to be paid off. Juan was a quick study and he had learned the routine necessary for these special runs, and so far he had not encountered any glitches. He was glad of the work, especially since his wife was expecting their third child. And this trip would be his last one. He'd been promised his debts would be paid, his freedom bought.

Juan glanced in his mirror, checking out the passengers behind him. This group was smaller than most of these usual private charters, especially one with the day's mark on board. The two youngest passengers were asleep, their bodies draped across each other – a man and woman in their mid-twenties, probably university students, their backpacks stuffed into the overhead bins.

A handsome middle-aged man who looked like an ex-rugby player sat alone at the rear of the bus with headphones on and his computer open on his lap. Of all the passengers, he looked the least like a tourist in his tan summer suit and blue shirt open at the collar. But his manner was relaxed, and Juan was sure he would not be a threat when the time came.

Juan guessed this was a man who'd been on this trip before because he was paying no heed to the spectacular sea views as the minibus climbed up the mountain to the mesa. Perhaps, Juan figured, the man was a tour planner, checking out arrangements for a future group.

Too bad the tour wasn't going to end the way his travel books predicted.

A man and woman in their early thirties were each reading guides to the Inca trails that Juan's brother-in-law had sold them at the terminal before they boarded the bus. They seemed like an odd match. The man, who looked like he'd never left the beaten path a day in his life, was dressed from head to toe in hiking gear from an upscale outdoor catalogue; everything matched and fitted perfectly. The woman had long dark hair, a face of freckles and the palest white skin Juan had ever seen. She'd been sleeping on and off since they boarded. They had different accents, although one was as thick as the other's. Juan thought the man might have been from Louisiana. He'd been to the casino once in New Orleans. The woman, he thought she might be Irish or Scottish. He wasn't sure. Those accents sounded the same to him.

Sitting directly in front of the couple was the morning's mark, the one at the centre of today's events, a middle-aged Brazilian male, trim and fit, the CEO of an international liquor distribution company and a man with close ties to power of all kinds. He was travelling with his third wife, also Brazilian, athletic, bronzed and beautifully enhanced, and she, Juan knew, was fronting the morning's enterprise.

She caught Juan's gaze; he averted his eyes.

The last passenger Juan considered was the one sitting directly behind him, a good-looking man, hard to peg his age, military grooming, dressed in desert combat fatigues, the insignia of a United Nations security force stitched on his shirt. Gazing out of the window, he was lost in his thoughts. He'd spoken to Juan in Spanish when he'd boarded the minibus at the last minute, squeezing through the closing doors as Juan was pulling away, making it impossible for Juan to insist he wait for the next one, which he should have.

A soldier in the mix was not something Juan was comfortable factoring in to the carefully crafted plan. The soldier's grey eyes had a lot going on behind them, Juan decided. He'd have to watch him closely when the time came.

Two hours south of Lima, the van turned off the Pan-American highway and onto the narrower canyon road that began the climb to the Hacienda del Castenado. The dramatic change in the landscape perked up the sleeping passengers and the odd couple. The man in the back closed his laptop, popping out his external drive and slipping it into his pocket.

Juan had only ever seen la Madre Montâna once from a plane, and when he had he'd thought it looked like an upside down bowler hat that the gods had carved out of the ground – the coastal road circumnavigating the narrow brim of the mountain. Driving to the hacienda, cut into the rock halfway up the mountain, was like driving in a trench. There was no space for error on either side, which meant that once the minibus reached this part of the journey there was no going back, no getting on or off until Juan came out the other side onto the terraced landscape of the Gran Tablazo de Ica and the hacienda.

Once the van reached the canyon road, the surface evened out, widening a little to accommodate the rows of terraced olive and grape vines on one side and to provide a safe distance from the sea crashing beneath them on the other. On this first leg of the climb, every Pacific wave sprayed water over the van. The students laughed as if they were on a ride at Disneyland. The soldier had closed his eyes, the businessman was reading and the Brazilian couple was arguing. Let the poor sucker win this one, thought Juan, watching the Brazilians in his mirror. It'll be his last.

Juan shifted his gears, compensating for the surface changes of the now unpaved road and the gradual incline as the minibus climbed even higher above sea level. With these first few miles of the coastal road, he needed all his concentration. He'd shift his attentions to the real job at hand once he and his passengers were safely at the top.

7

Aiming her binoculars out across the landing strip, Isela tracked a plane coming in low through the mountains. It was still a speck, shifting in and out between the snow-capped peaks. She turned her attention to the canyon road, watching for the minibus that would soon be visible on the horizon. Then, shifting herself out of the sun, she turned her binoculars to one of the guests at the hotel who had been reading in the shade of an umbrella at the café since early morning.

According to one of the hotel's sous chefs, the man had simply appeared the night before when the town was locked up tight against a raging Pacific storm. The weird thing was, the man hadn't banged on any doors, hadn't shouted for anyone to open up, had made no anxious cries for shelter. He'd simply pulled up his coat collar and huddled against the front gates of the hacienda, the lashing rain and buffeting winds pelting him for hours.

According to her mother, this man was charismatic and charming and cursed – she could smell it on him. That morning at breakfast, after her father had excused himself to his study, her mother had insisted that the stranger smelled of death. Isela rolled her eyes as she remembered

41

her mother's admonition to stay away from him.

'This stranger has the soul of *El Cóndor*, the ancient one fallen from the heavens, unable to return,' said her mother in the tone of voice she reserved for North American tourists and Isela. Her mother lifted a pewter goblet to her full red lips. '*El Cóndor* carries darkness inside him. His burdens are pressing on his soul. You must stay away or the darkness will suffocate you.'

'How do you know this?' prodded Isela, well aware that this conversation was shifting into territory that forced her mother to remember her roots, to have to say out loud that she was also Cuari, like her mother and her mother before her, a line stretching back to the Sun King, one of the chosen tribe of women meant to protect the mountain. With three marriages, and a considerable amount of make-up, Isela's mother had managed to conceal that part of her identity. Until recently when the first tremors began and the mountain got angry.

'I am not stupid, Isela,' said her mother. 'I know how you think you can goad me so easily, but mind my words. One day, you'll understand. Yes, I am a Cuari, and so, my love, are you. So beware.'

Her mother lifted her goblet and moved to the tall arched window that looked out over the family's private gardens. Gazing up at the mountain's plateau, she shivered. Turning to face her daughter, she said, 'I'd hoped the burden of the mountain would never be yours to endure, but I'm afraid it may be your destiny after all.'

Directly beneath them a fountain bubbled, its water drawn from an underground spring that was part of an ancient aquifer that kept life in this high desert. Dotted around the hacienda were similar fountains, each one considered sacred, and, according to the stories reprinted in every brochure and website for the hotel, had been flowing continuously since the area was first populated in ancient times.

Next to the Inca trails that began a few kilometres from the hotel and the nearby Nazca lines, the baths were a tourist draw. The water from the sacred valley was believed to have properties that made men swoon and women shiver; that made love sweeter and bodies more alluring.

Now, crouching alone behind the tower wall, her binoculars resting on the crumbling surface, Isela finally spotted a cloud of dust on the far horizon.

At last. The mark.

The first bus of the day from Lima was coming off the highway and climbing up onto the canyon pass, and this one was bringing her ticket out of this stifling town.

Picking up her automatic rifle, Isela checked the cartridge, sighting it into the shadows above the café.

The *cóndor* was staring up at the tower. Isela ducked out of sight.

¡Que huevón!

Gaia

8

Southern Coast of Peru, 1930

Gaia's sensitivity to the world outside the temple had been further proof to the Cuari that she was indeed their guide, their star scout, the sacred spirit described in the ancient prophecies as the one to come before, the one who would prepare the way for the deity when he returned to begin the end of times. For the High Priestess, such affirmation had never been necessary. For she had known that Gaia was a spirit guide since the night of her birth, which she had witnessed: Gaia's first howl, her mother's last breath. Gaia had burst from her mother's womb, limbs and tail first, encased in a thick membrane.

The Priestess, an old woman even at Gaia's birth, had become her guardian and her teacher. From early in her childhood, Gaia could hear when the crops should be harvested, could taste the wind before it blew, and feel the rains from the sea before the clouds scudded the storms inland. Gaia felt pain when she was not hurt, heard singing when it was silent, and at night she travelled beyond the mountain to the stars.

Gaia had learned divination from the rocks and the birds and even as a child she had demonstrated her quick wit and her eidetic memory. The old Priestess had taught her to read the ancient scrolls when she was barely able to walk to fetch them. Gaia could hold the Cuari's stories in her head, glyph for glyph as she read them, remembering the names of every child born in the village since the conquest.

How many nights had the old woman bathed her in oils to quiet her spirit when it raced across the heavens, her body convulsing against the ground, her being so sensitive to the material world that her screams could wake the gods.

Perhaps they finally had.

For her part, Gaia knew her place in the Cuari was a special one, but she also knew that her place in the cosmos would be even more acclaimed. Gaia and the old Priestess had been watching the signs from the mountain since the winds had sheared off its crown during the cold season.

If this man who had fallen from the heavens was the being prophesied since ancient times, then the oracle had told the truth and Gaia must prepare to fulfil her purpose. Gaia could barely control her excitement as she finished dressing, sticking wax plugs into her ears, her excitement filling her head with music.

The old woman placed her rough hands, the hands of a farmer as well as a holy woman, gently on Gaia's shoulders. Even a priestess had to work to sustain life in the tribe. No matter how sacred their purpose, they still had to eat.

'The elders will go with you to bring him back. Can you manage the climb?' The Priestess looked at Gaia's feet.

Gaia nodded, quickly braiding her hair and pulling her cowl over her head, leaving only her dark eyes and dimpled chin visible.

'If this fallen man is the prophesied one,' said the Priestess, 'then he must be sacrificed to the mountain as has been foretold, but, Gaia, if he is not...'

The Priestess did not finish voicing her doubts, fearing

what it would do to Gaia if this man was not the one from the prophecy. Gaia's quick mind had no space for uncertainty in this matter, no crevices for doubt. This was her destiny. Her reason for existing. The Priestess sighed. Gaia may have been born an ancient star guide, but in the old woman's eyes she was still a child.

'Remember what you've learned. He must be examined on the mountain, Gaia, and if he is not the one, you must do what you have been trained to do. He must not return here with you. We must not be discovered until the prophecy can be fulfilled.'

The Priestess lifted down a long wooden case from a stone shelf. Her knees popping as she bent to lift a sword that rested inside on red satin, its silver hilt carved in the image of the puma with jade for its eyes and a collar of pure gold.

The Priestess eased the heavy sword into a leather sash fastened across Gaia's chest. 'If he is not the one, his head must return to the mountain.'

Gaia nodded. 'But if it is him?'

'Then as it has been foretold, you will assist his return to the stars.'

'And mine?' she asked, lifting her head, her eyes blazing, her hand resting on the hilt of the sword.

'You will be his guide,' the old woman replied.

9

A copper bell forged at Chavin de Huantar had once hung over the entrance to the temple. Its chime would have brought everyone immediately, its particular pitch heard by a Cuari no matter where she was on the mountain. But when it had last been rung, a decade earlier, its chimes had sent Gaia into a madness that it had taken her months to recover from, and her sensitivity to the world was increasing the further she crossed into womanhood.

Instead, the Priestess sent two girls scurrying to call the rest of the Cuari from the mountain above the village. The pair dashed up into the mountainside. The women set down their tools, hitched up their llamas and all of them processed down the lush green slopes, their chatter like birdsong in the wind.

The Cuari gathered quickly and quietly in front of the Priestess. Propped at the old woman's feet was a lavishly embroidered pouch, concealing something that was the shape and size of a head.

'*Mujeres de la montaña*,' said the Priestess, raising her arms to the sky, speaking in the language of their Cuari ancestors. 'As the oracle has foretold, the deity has made his escape from the heavens. We must prepare him for his return to Uku Pacha so that time may be free.'

The Cuari glanced at each other, excitement in their eyes. A few whispered among themselves, one or two nodded and looked to the heavens in silent prayer. No one chanted or shouted or praised the heavens aloud. They were far too close to the temple and to Gaia for any vocal demonstrations of their faith.

'Gaia will lead you to him,' said the Priestess, addressing four of the strongest Cuari kneeling before. They were dressed in colourful tunics, with the tribal symbol, three interlocking circles, raised to a point tattooed on the backs of their necks. Their feet were bare, their hair neatly braided, their brown faces mapped with sun and suffering. 'Remember that if he is indeed the one from the stars, he must be returned here before nightfall, before the heavens discover that he has gone.'

The Priestess lifted the heavy screen from the temple entrance and Gaia stepped out into the sunlight, her cowl protecting her eyes from the dazzling light. The entire village prostrated themselves in front of Gaia and the Priestess. A few of the younger women who had been children when Gaia had first gone into the temple had never seen her before, and they gasped at her ethereal beauty, their voices tickling Gaia's toes. She looked across to the younger women and smiled broadly at them.

The Priestess motioned Gaia to step forward and hold out her wrapped hands. She anointed each of Gaia's fingertips with balsam oil in a blessing to the mountain for Gaia's safe passage before handing her the head-shaped pouch, which Gaia accepted with a curt bow. Then, with the help of another Cuari, Gaia slipped the pack over her shoulders with great care, balancing its weight against the tilt of the sword in the sash across her chest. As a guide, Gaia knew she and the Priestess were the only living beings who could have any direct contact with the deity from the heavens. With all her heart, Gaia prayed he was the one – his presence among them, his return to them, would allow her to bring an end to her suffering without bringing dishonour to the Cuari from the gods.

Before Gaia and the elders began their ascent to the mountain's flat top, one of the village women passed Gaia a pouch filled with water, two warm tortillas and a lump of goat's cheese. Knowing they would not be stopping until they reached their destination, Gaia tore into the sparse meal as she led the procession up into the canyon towards the billowing smoke.

For anyone else the climb would have been a difficult one, but the Cuari had spent their lives on this mountain and they were as agile in their movements and as skilled in their climbing as any mountain lion, especially Gaia. She kept a safe distance ahead of the elders so that their odours and the low hum of their conversation caused her as little discomfort as possible.

When the narrow pass began to flatten out towards the plateau and a field of ice was visible like glass on the horizon, the temperature dropped drastically. The cold chimed in Gaia's ears like distant goat bells. Despite the wax plugs, Gaia could hear a long low moan of anguish in an outcropping of rocks directly up ahead. Gaia tasted saltwater and her fingers tingled. She knew they were close to him.

Gaia raised her hands and stopped the elders, pointing up ahead to the sagebrush and the rocks where the man's mangled legs and twisted feet were visible, twitching against the ground.

The Cuari stopped, not shocked at the sight of the shattered body and broken limbs caught between the rocks – they had seen enough slaughtered animals in their lives –

but at the feral moaning that was emanating from the man. It was terrifying. If this man came from their gods, one of the Cuari elders thought, he was not happy about leaving.

Gaia was about to run forward when the same elder reached out and grabbed her from behind. Gaia flinched as if she'd been struck with a whip.

The elder pulled away her hands immediately. 'Forgive my touch,' she whispered. 'But he may be dangerous.'

'He will not be,' replied Gaia. Her own voice tasted like ginger root on her tongue. Gaia was far too curious to see what the gods had sent to wait any longer. The elders drew their swords and formed a horseshoe round the rocks, making sure they could not look upon the man, but they could assist their guide if she needed protection quickly. Gaia tiptoed closer to the body. The mist had lifted from the mountain and the sun was at its peak, long shadows poking like curious fingers between the rocks.

Gaia untied the pouch and set it on one of the larger flatter rocks, halting a few paces from the soft brush where the man had landed. She stared down at him and prayed he was the god who would be the mountain's salvation. And her own.

He was broken in too many places for Gaia to count, his body lying at odd angles, his arms dislocated from his shoulders, his head lolling to one side on a pillow of blood. The back of his skull had flattened in the impact. His face was so swollen that his eyes were slits sliced into his ballooned skin. Teeth had stabbed through his lips and they were still oozing blood.

This is not the prophesied one, Gaia thought. This is a mortal man. She turned to the elders. 'He is not the one the oracle foretold.'

Gaia leaned forward, and tilted the man's head back, exposing the torn skin and ragged bone of his broken neck.

Turning her body, she unsheathed her sword, holding it steady at her side. Living a life cloistered from the world had given Gaia all the time she needed to master most of her ancestors' fighting skills. She was as adept with her sword as any knight had been. The jade on her hilt caught the sunlight, sending triangles of light bouncing off the rocks and a melody of flutes in Gaia's mind.

The man moaned.

Gaia lifted her sword above her head.

In the seconds before Gaia brought down her blade, the man turned his head and Gaia watched in astonishment as his neck healed and the back of his skull filled out.

Letting her sword fall at her side, she dropped to her knees. Without knowing why, the elders followed their guide's lead, and they too knelt.

'Forgive me,' she said to the man's swollen face, his lips repairing themselves as she stared.

He howled again. With every small tear that healed, every bloody wound that dried up, some agonising, mind-blowing pain seemed to be shooting through his brain.

Recognising his suffering, Gaia reached into the pack the Priestess had given her. She slid out a gold mask like the helmet of a Conquistador, with a faceplate shaped like the sun soldered to it.

He seemed to be aware of Gaia's movements and the soft melodic lilt of her soothing voice, and his howls quieted. Crouching next to his head, Gaia slipped two cacao leaves from her sword's pouch.

She looked up at the sun. They didn't have much time. The sun was already making its descent to the underworld, and when it reached Uku Pacha the gods would know this deity had escaped. They had to move quickly if they were going to get him safely to the village before night and prepare him for the mountain.

She gently opened his mouth wide enough for her to press the two leaves on his swollen tongue. She poured water into her hands from her canteen then trickled the cool liquid from her fingers into his mouth, lifting his head slightly so he could swallow. Dripping more water onto her wrapped hand, she mopped his forehead and bathed his swollen eyelids. Then she rubbed soft wax across his cracked lips. He moaned again, softly, less agitated this time.

Gaia thought he was trying to smile.

She stayed at his side until his anguished moaning ceased and the coca leaves had calmed him. When he was silent, she was aware that his legs had healed themselves, bone no longer cutting through his torn trousers. Gaia lifted the mask from the rock above him and eased the golden sun over his face.

Her task completed, she nodded to the elders that she was ready. The four women spread the sling open next to his body and then carefully rolled him onto the sturdy skin. Gaia noticed that his arms were no longer dislocated. The revelation that this man was able to heal his own body did not shock her. He was after all from the heavens.

Lifting the poles onto their shoulders and with Gaia leading their descent, the women raced the setting sun down the steep canyon pass to the village.

10

Darren Crowder had been a journalist before the Miracle, a good one. He'd been working on the health desk of the *Washington Register*, an online weekly read mostly by policy wonks and government agency bureaucrats. As tragic as it had been, the Miracle had given Darren and his colleagues lots of 'I told you so' opportunities as the events of those terrible months had exposed flaws inherent in America and the world's healthcare policies. When people finally began to die again, two significant global changes occurred as a result: governments increased the personnel in their clandestine agencies in the hopes of avoiding another such event; and, within these agencies, they covertly invested resources to track the three families who were behind the near apocalypse.

Many months and far too many international tribunals and governmental hearings later, the anger and horrors surrounding the Miracle had dissipated, and blame had been spread evenly among governments, corporations, health organisations and NGOs for the catastrophic administrative and leadership failures that had led to such terrible lapses in global morality. Ordinary men and women just wanted their lives to return to some kind of normal. Their deaths, too.

Darren Crowder had been recruited for the Special Activities Division of the CIA. The Deputy Director had read and appreciated Darren's work post-Miracle Day, and had personally hired Darren as an analyst. The new agency was known publicly (and any time the Deputy Director was within earshot) as the Office of Geo-Global Affairs; the rest of the time, it was known as 'the Morgue', because their mandate was the result of death's comeback.

Looking across the crowded room, Darren decided that, although this was a branch of the CIA, the space had all the characteristics of a newsroom. Its mandate was unique but its approach was no different – smart men and women gathering information, raking through reports and records to uncover patterns and relationships. In the case of the men and women in this particular room, sifting to discover how deep the power of the three families ran, whether or not they continued to pose a threat, and perhaps the most important question of all, as far as Darren was concerned, who the hell were they?

Darren's computer beeped an alert. He typed in his access code and a satellite map popped up on his screen. At first he distrusted his own eyes. He couldn't possibly be seeing what he was seeing. Zooming in on the image, he stared at the screen for a good ten minutes before saving the file to the department's server, logging off and dashing into the narrow hall. Skipping the elevators, he took the stairs instead, leaping down three at a time.

Breathless, he rushed into the Deputy Director's outer office. The Deputy Director's assistant jumped up from his seat, attempting to block Darren's entry into the inner sanctum.

'I need to see the Deputy Director immediately.'

'Let me see if he's available.'

The assistant sat back down, waving Darren to a leather

couch where he realised a young woman was sitting, flipping through a magazine, obviously waiting to see the Deputy Director. She looked familiar, but he dismissed the feeling, realising that everyone applying for a position with this unit had the same look about them: grey suit, grey expression. No one had a sense of humour any more. It was as if society had lost its ability to mock, to poke fun at life, because death had left for a while.

The assistant hung up the phone. 'He's in the middle of important interviews, Agent Crowder. I'm afraid you'll have to wait like everyone else.'

'This really can't wait,' said Darren, pushing past the assistant, who couldn't get to the emergency lock on the Deputy Director's door in time. Darren charged into the office, but not before he noticed the woman on the couch was still flipping through her magazine, unfazed by his brash actions.

Inside the expansive office with its view of the capitol building, the Deputy Director looked up, snarled, and with a wave of his hand dismissed a new recruit who was seated in front of his desk. His assistant shut the door with more emphasis than necessary.

'You have to see this, sir,' said Darren, placing his palm on the top-left corner of a wall-mounted computer screen. After his access was granted, Darren called up the file that he'd viewed at his desk.

'This better be something,' said Rex Matheson, the agency's most recently appointed Deputy Director, stepping out from behind his desk and closer to the screen.

'It's from the Castenado operation in progress in Peru, sir, the one tracking our lead to the three families.' Darren paused before adding, 'And it's way more than something. It's someone.'

Isela

11

Southern Coast of Peru, Hacienda del Castenado, present day
Through her binoculars, Isela watched plumes of dust trail behind the minibus as it climbed along the canyon road towards the hacienda. It would be close enough for her in ten minutes, max.

She peered over the top of the tower wall, signalling to Antonio who pushed off from the tree, and jogged inside the wooden gates of the hotel's tropical courtyard. A few minutes later, the speakers on the pink adobe wall that faced the square emitted the lyrical strains of Andean charango music, the high-pitched guitar sounds loud enough for even the footballers across the airstrip to take note. The market came to life when the music filtered from the hacienda. The vendors opened their stalls, the women on the church steps haggling with each other for the best spaces.

Isela stared at the boys playing near the airstrip and realised that she could no longer see the approaching plane. Had it landed and she'd missed it?

No, that wasn't possible. But if that wasn't possible, where had it landed? The hangar, tucked into the trees next to the landing strip was where her father kept his planes, and she could see that it was still secured.

Focusing her binoculars on the tree line, Isela scanned the area at the start of the hiking path that led deeper into the canyon and up to the mountain plateau. Tourists usually took the other road, the one to Lake Aczuma, a man-made oasis that filtered the spring waters for the travellers who came to the hacienda for something more authentic than the hotel's swimming pool and the guided tours of the nearby Inca ruins.

With the music blasting, the men and women dotted around the market place were suddenly livelier, their movements choreographed in response to the hotel's demands to entertain arriving tourists. Not that these villagers didn't benefit. The Hacienda del Castenado was the envy of many of the region's bigger towns, with its community buildings, including a state of the art primary school completely rebuilt after the devastation of the 2007 earthquake, a disaster from which lots of villages in the area had never recovered.

But hotel or not, beneath the strains of the music and the colourful costumes of those crowding the square, Isela knew these peasants were all still slaves to the owner of the hacienda, her father, the drug kingpin and kidnapper extraordinaire, and her mother, the matriarch of the mountain.

Beyond the concrete structure, Isela focused on a cluster of round thatched roof huts, brick cairns, built by her ancestors centuries ago for ritual sacrifices to the gods for a rich crop. Her father had kept the outside structures intact, but renovated their insides to create saunas and meditation huts for the New Agers who would make their pilgrimages to the resort in the tourist months. These cairns dotted the landscape, forming a line up into the mountains.

Forgetting about the plane, Isela zoomed her binoculars in on the last cairn bordering her father's land.

Was that movement she could see behind the structure?

She held her gaze on the spot for a beat, reassuring herself that she had imagined it.

The minibus was right on schedule, having passed the first cairn on the canyon road, then the second, and was now close enough for Isela to see the driver with her binoculars. She recognized Juan at the wheel.

Shit, why did it have to be Juan? She liked him. He was loyal, which meant he would not give up the mark without a fight.

Eight minutes to go.

Isela turned her attention to the *cóndor* in the café, who was getting to his feet. He threw some money on the table and jogged along the cobbled sidewalk behind the café towards the airstrip and the boys playing football. Isela narrowed her focus on the scene. The boys stopped playing, and watched the man walk towards them.

He said a few words. They replied. From the hand gestures and the body language, Isela knew that they were negotiating. It was a skill everyone in the hacienda had perfected. The man passed money to Enrico, who Isela knew was her age and the oldest of the group. Enrico handed the ball to the man who tossed it in the air in front of his feet, booting it across the airstrip and over the flat roof of the hangar.

Why would he buy a football from them only to kick it into the trees? The boys sprinted after it, disappearing into the jungle behind the concrete hangar.

A piercing whistle broke Isela from her reverie. Peeking over the belfry wall at the piazza, she saw Antonio signalling to her to begin her countdown.

Isela nodded. Finally, she was going to get out of here. Get away from the madness and the sway this mountain had on her.

Setting her rifle in a tiny trench she'd dug out of a stone on the ledge, she sighted on the canyon road and waited her chance to be free of the mountain.

Gaia

12

Southern Peru, 1930

The sun was a blazing orange ball dipping into the sea as Gaia led the elders down from the mountain. They were carrying the man between them.

A young girl had met the procession midway with water for Gaia and the elders. Now she darted out ahead of them to alert the High Priestess. As soon as she knew of the procession's proximity, the Priestess accepted a bouquet of condor feathers from another elder. Soaking the feathers in a clay bowl filled with goat's blood and with another elder pacing behind her holding the pot, the Priestess marked the walls of the temple. It was a necessary part of the ritual so that when the underworld discovered the man from the heavens was missing, the temple would be protected from the wrath of the gods.

Every three steps, the Priestess stopped, prayed, and then brushed the Cuari symbol of the three interlocking circles on the stone blocks of the temple. While she marked, her chants called on the gods of the three worlds – the underworld, Uku Pacha, the overworld, Hanan Pacha, and the world of man, Hurin Pacha – to join as one as they once had been. The three must be united when the prophecy was

63

fulfilled.

Gaia halted at the end of the canyon, letting the Priestess finish her ritual. When she had walked the perimeter of the temple, the Priestess placed the feathers into the bowl and then waved for Gaia to proceed. The twilight made it possible for Gaia to drop her hood as she crossed the dusty clearing, her shining eyes absorbing as much as she could withstand before hiding herself away to prepare herself and the *cóndor* for their journey. As soon as Gaia walked out of the canyon, the villagers dropped to their knees, prostrating themselves on the ground, pulling their small children beneath their bodies, terrified of seeing the man who had fallen from the heavens.

With Gaia still leading the way, the four elders carried the sling through the channel created by the villagers and set it down inside the circle the Priestess had made. Only the Priestess and Gaia were permitted to cross the circle.

Leaving the man wrapped in the sling, the Priestess and Gaia each gripped a wooden pole and awkwardly dragged his inert body into the temple. They stopped next to the reed mat Gaia had rolled out earlier.

'I am sorry,' said the Priestess, breathless from the task. Gaia waited until the old woman had caught her breath and mopped her forehead dry. Gaia tasted potatoes from the old woman's sweat.

Lifting a roll of black cotton gauze from a basket next to the door, Gaia wrapped the thin fabric round her head, covering her mouth and nose. She looked like a *bandito*.

'We must follow the prophecy as precisely as we can,' said the Priestess.

Gaia nodded, swallowing the high sharp chords shooting across her skull and the aching in her joints from the odours of blood and sweat emanating from the man. She had become skilled at carrying her suffering because she knew it was a gift from the gods. This day would fulfil her destiny. Soon she'd be dancing on the stars.

Placing a bowl intricately patterned with bands of red and black next to the man's head, the Priestess knelt and untied the leather straps binding the sling. She glanced up at Gaia, who nodded, and then with a graceful flourish the Priestess threw open the sling.

The old woman fell back on her heels, knocking over two of the clay pots, their oils absorbed instantly into the soft wool rugs carpeting the temple floor.

The man's clothing was torn and bloodstained, but his bones were no longer broken, and the mass of tears and cuts to his legs and arms were almost healed. Gaia lifted the golden mask from his face, and both women looked at each other in astonishment, tears of awe filling Gaia's eyes.

The man's face remained bruised, his eyes swollen, his lips cracked, but his face had no other injuries.

'Have you ever seen anything like this... like this *being* in your experience, Gaia?'

'Never,' said Gaia, kneeling at the other side of the man, stroking the dark hair away from his forehead.

Both women remained at his side, sitting cross-legged in silence until the sun fell completely from the heavens and dropped into the sea, and beams of moonlight filtered into the hut through the slits in the stones. The fire had long since gone out. When moonlight touched the top of his head, the Priestess slowly rose to her feet, her bones creaking. Gaia remained seated, her eyes closed, drifting in and out of sleep.

The Priestess relit the fire, then touched Gaia's shoulder. 'It is time. Uku Pacha has opened. We must prepare for your descent.'

For all of her young life, Gaia had been practising and praying for this honour, to be the one to guide the star man to the underworld so that the ancient prophecy might be fulfilled. Since the beginning of time, the Cuari had been the protectors of the mountain, first waiting for a guide to be born among them and then, when she was waiting, preparing her to accompany the deity.

Gaia accepted a bowl of warm milk from the Priestess, drinking all of it without even noticing the dots of colour that danced before her eyes as she did. Returning the empty bowl to the Priestess, Gaia slipped her ceremonial hunting knife from its sheath. With trembling hands, she began the ritual that until this day she had only dreamed about.

First, Gaia sliced the blade through the sleeves of the man's coat, peeling back the cloth, exposing his shirt, braces and trousers. While the priestess removed his boots, Gaia stripped off his bloody clothes, tossing them into a pile near the temple door. The Cuari elders would take the clothes up to the mountain where they would burn them, sending the smoke into the mountain as a sign that he was coming. When he was naked, Gaia soaked a piece of cotton in warm eucalyptus oil, bathing his face and his body.

Gaia had never seen a naked man until now, but the images on the walls of the temple and the glyphs on the ancient scrolls had prepared her for the sight. When she finished, she spread a blanket she had spent most of her childhood embroidering with a sleek black puma circling a giant condor. She spread the blanket across the man's naked body.

The Priestess crouched behind Jack's head and painted the Cuari symbol on each of his temples using inks from the row of clay pots, while Gaia washed the man's feet.

Soon the air in the hut was thick and pungent, the aromas from the oils and the steam from the water basin clouding the space. The man moaned and stirred under the blanket.

The Priestess looked at Gaia. 'The time has come.'

13

Jack Harkness opened his eyes. He sat bolt upright and inhaled. He was not breathing.

Dead. Again.

He had experienced this awakening too many times before. He knew what to expect.

He inhaled. He exhaled.

Nothing.

No gasping. Nothing.

Cupping his palm at his mouth, he exhaled again. Nothing. He wasn't breathing. What the hell?

Renso. The Hornet. The mountain. Jack's chest felt light. He pressed his hand on his heart. Still beating. So maybe not dead.

In limbo? Still healing?

Strange.

Jack took deep breaths in and out, but nothing went in or wheezed out from his lungs.

So did that make him dead?

Confusion rushed over Jack in a cold wave. Never experienced this before.

And then the wisp of an image – a girl, the sun, a kiss, darkness.

And so much pain. Jack gasped, the memory flitting away.

Sitting up, Jack could feel he was lying on a platform of rock. He squinted, running his hands over the surface, eventually seeing he was on a lip of rock that ran the circumference of a massive stone chamber. The walls were black granite marbled with veins of silver that were pulsing in the darkness. Above him the chamber formed a square opening, a faint glimmer of moonlight filtering down. Far below him the ground rippled like a satin robe in a soft breeze.

Could rock do that?

Jack was acutely aware of his body, of the fact that he was wearing nothing except a long, intricately embroidered tunic, that the soft wool was caressing his skin, that he was enjoying the sensation immensely, that he was hearing water flowing somewhere in the distance, that despite the darkness he was now seeing clearly, and that in the face of an overwhelming thirst he was tasting lemon and ginger and a hint of chocolate.

Had he fallen from the plane to this place? Into the mountain itself? The plane exploding on the ground flashed in front of Jack, Renso's last moment like a black and white newsreel running above Jack's head. He reached out a hand to touch him. The image dissolved. Renso. Poor Renso.

Jack heard himself think the words, but he felt no sadness, no ache in his loins or his heart. He adored Renso, had adored Renso, and yet Jack couldn't make himself feel even a fleeting moment of grief.

Staring down at his hands, Jack turned them over and over. Long fingers, no calluses, flat round nails. Definitely his hands. Then he pushed up the wide sleeves of the tunic and stared at his arms. He parted the tunic, running his hands across his skin. No puncture wounds, no damage anywhere on his body.

So he had healed from the fall.

But did he fall? When did he fall? Minutes or months ago? The memory of it felt small and thin and kept darting from him.

'I'm Jack Harkness,' he said aloud, his voice carried no echo. In a stone chamber of this size, it should have. Strange.

'I'm a Time Agent, a time traveller.' Jack smiled. His voice felt soft and sensuous in his throat. 'I know a Time Lord, the time of the day, the time of the night, tea time, two times two is not too many times,' he said, laughing, the words bouncing playfully in his brain.

His laughter echoed, but his voice had not. He laughed again. The silver veins in the walls pulsed brighter each time he did. Jack had never seen anything like this place, and he had been strapped into and locked down in a lot of strange places. This had to be one of the most fantastic.

Leaning back against the rock wall, Jack felt a warm rush of desire flood his being. He felt himself grow hard beneath the tunic. Wow. His body felt ethereal, weightless, but grounded, experiencing this moment, substantial. The silver veins from the rock, reached out like long probing fingers and they danced across his body.

Jack closed his eyes, but instead of darkness he saw himself languishing on the platform of rock experiencing a powerful rush of pleasure.

For a beat Jack realised the chamber was inside his head and outside it. Behind him and in front of him. He laughed at the absurdity and let himself sink back into the rock. The silver veins threaded themselves across every muscle, every limb, every part of him. Closing his eyes again, he could see himself being folded into the rock.

The sensation was wonderful, yet Jack heard himself thinking that this was not a good wonderful. It was a bad wonderful. It was the wonderful at the end of a thrilling journey. It was the wonderful after intimacy. It was the last hurrah, the final chapter, the kiss goodbye, the beginning of the end.

Jack lifted his arm and tore it away from the wall, snapping the threads.

He heard a sob. It tasted like ginger.

Maybe this was a good thing after all. He let his arm fall to his side again. The threads slithered over his hand instantly. Jack's body had never felt so warm, so wholly satisfied, so welcomed, so at peace.

'Jack, move!'

Closing his eyes again, he saw himself closing his eyes again, and closing his eyes again, and closing his eyes, his mind in a fun-house mirror of its own making. He spoke out loud, he yelled, he howled, the sound of his own voice keeping him aware, forcing him to be aware that he was not ready for the end.

He was inexplicably conscious and unconscious at the same time. Self-aware, trapped in a chamber, somewhere underground, and more than a little freaked out.

'The time of the prophecies is at hand.'

Jack glanced up. Not his voice. The opening in the top of the chamber was widening. Jack could see the full moon. Jack liked the moon. He smiled at the thought, the veins pulsing as they tightened their grip on his legs, his thighs, his cock, thousands of them now like thin threads of electricity pushing and probing through his hair, pouring out of the black rock, engulfing Jack, absorbing him. Suddenly the veins were wrapping his body, mummifying him, swarming and slithering, engulfing Jack's shoulders, his neck, his head.

A low growl, seductive, echoed in the chamber. Jack licked his lips. He tasted mint. His hands tingled. Jack's head was almost fully covered in silver threads, and he could see in front of himself, behind himself. The universe floating around him. He was in the stars. He was home.

'Hey! Hey! Are you OK?'

'Wait,' shouted Jack. He felt hands pulling his head and shoulders from the soft rock. 'I'm not ready.' They were his hands.

Jack watched the silver veins retreating, screaming, into the granite.

Looking down, Jack could see a school of blue fish with bulging marble eyes and spiny scales gliding in and out of his line of sight.

The growls were louder, less seductive, angry and feral.

Jack stared at the fish, mesmerised, a memory from his childhood playing out before him like a hologram inches from his eyes. Jack was a teenager, running into the Boeshane Sea with his brother, Gray, trying to catch blue anchoa. An almost impossible feat, but if you caught one when its eyes were open then you could see your future.

Had we caught one that day? Am I still a boy and this is my future?

Jack looked down. The fish were gone, and Gray, and their past too.

The growling became a word, '*Fall!*'

The word pulsed from the veins shooting like electricity from the granite again, attaching to Jack's head. A thunderous roar erupted from beneath him.

'*Come on, Jack. We've got no time left.*'

The roaring was getting louder and as it did the taste in Jack's mouth was intensifying, ginger and lemon and eucalyptus.

'*Fall!*'

Jack stood and took a step towards the precipice, staring down at the three rings of fire, all circling in unison, chasing each other, the end of one the beginning of the other.

'*You must fall together,*' howled the voice, animalistic, deep, and not human. Like Jack was hearing an electrical charge, a sound wave, a force of nature.

The veins throbbed brighter and pulled tighter around Jack, even as he stood on the edge.

'No!'

Jack tore himself from his cocoon and when he did the entire chamber began to crumble around him. Jack threw himself across the ledge as a massive rock crashed down from the wall behind him. Jack rolled from its path, but as soon as he did, the rock raised itself up on the ledge. Shifting its shape into a petrified version of Jack, it lunged at him.

Jack locked his fingers together into a double fist and swung at the monster's head. The rock crumbled in front of him, sending pieces of smouldering rock and ash into the abyss below.

Jack felt as if his skull was cracking. He stared at his hands, willing them to move again. He ripped the rest of the silver vines from his head, his chest, his arms, and his legs. The mountain screamed, the rock rumbled, a thunderous roar burst from the rings of fire, sending a flaming serpentine fissure up from below. The fissure shot along the lip, chasing Jack across the ledge. The chamber shook. Jack skidded, scrambling for a foothold. Hot bubbling lava began rising from the rings beneath him.

'*Fall!*'

'No!'

The keening shriek whistled angrily from every crevice. '*This is how it must be.*'

14

Jack's eyes flew open.

'Jesus, amigo,' said Renso, tossing a bloodied rock down into the dark abyss of the mountain. 'How the hell did you get all the way down here?'

Jack stared blankly at Renso. He felt as if he'd been in a bar brawl and he had not won. Every muscle ached, his head hurt and he smelled of sex. A heavy gold blanket was draped across his waist. He kicked it away and stared, stunned, at a beautiful dark-skinned young woman curled next to him.

Jack shook her. She was unconscious, a cut on her forehead bleeding onto Jack's tunic.

Confused, Jack looked up at Renso. 'Where am I?'

'You're on some kind of altar,' said Renso, helping Jack sit up. 'Like a grotto that's been carved into the inside of the mountain. There are three of them all round the perimeter down here. I think that's what we were seeing from the Hornet jutting out from the inside the mountain's basin.'

'The what?'

'My plane, which, by the way, is nothing but melted rubber and tinder now. You owe me so badly, amigo.'

Jack wobbled to his knees. He felt Renso shaking him.

Panic and bewilderment crashed Jack's psyche. Renso wasn't touching him.

The ground was shaking.

He was shaking.

'Easy does it, my friend.' With two good hands, Renso grabbed Jack's arm. 'It's a long way down.'

'When am I?'

'What?' asked Renso, not understanding Jack's question.

'Time?' stuttered Jack. 'When is this?'

'Well after midnight of the day we went flying, if that's what you mean. I've been searching for you for hours.' Renso handed Jack a canteen. Jack gulped and gulped until water was dripping down his chin.

'My chute caught in the trees so I was out for a while too. But, Jesus, how on earth did you get down here?'

Renso peered inside the grotto. The walls were covered in rows of colourful glyphs and drawings. Renso waved his flashlight over one of them. It was a detailed drawing of a man riding across the stars on the back of what Renso thought looked like a mountain lion, a puma to be precise. Renso tilted the light up to a series of interlocking pointed circles carved across the grotto's arch.

'What is this place?'

'Renso? Is that you?' Jack grinned, as he finally grasped who was with him. 'Renso, I'm so glad to see you. I thought you went down with your plane.' Jack lifted his hand, caressing his friend's rough beard.

'I'm happy to see you too, Jack, and I did go down with my plane, only not all the way to the ground, thank God.' Jack handed him back the canteen. 'But we need to move, Jack. We've not got much time.'

'Time for what?' Jack stood up, instantly feeling dazed, confused and nauseated again. What the hell was he wearing? He held up the sleeves of an embroidered tunic, the wool itching his skin. His legs were covered in scratches, long sharp claw-like scratches, blood was dripping from a cut on his arm, and all the way from his ankles to his groin his skin was covered in thin red lines, like rope burns.

Renso helped Jack to his feet, guiding him along a ledge towards the shortest section of the rock that he had climbed down.

Jack looked up. They were about ten metres inside the mountain.

Without warning, a thunderous rumbling shook the entire basin. Jack pitched forward. Renso grabbed him and pinned him against the wall until the tremor settled.

'This volcano is about to blow again, Jack. I don't know how you got down here or what you were doing with that... that animal over there, that's none of my business,' Renso pointed back to the grotto at what was curled beneath the blanket with Jack.

'We've got to get out of here. Now!'

Suddenly a geyser of black steam exploded up through the mountain, firing chunks of flaming rock out through the top, pelting Jack and Renso as they shuffled towards their way up. Renso half-carried, half-dragged Jack to where he'd left his rope. The air was thick with tar and sulphur.

'Renso, we should dance and then we should have a drink and then... who knows.' Jack chuckled, grabbing and shaking his friend's hand.

'My friend, I don't know much about what happened during these last few hours, but one thing I do know. You, Jack Harkness, are stoned.'

'I thought you died, Renso,' exclaimed Jack. 'I'm so glad you didn't.'

'No thanks to you,' said Renso, wrapping his rope round Jack's waist and tying it off in two thick knots. 'You were a man possessed this morning. Eyes bleeding, weird sounds coming from your mouth and then you attacked me. You leapt over into the cockpit and you tried to snap my wrist, ended up tearing the hell out of my skin.' Renso held up his wrist, showing Jack three raw patches where his skin had been scratched away. 'Then you knocked me out.' Renso tested that the rope around Jack's waist was secure. 'Next thing I know, you're flying through the sky like a bloody big bird and my Hornet is about to meet the mountain.'

Jack grabbed Renso's shoulders, pulled him forward and tried to kiss him.

Renso slapped him upside the head. 'Jack, no time. I'm going up to the top and then I'll pull you out.'

'I can climb. I'm a seasoned climber. I once raced Hilary to a summit... now where was that? Wasn't Everest, I know that.'

'You're in no condition to climb without my help. Stay here.' Renso pushed Jack against the wall.

'Just for a few more minutes. OK? I'll get you out of here soon.'

'Okee dokee, my fine fine friend,' Jack giggled.

Winding the extra rope over his shoulder, Renso began to climb the rock.

In the grotto, Gaia stirred.

Jack watched, mesmerised, as the beautiful young Indian woman shook off the blanket, stretched her naked body and began walking along the ledge towards him. Her movements were graceful, her smile inviting. Jack could taste ginger. He could smell her pleasure. She lifted her arms enticing Jack into an embrace. In the thin beam of moonlight, her eyes shone like cobalt. Jack could feel his loins ache for her. He took another step.

'Jack, stop! Snap out of it, Jack!'

Jack looked up. Renso was standing at the precipice, paying out the rope. Behind him, Jack heard a low feral growl. Without looking back, he tugged on the rope.

Jack was yanked off the ledge. For a second, he was swinging loosely over the precipice.

'Jack,' yelled Renso. 'A little help would be good.'

Grabbing the rope, Jack used the momentum to climb.

Then he looked back and saw the Indian woman, her arms outstretched, her dark eyes pleading with him to return. Jack hesitated. The rope released a little. Jack slipped back towards the ledge.

In that instant, Gaia whipped her sword from behind her back and swung it at Jack's neck.

'You must not leave!'

15

Renso had found enough crevices in the rock face to move with speed and efficiency, which was good, because the air inside the mountain was heavy with ash, and the stink of sulphur made his eyes water.

When he was almost at the top, Renso looked back down. Jesus, no.

Jack had moved. Behind him, the creature was slinking along the ledge, and Jack was walking to meet it, his hand outstretched. It was a mountain lion, a sleek black puma, animals that used to be everywhere in the Andes and were now extinct in this region. The beast had a pulpy cut above its eye where Resnos had thumped it, which was still bleeding into the surrounding rock.

Renso dug his foot into a crevice near the top and hauled himself up and out, rolling quickly away from the opening, unwinding the rope as fast as he could. The moon was full and the plateau was bathed in its soft white light. Scrambling to his feet, Renso ran to an outcropping of rocks, tied off his end of the rope, then sprinted back, wrapping two loops around his own waist.

Bracing himself above the basin, Renso slung the rope down and called to Jack. The puma was poised to leap. Renso knew that it would take Jack with it down into the volcano.

'Jack, stop! Snap out of it, Jack!'

He felt Jack's tug on the rope.

He saw the mountain lion pounce.

He hauled on the rope. For a second, Jack was swinging against the precipice, the puma snarling and snapping at his bare feet.

'Jack,' yelled Renso. 'A little help would be good.'

Thank God. Jack was climbing. Renso relaxed.

A sudden tug on the rope, and Renso knew that Jack had fallen back. He heard the roar of the puma.

Renso pulled his pistol, firing into the darkness.

'Jack! Are you OK?'

Jack was staring down at the creature lying on the ledge, her shoulder bleeding. 'You shot her. She was so beautiful.'

'You're hallucinating, Jack. You're stoned. What I shot was not a woman. It was a mountain lion. Now move before the damn thing gets up again and wants to eat you.'

Minutes later Renso pulled Jack out of the basin. 'We need to get back to civilization and fast.'

Jack stared back down at the body, a deep despair washing over him. If he was hallucinating, why did this all feel so real, and why did he feel that he should remain here with her?

After Jack's slow clumsy climb, Renso hauled him from the maw of the mountain. By this time, the ground was trembling so violently, the smoke and sulphur so strong, that even Renso was having a difficult time remaining on his feet as he pushed and cajoled an unsteady Jack towards the steep canyon pass.

About halfway down, Renso spotted a clearing and a deserted pueblo village. 'At least whoever lived here got out safely.'

A stone temple, shaped like a round pyramid, had been

built in the centre of the clearing. If the mountain was still standing when this eruption stopped, Renso decided, he'd come back. Might be Inca treasures still buried in this place.

Jack stopped outside the cairn. 'I think I was here.'

'How's that possible?'

Jack pressed his body against an irregular block of stone that was obstructing the entrance to the temple. It wouldn't budge. He began to laugh. 'Hey, a little help.'

'No time, Jack. We need to get off this mountain before she erupts.'

Jack kept pushing, the stone moving a few inches then sliding back.

Renso kept going until he realised Jack wasn't behind him. Renso was starting to get angry. He loved Jack. They'd known each other since the Great War. Jack had saved his life. Twice. And he was certainly the best shag he'd ever had, but right now, stoned or not, he was a real pain in the ass.

Renso got behind Jack and pushed. The block of stone shifted enough for their passage. On shaky legs, Jack stepped through the antechamber and into the main temple.

'I've definitely been here.' Jack could feel it, but he couldn't get the memory of it to form.

Following Jack inside, Renso was astonished to see that the chamber was furnished as if a queen had lived here not centuries ago, but today. The fire was still smouldering.

Another deep throaty rumble from inside the mountain shook the chamber, knocking both men off their feet. Jack fell into a stack of pillows in the corner. He didn't try to get up.

'I remember an old woman with white hair, and…' Jack's voice drifted off as he tried to find words to get back what he couldn't remember.

The ground rumbled again, this time freeing two large triangular stones loose from the roof, crashing them onto a wooden trunk, cracking its lid open, exposing an array of ceremonial knives. Renso picked one up, admiring the jade inlaid along its hilt. No point in leaving all of this to be raided by poachers before the villagers return, he thought. Plus some evidence might encourage investors to sponsor a return trip. He slipped two of the gem-encrusted knives under his belt.

Jack rubbed the heel of his hands against his bloodshot eyes. 'Man, I'm fried. I can't get my brain to focus on anything for more than a second.'

Renso stepped to the fire pit, kicking over some clay pots as he did. He lifted one, and shoved that into his pocket.

The mountain roared. The ground trembled. A fissure shot across the stone walls.

'Why are we here, Jack? This morning I survived a plane crash. I really would rather not be buried alive in the middle of the night. I need a shot of tequila and sleep. Make that a lot of tequila.'

'And I,' said Jack, getting up off the pillows with some difficulty, bowing slightly, holding the edges of his tunic, laughing. 'I want some trousers.'

After a few minutes of digging in the baskets and wooden trunks around the chamber, Jack found his coat in shreds under a mat next to the fire. He held up one of its sleeves.

'Looks like someone took a sword to your coat.'

'Thank God I've got more than one,' said Jack.

A deep rumble knocked both men to the ground, the smell of sulphur getting worse, smoke and ash drifting in through the opening in the roof.

Jack scavenged around his shredded clothes, finding none of them in one piece. His boots, on the other hand, were wearable. He sat down next to the hissing fire and pulled them on.

When he stood, even Renso couldn't contain his laughter.

'You look like you've escaped from a sanatorium.'

Jack looked down at his boots, at the deep scratches, like claw marks on his legs from the Indian woman and a strange feeling of déjà vu came over him, snagging part of his mind and focusing it. With an urgency that he couldn't explain to Renso, he knew he had to remember the feeling, remember what had happened today, if it had happened today. The mountain, the woman, the old woman, the sun in his eyes, the cave… Already the memory was peeling off, drifting away like ash.

He had to write down what he could remember. It was important. He didn't know why, but he could feel in his bones that it was.

As the mountain shook, Jack rifled through remains of his coat, feeling some sadness at its destruction.

'What are you doing?'

'I need to find something to write on before I lose what happened completely. This mountain is doing weird things to my brain.'

'Maybe not just the mountain,' said Renso, lifting a bowl layered with cacao leaves.

'I know that's part of it, but I feel different, like I'm watching myself think.'

'Here,' said Renso, pulling Jack's notebook from his breast pocket, handing it to Jack. 'Use this.'

'How did you get my notebook?'

'I found it when I was looking for you – after the Hornet crashed.'

Jack opened to a blank page, scribbled across the pages, not sure what he was writing but feeling an intense need to put his thoughts on the page, to capture all the weirdness that was flitting across his mind. Jack made notes about the two women, about this chamber, the crashing of the Hornet and the strange seduction inside the mountain. He wrote while all around him was crumbling because at that moment, in that place, Jack believed he had lost all sense of what was real and what was not.

16

An earth-shaking crack shook shards of rock from the stepped roof of the temple, pelting both men. Renso grabbed the notebook from Jack's hands, shoved it into his shirt pocket and, yanking Jack's arm, dragged him out of the temple.

Above the terraced fields, the two men watched as the top blew off the mountain in an explosion of noxious gas, smoke and flaming rock.

'Jesus, did you see that?' asked Renso, pushing Jack ahead of him out into the clearing.

'I wonder what happened to all the other women who were here earlier?' Jack asked, while they were zigzagging across the clearing, their hands covering their heads as the mountain spewed pieces of itself at them.

A tree whipped from the ground near them, its massive roots tearing from the ground in front of Renso, catching his feet and sending him splaying across the dirt. As Jack scrambled to help Renso, they watched in awe as the ground beneath the temple swelled up as if air was being pumped underneath it. A mound of earth lifted the structure higher and higher. The ground roared, then the mound ruptured, swallowing the entire stone structure into the earth.

'Jesus,' said Jack, pulling Renso to his feet as they made for the canyon pass at the other side of the clearing, their only way to reach the bottom of the mountain.

Renso could hear Jack laughing a few steps behind him. 'What's so bloody funny?'

'That.' Jack pointed to the smoking basin where the temple had been. A fissure as wide as a trench was pushing out from the swallowed temple and reaching along the ground towards them. Breathless, Jack watched the fissure circle the pueblo village shaking it to its foundations, the adobe huts, the nearby olive trees, the fire pits folding into the ground. And then it shot directly towards Jack and Renso.

'That... that fissure is chasing us,' said Jack.

'Jack, you are certifiable,' said Renso, breathless and sceptical.

Leaping over trees being torn from their moorings, ducking from rock projectiles flying off the temple, the two men charged across the clearing to the jungle. All around them what was left of the village was filling quickly with the smoke and fumes from the volcano that was oozing lava.

'I think the mountain is trying to stop us,' shouted Jack, knocking Renso out of the way of a falling tree.

Gagging from the smell and the smoke, the widening maw chasing closer and closer, Renso yelled back at Jack, 'I think it may succeed.'

Every hut and tree the fissure snaked beneath was sucked into it, chewed up, and then dragged along, crushed and crumbled in its wake. Jack's lungs were aching, his bare legs tattooed with cuts and burns from the flying ash and hot coals spewing from the mountain. He knew that they had to get to the canyon through the jungle but he was afraid that it was going to be impossible to navigate in the fading moonlight.

With no idea where they were heading, side by side Jack and Renso crashed into the thick jungle, ducking, dodging, weaving through the thick foliage as it slapped and slugged and assaulted them.

Jack paused to get his bearings. Wiping blood from a cut above his eye, the fault line crashed into the jungle behind them, its progress marked in the crushed and collapsing trees as if an invisible monster was stepping on them. Renso stopped and stood at Jack's side, the fissure charging closer and closer.

Jack smiled at Renso, grabbing his face and kissing him hard on the lips. 'It's been a pleasure in so many ways, amigo. Now run. I know this sounds crazy, and I know I'm stoned out of my mind, but I think the mountain only wants me.'

'But… I'm not going to leave you to die. Not when I just found you again.'

'Trust me. I'm not going to die. Now run. Run!

Renso looked into Jack's blue eyes and saw something that made him realise he'd never really known this man. But even back in the trenches, he'd been able to trust Jack's word. Renso turned and he ran, knowing in his heart it was the last time he would ever see Jack Harkness.

Jack watched until Renso was out of his sight, then he took one, two, three steps towards the oncoming rift. With only inches before the gaping chasm touched Jack's boots, the ground stopped shaking, the cleft in the jungle began to close, the ground healing itself, leaving a path of destruction that looked like nothing more than a heavy wind had been trailing behind them.

Puzzled, Jack followed the line of destruction back to the village. He looked up at the top of the mountain, calm now, no longer erupting, a thin sliver of the sun rising behind it, capping its peak, washing it in the pale light of dawn.

Jack's headache was no longer raging. He sat down on a pile of loose mud bricks that had once been someone's hut. He stared at his tunic, at his scuffed boots, at his legs that were already healing. He glanced at the shell of a pueblo village, at the terraced fields behind it that had been churned into mulch, and he started to laugh. He ran his fingers through his hair and he howled.

'Where the hell am I?'

17

Langley, Virginia, present day

'Hold my calls,' Rex Matheson yelled into his intercom. 'And get rid of my next interviews.'

He glared at Darren. 'How did this mission become such a goddamn cluster fuck?'

The computer screen in front of them was displaying a satellite image of the piazza at Hacienda del Castenado an hour earlier.

'Everything was going according to plan until—'

Darren used the track pad and zoomed the video image in on the belfry and Isela taking her shot. Darren forwarded the image and they watched the minibus careening off the canyon wall, flipping over, a body flying through its windshield, then the van skidding to a halt at the mouth of the canyon.

'As far as I can figure, the girl must have been in on it with Castenado, but I think Carlisle dismissed her as a threat because of her age. We had eyes on everyone else in the piazza. Just not her in the belfry.'

'What happened to Agent Carlisle? He was driving the minibus, right?'

'He was, but he never gets out. I think we have to assume

the worst, sir.'

'Shit,' Rex rubbed his hand over his shaved head. 'So what happened to our mark, to Donoso?'

Darren used the remote to forward the satellite. 'We don't know yet, but it gets worse, sir.'

'How could it get any damn worse?' yelled Rex, pacing in front of the screen.

'Watch.'

Part Two

'The mind is its own place, and in itself can make a heav'n of hell, a hell of heav'n.'
John Milton, *Paradise Lost*

Gwen

18

Gwen Cooper spotted the madwoman waving her hands in the air shouting, 'Distaw! Distaw!' in the tea and coffee aisle. Glancing at the woman, Gwen immediately dismissed her as a 'nutter' and returned to her struggles, getting Anwen to sit in the front of the shopping trolley. The madwoman eventually wandered over to the breads and cakes, her shouts of 'Quiet! Quiet!' echoing in the warehouse-sized supermarket.

'No! No! Uppie,' Anwen demanded, grabbing a handful of Gwen's hair when she leaned forward to hook the safety strap round her daughter's tiny waist.

'Not this time,' said Gwen, untangling her contrary toddler's sticky hands from her hair. 'We've got a lot of shopping to do.' Gwen manoeuvred her trolley towards the fruit and vegetables.

Anwen was not giving up this battle quite so easily. She began to scream, arching her back, stiffening her body and at the same time slamming her arms and feet against the side of the trolley.

Gwen pressed her hands on her daughter's scissoring legs in a pathetic attempt to squelch the tide of the coming tantrum. It never ceased to amaze Gwen how quickly this beautiful baby girl could morph into a monster child.

'Please, not now, Anwen,' Gwen pleaded. 'We've got to get back home before Daddy does or I'll be in big trouble. Again.'

Anwen continued to thrash and scream, calling attention to the two of them from the queue at the meat counter. In the middle of the afternoon, Swansea's shoppers were not sympathetic to the squalls of a spoiled toddler. They snarled and tutted. Gwen swore under her breath.

'Bugger off,' parroted Anwen.

Gwen gawked at her daughter. 'No. Bad word, Anwen.'

Great, now she's learning to swear, thought Gwen. One more thing to add to her list of bad mummy traits. When did she start such a list? Gwen couldn't remember and because she couldn't remember she was annoyed with herself for even holding such a sentiment. She was a good mum. She was home all day with Anwen. She was getting more quality time with her daughter than any of her working-outside-the-home friends with their suits and their shiny, styled flat-ironed hair. Gwen couldn't recall if she'd even showered today.

Get a grip, girl.

Gwen guided the trolley towards the cereal aisle. 'How about some puffs?'

'Puffs!' squealed Anwen, the tantrum stopped in its tracks.

Gwen laughed. Bribery as a child-rearing strategy. It worked every time.

'Maybe you'll only need a couple of extra hours of therapy,' said Gwen, kissing the top of her daughter's head. She took out her phone and touched the photo icon, passing it to Anwen, who tapped the screen knowingly, flipping through the family photos.

Turning into the cereal aisle, Gwen wondered if the fact that Anwen could already use a touch pad successfully was another sign of her flawed parenting. What next? She'd be on the internet, sexting. Seriously, Gwen, get a grip. And then she spotted the madwoman again. This time pacing directly in front of her.

The woman was halfway down the breakfast aisle, tearing open boxes of cereal, holding them up to her ears, shaking them aggressively, and then dumping them onto the ground at her feet. Surrounded by piles of cereal, she looked like she was building a nest.

Definitely need a clean-up in aisle six, thought Gwen, pushing Anwen towards the mess. Surprised, Gwen noted that the woman did not look homeless or destitute in any way. She was dressed in dark jeans, a white blouse and a navy suit jacket. Her purse hooked over her shoulder, a designer brand, was covered in crumbs of Weetabix. The woman was muttering to herself and every few seconds she'd stomp her feet and yell 'Stop it!' to some imaginary person behind her. Somewhere along the way, the woman had lost her shoes.

Gwen wheeled her trolley closer and noted that the woman was not much older than she was, in her early forties perhaps, and she felt a pang of guilt for earlier dismissing the woman as some elderly nutter.

The woman spotted Gwen. 'Can you hear it?' she asked. Her lips were pale and her mascara was smudged. She'd been rubbing her eyes – a lot. Her neck was covered in red blotches and she'd lost one of her hoop earrings.

'You all right, luv?' asked Gwen.

'Do I look like I'm all right? I can't get a minute's peace today!' the woman yelled, tearing the top off another box, shoving her hand inside and pulling out a sleeve of cereal. 'I can hear something moving inside these boxes. The manager needs to know about it. Someone should tell him.' The woman's voice cracked and she began to sob hysterically.

Gwen picked up a box and held it to her ear, feigning interest and hoping it might calm the woman. The woman stared expectantly at Gwen, who smiled reassuringly. White specs of saliva were gathering at the corner of the woman's lips. Gwen held the cereal box up to her other ear to reinforce her concern in the woman's plight, while gently sliding her phone from Anwen's hands.

Anwen immediately began to howl in protest.

Startled, the woman dropped the cereal box she'd been examining and began bouncing on the souls of her bare feet. 'Make her stop! Make her stop! It's hurting my toes.'

Gwen tried to reach for the woman, to calm her, but she leapt away. Now Anwen was squirming in the seat, her cries getting louder. An elderly couple began down the aisle towards them, observed the scene and backed away.

'Cowards,' said Gwen, snatching a box of puffed wheat from the shelf, and thrusting it into Anwen's hands. Immediately, Anwen's howls dropped to a low fuss while she negotiated the top of the box, her tiny hands tearing into the cardboard.

When Gwen turned back, the woman had dropped to her knees on the tiled floor and was rocking back and forth, mumbling nonsense about her feet.

Gwen crouched in front of her. 'Is there someone I can call for you?'

'I just want it all to stop.' She cradled her head in her hands. 'Everything is too loud. Everything. I can hear myself blink. My feet ache. They hurt so much.'

Poor thing probably stopped taking her prescriptions, Gwen thought, putting her hand on the woman's shoulder and gently squeezing. The woman screamed and crab-walked frantically away from Gwen's touch.

'Don't yell at me!'

'I'm sorry... I'm sorry,' said Gwen, raising her hands in the air. The woman backed herself against the corner of the shelves at the end of the aisle, tucked her head between her knees and tugged her jacket up over her head.

'Listen, I'm calling someone for you,' said Gwen, cereal crunching under her feet. 'I'll wait here with you until they come. OK?'

The woman let out a long sad moan. Gwen took the sound for a yes and put her phone to her ear, quickly calling 999. While she patiently explained the situation, Anwen steadily covered herself in a rain of cereal.

Meanwhile the woman was thumping her feet against the shelves behind her, but she was no longer shouting or even moaning, she was humming, not a tune as much as a chord of peculiar-sounding notes that slowly became a low chant in Welsh of 'Distaw! Distaw!'

'Thanks,' Gwen said and slipped her mobile into her pocket. She knelt in front of the woman. 'It'll be ok, luv, someone's coming to help you. I'm sure they'll make the noises stop.'

19

The shop manager and a security guard charged down the cereal aisle, taking in the piles of crushed grains, the empty boxes scattered on the floor, a toddler in a trolley eating from a ripped-open box like some kind of wild animal, and two women crouched on the floor, one of them hidden under a jacket, singing and rocking on the balls of her feet.

'Oi! What are you doing?' the manager yelled, pointing angrily at Anwen. Blissfully unaware of her surroundings, she dug into her puffed oats. 'Christ, you'll have to pay for this mess you know. This isn't a... a play school,' he blustered, nodding to the security guard, who pushed Gwen's trolley off to the side, blocking her passage back down the aisle to the front of the shop.

At both ends of the aisle, small crowd of shoppers were gathering, some taking pictures of the bizarre scene with their mobiles.

Gwen tried to squelch the rage she could feel rising in her chest as she stood and faced the manager. She clenched and unclenched her fists, banging them against her legs, taking deep breaths and hearing Rhys's voice in her head before he left for work that morning.

'Please don't pick any more fights, Gwen. We already

can't go to Boots or to the butcher's and you're getting a bit of a rep at the Cwm Deri bakery, and it's not for your taste in muffins. Try to stay calm. Please. Keep Mrs Angry in check.'

Gwen forced Rhys out of her head. 'Mrs Angry'. Who the hell did he think he was talking to? Anwen? I'm in control. I'm always in control. She could feel her chest tightening and she could hear the manager speaking into his mobile and for a brief moment she thought she could see his words, pink and opaque, floating across her field of vision then exploding into a test card of white noise.

Really, Gwen, get a grip.

She started to count to ten. Rhys was right. This was the closest supermarket to home. Gwen was aware that her temper had been riding close to the surface for a few weeks now. Since the terrible final days with Jack, she'd been seeing red a lot, but, shit, this poor woman was so obviously ill and that big tool of a bloke had just wheeled Anwen – her daughter, and at the rate she and Rhys were drifting apart it may be her only daughter, ever – without her permission, and here she was only trying to help, trying to be a good citizen, a helpful neighbour. No one appreciated her efforts at anything any more. This woman needed her help. She did. And when was the last time anyone had needed her help for something important? Hell, when was the last time she'd done anything meaningful other than play with wooden blocks and watch bloody CBeebies all bloody day.

'The police are on their way.' The manager pushed passed Gwen and reached for the cowering woman's arm.

And that was all it took. Gwen grabbed his wrist and twisted his arm up behind him, flipping him to his knees and banging his head against the shelves. 'I know they're on the way. I frickin' called them!' Gwen was swimming in red. 'And this mess isn't mine, you bloody idiot. It's hers.'

Gwen's sudden violent reaction, stunned the security

guard who froze in place for a beat, then came to his senses enough to wrestle his boss from Gwen's grip, pushing Gwen closer to the woman, who was rocking and mumbling more aggressively on the floor.

The guard had completed his training only two days before, and he had learned that you do not touch a customer unless you absolutely have to. Did this count as one of those times? He stared at Gwen. This woman looked really pissed off. He looked to his manager for some guidance, but his boss had backed up against the shelves, trying to regain some of his dignity, and holding his mobile in front of him like a weapon.

'I'm filming you,' he yelled at Gwen, 'so... so you'd better back away.'

Gwen ripped the phone from his hands and dropkicked it into the dairy section. Then she pivoted and faced the guard, who instinctively raised his hands in surrender, taking two steps back.

Behind the guard, Gwen could see customers' arms stretched in the air and mobiles flashing pictures. Beyond the crowd outside in the parking lot she could see the lights of an ambulance and a panda car, but worst of all she could see a look of sheer terror on Anwen's face. God, what am I doing? Gwen inhaled and exhaled and the red at the edges of her vision began to fade, the crunch of the cereal at her feet softened, the lights above her seemed to flicker and dim.

Holding her hand out to the manager, she said, 'I am so, so sorry. I... I felt... I thought you were going to hurt her. This woman needs help.'

The manager slapped Gwen's hand away.

'And so do you, missus.'

Anwen started to cry again.

'Sorry. I'm so sorry. I don't know what came over me,' Gwen said, lowering her voice and her hand. 'I was just protecting the woman. She's obviously having some kind of seizure and you just didn't seem to care.'

Gwen could feel the anger churning in her stomach. She felt sick.

Ennobled by the sight of the police entering the shop, the manager puffed out his chest and poked Gwen's shoulder. 'I want you arrested.'

'Mummee!' screamed Anwen. 'Uppie!' Then Anwen threw the box of puffs at the guard's head, who turned and took a step towards her.

'Don't you bloody dare,' shouted Gwen, her blood boiling again. She slammed her chest into the guard, who fell against the trolley, causing Anwen to scream even more.

'I want you out of my shop this minute,' hissed the manager, pushing the guard towards the entrance. 'Go get the police!'

'Fine... that's fine,' said Gwen, catching her breath and unclipping Anwen from the trolley. 'Please, let's at least take care of this woman first. She really is in bad shape.'

The security guard turned and glared at Gwen while negotiating his way through the crowd of shoppers to the front doors.

While keeping an eye on Gwen standing behind him with Anwen in her arms, the manager crouched a safe distance in front of the madwoman, who was now howling in anguish and trembling violently, her head wrapped and hidden under her jacket.

'I think she's having some kind of epileptic fit,' said the manager.

'No shit, Sherlock,' snapped Gwen.

'Listen, you... bitch,' said the manager, finally losing it. He stood up, pointing at Gwen. 'You're a bloody menace and for all I know you did something to this woman and that's why she's in such a state.'

A ball of white, like the after-burn of a camera flash, burst in front of Gwen's eyes. She was about to charge the manager again, but Anwen squirmed in her arms. Gwen blinked hard and the anger settled back in her chest.

The madwoman's howls had shifted to screams of terror, jolting the manager and Gwen from their face-off.

'Is that blood?' asked the manager, noticing a small puddle forming under the madwoman.

Two paramedics wheeled a gurney piled with bags of equipment down the cereal aisle, forcing the manager and Gwen to step aside. The manager took the opportunity to get clear of this insane mother. He marched down the aisle to greet the two constables who'd arrived with the ambulance.

'Don't you dare move!' he yelled back at Gwen. 'You're not leaving here until I say so.'

'Piss off,' muttered Gwen, sliding Anwen onto her hip, watching with concern as the paramedics tried to get a blood pressure cuff on the madwoman who was now prostrate on the floor, breathing heavily, her body stiff as a board, blood pooling under her head, which along with her hands was still wrapped in her jacket.

'Did she ingest anything?' the female medic asked Gwen while her partner tried to untangle the jacket from the woman's head. She slapped away his hands, struggling against his ministrations.

'I don't know who she is,' said Gwen, tightening her hold on Anwen, aware of the manager waving his arms while one of the constables stared at her and the other unclipped his radio from his lapel, requesting back-up. This day was not going to end well.

'She was already really agitated when I spotted her,' Gwen told the medic. 'I think she came into the shop that way.'

The medic was cutting the jacket from around the

woman's head, her long hair matted to the fabric with her own blood.

Gwen shivered, her anger becoming a dull ache in her limbs, the nausea dissipating. Oh God, if they could track the madwoman's movements through the store then they could track hers and she did not need to give Rhys one more reason to be disappointed in her ability to lead a normal life. She was already on thin ice in that area. No, make that cracking ice.

Finally, the medics had the madwoman restrained enough to peel the jacket off her. Her hair was plastered to her scalp. Sweat soaked the woman's face. And blood. Lots of it. The woman squinted, confusion and pain masking her face. She held something up to the medic.

'It's all quiet now,' she said.

The medic fell back on his heels, frantically fumbling in his kit bag for an ice pack.

'Call it in,' he screamed to his partner, who couldn't stop staring at the side of the woman's head, at the pink pulpy flesh above her neck and the bloody ear gripped in her soaked fist.

The medic looked up to tell Gwen she'd better give the police her statement, but Gwen and Anwen were gone.

20

Cradling a mug of hot cocoa in her hands, Gwen stared out of the nursery window at the full moon. Behind her, Anwen was asleep, finally, and Rhys, finally, had headed to the local, for 'some sanity', he'd yelled.

Gwen had edited her role in the events of the day considerably, saying only what supported the brief mention of 'The Madwoman in the Supermarket' on the local news. Rhys claimed he was sick of her self-deprecating taunts about her domestic capabilities – had she really told him she thought she was a bad wife? Her complaints were exhausting him, he claimed. He refused to be dragged into another fight with her over why she was so unhappy, why she felt so useless and why she'd had this terrible taste in her mouth ever since she'd come home from the shops. She had told him it tasted like hopelessness, which, he hollered, was as ridiculous as she was becoming. Slamming the kitchen door, he stomped off down the road.

Gwen closed her eyes, trying desperately to let the silence calm her. How did she get to this place? To this point in her life where she had no idea who she was or what she was meant to do next? For a while, she had *been* someone – a member of a team, a formidable force, protecting the world from so many of the terrible things she hoped her daughter would never have to witness, and, oh she loved her daughter more than life itself. Why then was she so miserable, why was she so angry all the time and so, so terribly sad?

She sipped her cocoa, wiping the tears from her face. Hopelessness, that's what it tasted like.

Maybe she just needed some company. Gwen watched the thin clouds cut across the face of the moon.

'"The tide is full,"' she whispered. '"The moon lies fair upon the straits"... and I'm going right off my rocker,' she said aloud to herself, 'reciting a bloody poem I memorised at school.'

Behind her, Anwen rolled onto her side, kicking off her blankets, snuffling the way toddlers do, until she slipped back into sleep again. Gwen knew what her mum thought was wrong – the baby blues, post-partum depression. But Gwen knew that wasn't it.

PTD, more like. Post-Torchwood Depression.

Maybe she should talk to someone about what was happening to her? After today's outburst in the supermarket, she was sure that she needed some professional help, needed to find someone she could trust to help her make sense of her mixed-up feelings, to help her figure out the next steps in her life.

She set her mug on the wide sill of the bay window and curled her legs under her.

Where are you, Jack? I really need you. Something terrible is happening to me.

21

Gwen wasn't sure how long she sat at the window, watching the rising moon, but it was long enough for her self-pity to begin to piss her off too. She needed to take control of the situation. She stood up, knocking her mug to the floor, a decision made.

She tiptoed out of Anwen's room and into her bedroom, lifting the baby monitor from Rhys's bedside table and turning the volume to high. Anwen's breathing was steady and clear. Downstairs, she grabbed her phone from the table in the hallway where she'd set it on top of today's post, and a torch from under the sink. Grabbing her coat from behind the kitchen door, she dropped her phone into her pocket, keeping the baby monitor in her hand. When she got to the front door, she held the monitor to her ear to be sure she could still hear Anwen. She could.

Gwen hurried along the street, putting the monitor to her ear every few steps just to be sure. At the end of the road, she took a right turn, heading for a row of lock-ups and opening one of the garage doors. Satisfied that Anwen was still asleep and that she could still hear her, Gwen took a set of car keys from her pocket and clicked the fob. Directly in front of her in the darkness, something beeped and flashed twice. Gwen lifted up the bottom of a camouflage tarp and popped up the rear doors of a large black vehicle.

Leaving the rear doors open, the tarp draped over them, Gwen climbed inside the burned-out shell of the only surviving Torchwood vehicle. The back of the SUV was empty. The seats destroyed long ago, the smell of charred rubber, gunpowder and pizza of all things lingering inside. For a brief moment, Gwen was sitting in the back as the SUV sped through the streets of Cardiff, Jack driving, laughing, his hand resting lightly on Ianto's knee. Ianto serious as ever. Tosh and Owen taunting him from the back seats.

Anwen's soft cries from the monitor brought her back to the SUV and the shell it really was. Gwen waited to be sure Anwen settled back to sleep. When she did, Gwen crawled to the front of the vehicle, pulling up a thick plastic liner, swinging it all the way to the rear doors.

She pressed the key fob in a series of three beeps, a pause, and then another two, watching as a compartment opened in the middle of the SUV's floor, a computer screen and keyboard emerging.

Gwen set the baby monitor next to her, its soft static comforting her. She powered up the system. On the roof of the SUV, an antennae the size of a knitting needle revealed itself from the folds of the cracked skylight.

She logged in to the system, smiling as the familiar Torchwood logo appeared on the screen. After they'd been so easily discovered by the CIA a few months ago, and assuming that they might still be being watched, Gwen had agreed with Rhys that they'd keep computers and the internet out of their home. Every week, Gwen scanned the house and their car for bugs. So far they'd been left alone. If Rhys discovered this set-up, Gwen was sure, given everything that she'd put him through, that this would be the proverbial last straw.

'So we'll keep this our little secret,' she said, setting the baby monitor off to the side.

Gwen googled 'supermarket madwoman' and found six versions already uploaded to YouTube. After she'd played three of them and watched herself attack the shop manager from a variety of angles, she was embarrassed, but, she had to admit, she also felt a bit chuffed that she could still defend herself, that she could still kick someone's arse.

No, Rhys was right, she thought. She really did need an anger management class. By no stretch of the imagination had she been defending herself or Anwen. But still, she couldn't stop herself from grinning as she replayed, rewound and replayed again, the moment when she shoved the manager into the breakfast cereals and the look of terror in his eyes.

Pausing the video, Gwen leaned back against what was left of the SUV's dashboard, her heart racing. She'd snuck out here intending to use Torchwood software to delete all record of the incident, but before she did she decided to play the last of the four versions of the incident. This one had recorded from the other side of the aisle so it had captured Gwen, Anwen clutched to her chest, ducking out the emergency exit to make her escape. The person recording had darted back to the woman and the paramedic after Gwen had left. The local news had not shown any of this and when Gwen finished watching it she could see why. As the medic slipped the jacket off the woman's head, she gasped at the violence the woman had inflicted on herself.

Strange. Gwen's curiosity trumped anything else she had been feeling. She opened another program on the computer and sent the same message she'd been sending for the past three days, since she'd felt her life caving in on her.

Gwen heard Anwen cough, paused, listened for a beat, then she opened a number of windows and scrolled through screens, until she had access to the local CCTV cameras outside the hospital in Swansea. When she recognised the medics unloading the gurney with the madwoman strapped to it, Gwen zoomed in on the image. They must have sedated her, Gwen thought. The woman was unnaturally still, her eyes wide open, and a bandaged taped to the right side of her face.

Gwen noted the time stamp on the recording, closed out all but one of her screens and in a few minutes had hacked into the patient admission records.

Before she could investigate further, she heard a car door slam through the monitor. Shit. Rhys was home. He'd kill her if he discovered she had hidden all of this equipment, never mind that she'd left Anwen.

'Come on, come on,' she said, scrolling through screens until she found the admission files for the day's patients.

From the baby monitor, she could hear Rhys's footsteps on the stairs, and, of course, Anwen decided at that moment to stir. Gwen listened as her whimpers began.

She found the database. Her fingers flew across the keyboard, her adrenalin spiking. God, she missed this rush.

Anwen burst into full-scale crying.

From the monitor, Gwen heard the bedroom door creak open. Anwen's crib rattled, her screams increasing. Gwen heard the footsteps on the floor. She heard Anwen's blankets rustle.

Gwen stopped typing, her hands frozen in mid-air. What if it wasn't Rhys?

22

'Where's your mum then, luv?'

Gwen exhaled, not knowing what she would have done if the voice in the monitor hadn't belonged to Rhys.

Three patients' records popped on the screen one after another, two women and one man. She clicked on the man and scanned the A & E admission notes. Drunk and disorderly, he'd cracked his head open outside a pub.

Anwen's cries settled back to whimpers. Gwen could hear Rhys picking her up from her crib. 'Is your mum asleep, pet?'

She heard the nursery door open and footsteps going down the hall.

Gwen clicked on the other two admission charts, scanned their notes too. 'What are the chances of that?' said Gwen. Frantically, she emailed the charts to her phone.

'Gwen Cooper!'

Gwen jumped. 'Shit.' The static on the baby monitor crackled loudly, the anger in Rhys's voice palpable. 'Get back here. How could you leave Anwen by her bloody self?'

Gwen grabbed the monitor and was about to answer that she was in contact every second, but then remembered it wasn't a radio, a realisation that reinforced how much she missed her old life. How much she missed Torchwood.

She listened to Rhys's footsteps as he bounded down the stairs. She could not have him come outside and find her here. He'd take away the only things she had left that made her feel needed. Although, really, what could he do? He could lock her up in the attic like some wayward wife. He could take away her daughter. He wouldn't dare. Gwen's anger knotted in her gut.

'Gwen! Where are you?'

She was about to shut off the computer, when the screen filled with static. What the hell? Staring at the static, she ran her fingertips across the tracking pad, but the static remained. She tried to shut down the computer. The static remained. And then as if she'd stepped inside the noise, Gwen could see nothing but grey noise and static around her.

Yet a part of her knew she was staring at a computer screen inside a shell of an SUV in Wales. It was as if she was watching herself watching herself.

She shivered.

Somewhere ahead of her, Gwen could hear a low hum. Wait. Not a hum, a growl.

Gwen tore her eyes away from the static on the screen. She felt sick. She could hear the growling getting louder. What was it? Leaving the static screaming on the screen, Gwen crawled to the side of the SUV and stared out at the darkness. The windows in the SUV had been broken out ages ago.

This time she heard the low growl behind her.

Inside the SUV.

She whipped round, ready to attack, and found herself facing the most beautiful animal she'd ever seen. Its skin was crushed velvet, its eyes like polished stones – so black they shimmered blue. The puma went down on its front paws, holding Gwen's gaze.

Gwen could see herself in the puma's eyes, then it was no longer her face but the computer screen displaying a faint outline of an image, a geometric design of some sort. She stretched her hand out towards the puma; the air around its head felt dry and hot. It opened its mouth wide and took Gwen's hand inside.

'Bloody hell, Gwen. Where are you?'

Gwen's eyes flew open. She was alone in the SUV. When was the last time I ate or slept, she wondered. She looked down at her hand. It was wet and sticky and there were tiny tears of blood on her knuckles.

Behind her an image throbbed against the static on the computer screen. She tried not to stare at it again. In a panic, she sent a screen shot to her phone.

The rock in Gwen's gut shifted, pressing down on her chest. Her lips felt cracked and dry. Licking them, Gwen tasted peaches. She hated peaches. Soft and slithery in her mouth. Rhys loved peaches. Gwen hated Rhys.

She slammed the computer closed, hid it underneath the compartment in the floor again, brought down the antennae, and crawled from the SUV. Pulling the camouflage tarp back over it, Gwen slammed the garage door and sprinted down the street.

23

The only person making any noise at Gwen and Rhys's breakfast table the next morning was Anwen, who was enjoying the chance to practice her latest farmyard noises. Her squeals of delight were bouncing off the walls as well as the stiff cold shoulders of her parents.

'I don't know what's got into you, Gwen,' said Rhys, spooning oatmeal into Anwen's mouth whenever she paused long enough from her babbling to take a breath. 'It's not like you to leave Anwen alone.'

He handed the spoon to Anwen, reminding her how to hold it, laughing as she plunged it into the oatmeal, scooping an upside-down spoonful to her mouth, leaving most of it on her bib.

'I'm sorry, Rhys. I'm really sorry,' said Gwen, buttering a slice of toast. Her eyes were red-rimmed and puffy. 'I just had to get out. I've been feeling so cooped up here lately.' She paused and offered the buttered toast to Rhys, who arched his eyebrows but accepted it. 'Friends?'

He tore the toast in half, handing the other half back to her. 'Friends. But don't ever bloody well do that again.'

'For what it's worth,' Gwen said, 'I had the monitor with me and I could hear her the whole time. If anything had happened, I would have been back here in a flash.'

'All gone!' exclaimed Anwen with her hands in the air.

'That's not the point,' said Rhys, taking the tray off the high chair and lifting Anwen out. 'You heard me come into the house, but I could've been anyone. Could've taken her before you even knew she was gone.'

'I know. I know. You're right,' Gwen said, taking Anwen from Rhys's arms and setting her on the floor next to a pile of colourful plastic blocks. She refilled her mug from the coffee pot.

Rhys was right. Of course, he was right. But did he have to keep reminding her? She had said she was sorry. Many times. She had apologised last night when she had come rushing inside, her head thumping. She'd lied about where she'd been, blurting that she'd taken a walk to clear a headache, and this morning she had apologised at least ten more times before they'd even come downstairs for breakfast.

How many times did it take for him to get it into his thick skull? Really. How many?

Gwen noticed her hands were shaking. Too much caffeine. She emptied her coffee mug and put it in the sink. The clang sounded loud, like the noise her dad's welding gun made when he was in his workshop. Her dad. She missed him so much. He'd never had a chance to spend much time with his only granddaughter.

Anwen had waddled her way across the floor to the pots and pans cupboard and was in the process of emptying it.

'From now on, if you feel like getting away again, you need to tell me,' said Rhys, handing Anwen a wooden spoon from the drawer next to the cooker. Anwen banged the spoon against the pots, squealing with delight at the racket.

'God knows I would've stayed home if you'd told me,' added Rhys, shouting above Anwen's squeals and the radio news. 'And if you need a break during the day from being home with Anwen, just say so. You know your mum will help when she gets back, and mine would be round here in a flash.'

Gwen whirled round. 'Oh, you'd like that, wouldn't you, Rhys Williams! You'd like it if my mum or your mum had to take over because I'm doing such a bad job as far as you're all concerned.'

'No!' said Rhys, pushing away from the table. 'That's not what I meant at all.'

'Oh, isn't it? And I suppose I'm too stupid now to know what you mean? Poor Gwen, all cooped up in her own little world and making everyone so unhappy!'

Anwen was suddenly quiet. Rhys was stunned at Gwen's outburst.

'Don't you two look at me like I'm some kind of mental patient.'

Anwen whimpered. Gwen stepped next to Rhys, jabbing her finger in his chest. 'It's all right for you off all day at work, being treated like an adult, having real conversations with people who can use the toilet and chew their own food.'

Rhys couldn't help it, he laughed. This was his Gwen, his family-loving, alien-killing, arse-kicking Gwen, and her behaviour these past few days was beyond absurd.

Gwen shoved him against the refrigerator. 'Don't you dare laugh at me! I'm sick of being stuck home here with her. I want my old life back. I want Torchwood back.'

At that moment, Anwen called out, 'Mummy sad.'

Gwen slapped her hand to her mouth and fled from the kitchen.

Anwen threw the spoon across the floor and burst into tears. 'Mummee! Want Mummee.'

Rhys was in shock at how quickly this conversation, and his wife if he were being honest, had deteriorated. This was worse even than last night's confrontation. Rhys lifted

Anwen into his arms.

'Want Mummee! Mummee!' She was flailing in his arms, her tiny fists punching his shoulder, her anger rising.

Rhys carried Anwen into the sitting room and set her down. He gathered up some of her toys and books and placed them next to her.

Anwen picked up a book and lobbed it. 'No book!' Then she slammed herself onto her back and went into full tantrum mode.

Rhys crouched next to her, reaching out and stroking her forehead, holding out her favourite bear towards her. 'I know. I know. You want Mummy. I'll go find her. I'll go get Mummy.'

'Mummeee!' she cried, hugging her bear.

'What is going on with the girls in this house?' Rhys blew Anwen a kiss as he backed out into the hallway, closed the door on his sobbing child.

He could hear Gwen's sobs coming from the downstairs toilet. Shoving open the bathroom door, Rhys stared in, horrified by what he saw.

Gwen was leaning in front of the basin, her head bowed, her hands gripping its edges. Drops of blood were splashed across the mirror and dripping into the basin.

'Jesus, Gwen, what've you done?'

Rhys stepped slowly into the bathroom, edging behind her. But before he could reach over, calm her, help her, anything, Gwen raised herself up on her toes, whipped her head back, and smashed Rhys in his nose.

He toppled to the ground, slamming his wrist on the edge of the toilet. Gwen crunched her boot into his other hand as she fled from the bathroom.

For a beat, Rhys couldn't focus. He slouched against the stone floor, the pain worse than anything he'd felt. She'd broken his bloody nose. He lifted his hand to touch it, and worked out that his nose probably wasn't broken but his wrist might well be. He yelped in pain, cradling his arm against his chest. He could hear Gwen pounding up the stairs and all he could think of was something had possessed her. Had to be. An alien. A ghost. Something. Because this woman was not his wife.

From the sitting room, Anwen's screams were growing fiercer by the minute.

Ignoring Gwen's blood splattered in the sink, Rhys yanked open the medicine cabinet with his left hand, tearing through half-empty cough syrups, boxes of plasters and handful of hair scrunchies until he found a roll of bandage. After wrapping his wrist as best as he could with one hand, he made to bolt from the toilet, only to step into a pool of Gwen's blood, crashing his head against the basin this time.

Dazed, he lay with his cheek on the cold porcelain for a beat, and when he could finally see straight, he pulled himself up and carefully stepped out into the hallway. Anwen's screams had died to a whimper.

At least she was safe.

Rhys followed Gwen's blood trail to the bottom of the stairs where he stopped and listened. Gwen was moving around in the room upstairs. A wardrobe door banged shut, drawers opened and slammed closed.

What the hell was she doing?

Rhys's pulse was rising, his breathing shallow, and his wrist throbbing. Above his head, he heard a table being knocked over. Then the bed creaked as Gwen pushed it across the wood floor. Panic squeezed his chest, adrenalin spiking his system.

In that instant, terror gripped Rhys. He understood exactly what Gwen was doing. He had to stop her.

24

Sergeant Andy Davidson carried a cup of milky tea and two chocolate biscuits into the main Swansea squad room and settled at his new desk. This was his favourite time of the work day, before too many of his shift had arrived to fill the room and he had a couple of minutes to himself to review the night-watch sergeant's notes before thinking about the day's assignments. He'd been shuttled around South Wales quite a bit over the last couple of years, a series of temporary attachments following his unexpected promotion. He had a nasty feeling that the top brass now saw him as more trouble than he was worth. An unauthorised trip to London and a confrontation with some nameless MI5 spook had, Andy reckoned, led to this latest posting away from Cardiff.

Sliding his cup and saucer in front of his monitor, Andy set his hat on his desk, mussing his short blond hair. He dunked his biscuit in his tea and scrolled through yesterday's reports. Two burglaries, a rash of shoplifting, a fight at the cinema, disturbance of the peace at Bracelet Bay, an assault at the university library, an arson in a local stable, and a supermarket confrontation that had resulted in the store being closed for the rest of the day.

CID had been called in to the supermarket incident

and the assault in the library. The detectives were still investigating the latter, but an arrest warrant had been issued an hour ago in the former. When Andy read the name on the warrant, his biscuit slipped from his fingers and dissolved into his tea.

'Damn,' he said, licking the melting chocolate from his fingers. Pushing his cup aside, he clicked on the full report. The more he read, the more he thought the assault on the manager didn't sound like his Gwen. And the other woman, the one who'd ripped her ear off, well, she was obviously a nut job. Maybe escaped from the Dellmore Institute, he thought. Still, he'd have to bring in Gwen. He'd do it himself, first thing after morning roll call. It was the least he could do for his friend.

When he finished reading the supermarket file, something 'pinged' in his head. His new girlfriend, Bonnie from Blackpool, was taking psychology classes at the local college and she was teaching Andy to pay attention to his instincts, to be open to his 'buried tiger.'

Grrr! Andy grinned at the thought of her. What would Bonnie have made of Gwen, he wondered.

The old Andy Davidson would have taken his hunch to his superiors, then settled back at his empty desk with his tea and biscuits. But this was the new Andy, and just because he'd turned down a transfer to bigger police districts to stay close to his mum didn't mean he wasn't ambitious, a trait Bonnie was fiercely encouraging. Andy was doing his best to please her in every way and if she liked his buried tiger, then he was going to keep it roaring.

Andy scrolled back to the notes he'd read on the assault at the university. Something odd about that one, too.

Gulping down his lukewarm tea, Andy snatched up the rest of his chocolate biscuits and headed out of the squad room.

25

Rhys took the narrow stairs two at a time, slipping once on the carpet tread, forgetting about his wrist and putting both hands down to steady himself. Ignoring the pain that shot up his right arm, he crawled up the last few stairs on all fours. At the upstairs landing, he paused, steadying his breathing, focusing on Gwen's whereabouts.

He couldn't hear her movements now. Where was she? He tucked himself into an alcove at the end of the hallway and listened. Had she found what she was looking for?

Something heavy thumped to the floor and he realised that Gwen was tearing through the chest of drawers in Mary's room. Why was she looking in there? Rhys stood up, his head aching, his wrist throbbing. He was puzzled – pleased, but puzzled. If Gwen was in Mary's room, then she wasn't looking for the key to her weapons store after all – she knew exactly where that was.

Or had she lost her memory as well as her mind?

Gwen let out a shriek from the bedroom and then came flying into the hallway, spotted Rhys standing stunned at the other end and charged him. Rhys darted out of the way, tripped and tumbled down the stairs, finally able to stop himself before crashing through the banister at the bottom. He couldn't let himself waste time thinking about what new parts of his body were broken. Scrambling to his feet, he scampered like a wild animal back up the stairs, hollering at Gwen to stop. This time when he got to the landing, he could hear Gwen tearing up their bedroom.

His heart stopped when she stood laughing at him in the bedroom doorway, the key to her gun locker dangling from her hand.

With all his strength, Rhys threw himself at his wife. They fell backwards into the bedroom, careening off the wardrobe, and, with Gwen pummelling him with her fists and spitting obscenities at him, they crashed to the floor. Rhys's head smashed against the wooden base of the bed and for a second everything went black. It was enough time for Gwen to free herself from his clutches and dart from the room.

Rhys pulled himself up, the pain of his injuries nothing compared to the terrible fear that gripped his insides. Gwen had the key and he could hear her thundering down the stairs.

Anwen was silent, having finally cried herself to sleep.

Please God, let Gwen come after me first, thought Rhys.

He crawled out to the landing. Phone. The stairs in front of him were rolling and he felt like he was going to vomit. He had to get help.

Because what if he couldn't stop Gwen? Or worse, what if he passed out before he could even try.

Rhys patted his pockets. Shit. No phone. He remembered it was sitting on the kitchen table. Swallowing back bile, he peered over the banister. Gwen had dragged the gun locker up from the basement. It was on the floor near the front door and she was starting to unlock it. He wasn't going to be able to call for help; he'd have to stop her on his own.

No choice, mate.

By the time Rhys was halfway down the stairs, Gwen had popped up the lid of the locker. She glanced at Rhys when he leapt the last few stairs, landing in front of her. She lifted out her gun, and Rhys thought he was a dead man.

Gwen pointed the gun at his chest, screaming, 'You're not leaving me here alone any more! I will not smell peaches any more.'

'OK, love, OK. You can do whatever you want. It's your decision, but let's make it without the gun,' said Rhys, taking two steps closer, reaching his arms out to her, pain shooting to his shoulder from his swelling wrist, his voice hollow in his head.

'Don't you come near me, your words have too many points,' Gwen hissed, stabbing the gun at Rhys. 'You're hurting me.'

'Fine. I'll stay right here.' He backed up slowly. 'But can you please put the gun away, Gwen. You need help. Can't you see? This isn't you talking.'

From behind him Rhys could hear the creak of a floorboard, the scrape of a chair shifting, and then the living room door swung open and Anwen toddled out into the hall.

'Mummy! Uppie.'

26

On his way down the cracked tile stairs, Andy passed some of his officers on their way up from the ground-floor lockers. He greeted them distractedly, still puzzling over what he'd read in yesterday's incident reports. Two floors down, he stopped outside the security door to the video surveillance unit. Andy's mate Tommy Livesy, who played rugby with him on the over-30 team, was on duty. Good – Tommy would keep Andy's request quiet until he figured out exactly what his discovery meant. Andy may have been listening to his inner tiger, but he didn't think anyone else would listen without some persuading.

Swiping his identification on the keypad, Andy shoved the door open. A bank of computers in a horseshoe faced him with two officers watching a hundred screens of CCTV feeds and a few private security cameras in financial buildings in Swansea.

His mate turned when the door opened. 'Andy, my man. What brings you to our lair?'

'Nothing important. A couple of questions from last night's watch.' Andy nodded at the other officer at the desk. Tommy got the message. 'Jan, a minute. I'll keep an eye.'

Jan grabbed her cigarettes and lighter, but when she

passed Andy she stopped and put her hand out. Andy rolled his eyes and handed over his last two chocolate biscuits. She smiled and left.

'So what's up?'

Andy pulled Jan's chair next to Tommy's. 'Have you got the CCTV from that supermarket disturbance yesterday?'

'Give me a second.'

While Andy waited, he watched the men, women and children, moving across the screens in front of him. It was mesmerising and he wondered how anyone could keep track, and then he decided that maybe it was best if they couldn't.

'Got it. I'll send it to the screen on the top left.'

He did and it took Andy a few seconds to adjust his attention to what he was looking at. The camera was on the shop's front door, sweeping across the aisles every minute or two, which meant that Andy could only see the events in the breakfast aisle at a distance. Plus, the shifting camera made it feel like he was looking at a video flipbook, the sweep of the camera across the store far from smooth.

Didn't matter. Only a few minutes in, Andy was watching Gwen Cooper assault the store manager.

Andy reached for his notebook, quickly finding the page with the file numbers and names for the other two local disturbances. Tommy took the notebook up, glancing at the page before he passed it back to Andy. 'Did you want to see the video for that one, too? Strange times there and all.'

'What do you mean?' asked Andy, sitting back down.

'DI Horn was in here first thing this morning asking for the video for that file,' answered Tommy. 'Thought maybe you were working the case too.'

'Let's have a look, then,' said Andy, turning back to the screens. 'And if anyone asks, I'm working both cases.'

'This video's in colour so it's not as grainy as the first one.'

Tommy cued up the video and Andy realised immediately that he was looking at a floor in an imposing-looking building. 'It's the main library at the university. They've had problems with students having sex in the stacks.'

'I'd've checked out a book once or twice,' laughed Andy, 'if I'd known that was going on.'

'They installed a state-of-the-art surveillance system last term.' Tommy fast-forwarded the video. 'Check out the curly-haired dude with the droopy pants.'

Andy and Tommy watched as a young male student and his giggling girlfriend turned into an aisle of floor-to-ceiling books where they became a snogging frenzy of clumsy clutches and slobbering kisses.

The camera was angled in such a way that the students were never quite in full view, the camera catching them only when they moved out of the canyon of books and into the camera's full field of vision. Their antics were clearly not the main event, though – Tommy sped up the camera, hitting play when the students were attempting to loosen each other's jeans.

At that moment, a middle-aged woman in a tan shirt dress with a wide belt sprinted across the screen and charged into the couple, taking them both down.

'Jesus,' said Andy, 'where did she come from?' He knew from his notes that the woman was the head librarian.

'Oh, that's nothing,' said Tommy. 'Keep watching.'

At first the coupling students were too stunned to react, but after the young man got his jeans fastened and scrambled up from the floor, he grabbed the librarian and tried to haul her off his girlfriend. The older woman reached above her head, grabbed a hefty tome from the shelf and, with all her weight behind the swing, she smacked the book across the young man's head, splitting his lip and sending a tooth flying.

'Ow!' said Andy, putting his hand to his own mouth. 'That had to hurt.'

The young man crumbled to the floor, obviously in considerable pain. For a few beats, none of the three were visible on the screen until the young woman, screaming hysterically, came back into view, slammed into the librarian, pinning her to the floor with her knees.

'What the hell is she doing?' asked Andy, leaning closer to the screen.

'According to DI Horn, the student pummelled the librarian's face to a pulp.'

Andy kept his eye on the screen, trying to track the girl's movements separately from the librarian's, but it was difficult because of the camera's angle and their heightened frenzy. A few seconds later, the noise had attracted three nearby students, who charged the women on the floor, pulling the girl off the librarian, holding her back until university security rushed into the stacks and imposed control.

Tommy stopped the tape. 'According to Horn, all three are in the emergency ward at St Helen's. The boyfriend's had surgery on his jaw and the young woman's in shock. Horn's trying to sort out what happened.'

'Too bad we don't have another angle,' said Andy. 'I don't suppose we've got any students with their mobiles on this.'

'Nah. Horn said even the students who pulled them apart didn't see the actual assault. Just the aftermath.'

Andy stared more closely at the paused tape, at the young woman's back as she sat astride the librarian, her arms frozen in the air above her head, her knees pressed against the librarian's shoulders. Andy was thinking about the similarities that had caught his attention in the first place about this case. He could hear Bonnie nudging him to think.

The woman in the shop had ripped off the lobe of her own ear while Gwen and the manager were having their wrestling match, and here was this librarian with serious facial wounds, the result of an equally bizarre attack.

'Can you rewind to right before the librarian comes into the frame?'

'I can,' said Tommy. On the screen, the entwined couple shift in and out of the frame, their energetic coupling no longer Andy's focus.

'Stop,' said Andy, pointing to the corner of the screen as the librarian came into view. 'Can you get any closer?'

Tommy zoomed in on the librarian's shoulder's and the side of her face.

'Jesus! What the hell?' said Tommy.

'That girl didn't hurt the librarian,' said Andy, staring at the blurry angle of the side of the librarian's face, and what looked like the librarian's eyeball resting on her cheek. 'I think the girl was trying to restrain the librarian. Stop her from mutilating any more of her own face.'

'Now that's seriously messed up.'

'Seriously,' said Andy.

27

Gwen blinked fast, shaking her head, but she kept her gun pointed at Rhys, ignoring her daughter teetering against the door jamb.

'I think I need to go,' Gwen said, the words coming out in a strange squeaky pitch. But instead of taking a step back, Gwen took two steps towards Rhys, making any shot she took at him sure to hit Anwen too.

Keeping his eye on Gwen, Rhys shifted over to the centre of the hallway, his arm a dead weight against his side, his fingers throbbing. If he could keep Gwen talking, maybe she'd come to her senses, but he still had to get Anwen out of the line of fire.

'What're you thinking you want to do here, Gwen, love?' he asked taking two steps back towards the living room door where Anwen was playing with the fringes on the end of the carpet runner.

'You need to give me time to think. I need time to think!' Gwen said, her voice heavy with rage. 'Let. Me. Think!' She banged the side of the gun off the side of her head. One, two, three times, as if she was trying to pound sense into it. Rhys gasped, horrified the gun might go off, but before he could move, Gwen turned it back on him.

Holding the gun steady, she aimed at his chest, but her gaze was locked on a point directly over his shoulder. Gwen's concentration was so fierce that Rhys was sure someone was standing behind him.

Gwen was now muttering under her breath as if she was talking to someone, having an angry conversation that wasn't going her way. Gesticulating wildly, she began to toss the gun back and forth from her left to her right hand as if someone was trying to grab it from her.

With his wife's focus distracted, Rhys decided this might be his only chance to move. But which way? Forward to try to disarm Gwen, risk her firing the gun and Anwen becoming collateral damage? Or backwards, remove Anwen from the situation, and take his chances with Gwen and the gun?

Gwen steadied the gun at Rhys's head. She released the safety. Rhys made his decision. He pivoted, reached down and shoved Anwen onto the living room floor, then reached back, slamming the door quickly, praying she'd be safer loose in the living room than in the hallway with her deranged mother.

Gwen screamed, 'No! No!'

The gun edged up a little and she fired, shattering the mirror behind Rhys. He threw himself to the floor. Gwen fired again. Rhys rolled against the door to the basement, cracking his shoulder against the hard wood. Still screaming, Gwen fired wide and missed again.

Stunned, Rhys understood what she was doing. Gwen was fighting with herself, her face twitching madly, her eyes narrowed one second and then wide and panicked the next, trying desperately to stop whatever was in her head telling her to shoot her husband.

Cowering in the corner, Rhys watched helplessly as the angry Gwen took aim at his head. The Gwen who loved him, who adored their daughter, was not winning this fight.

A horrified expression crossed Gwen's face. Her shoulders stiffened, her head tensed, and with blood trickling down her arm, she tightened both hands on the grip of the gun. Her stance wavered a fraction of an inch. Gwen's face reddened, her concentration bulging the veins on her neck. She fired.

The shot went high. Rhys scrambled further into the shadows, broken glass stabbing into his knees. At least if she keeps shooting at me, he thought, she can't hurt Anwen.

'Stop moving, you stupid, stupid man.' Gwen's voice was a low growl. 'You're only making this harder on yourself.'

Rhys clambered up and stepped out of the corner. 'Gwen, you've got to try to fight this… whatever this is that's telling you to hurt me. You need to think about all of the good times we've had together and all of the good times that we can have with Anwen.'

'Will you please shut up, Rhys,' Gwen sobbed, the gun shaking in her trembling hands. 'It's just all so sour. Nothing matters any more.'

Gwen lifted the gun, aiming directly at Rhys's chest. This time there was no chance she'd miss.

'I love you, Gwen Cooper.'

Gwen fired. Rhys jumped. Gwen's shoulder jerked forward and she collapsed at Rhys's feet. He lunged for Gwen's gun, prising it from her fingers and tossing it over her body to the tall figure in the military coat who loomed in the doorway.

Holstering his Webley, Jack Harkness rushed to Gwen's side.

'Why'd you wait so bloody long?' screamed Rhys, clambering into the living room to rescue Anwen. 'I spotted you through the window when I put Anwen in here.' Rhys pressed his frightened daughter to his chest. 'She could have killed me, you bastard.'

Jack smiled and shrugged, kneeling next to Gwen, who had hit her temple on the floor when she went down and was moaning, drifting in and out of consciousness. Checking her pulse, Jack sighed with relief. It was strong.

Rhys glared at him. If it hadn't been for Anwen, he'd have bloody well punched the sod.

'I had to be sure she was really going to shoot you, didn't I?' said Jack, grinning. 'I couldn't risk shooting Gwen for no good reason. I like her better than you, remember?'

'You're still a bastard, you know that,' hissed Rhys, keeping his attention on Anwen who had spotted her wounded mother lying on the hallway floor. 'But thank you.'

'Mummy sleeping?'

'Yes, Anwen, your mummy's sleeping,' shushed Jack, taking off his coat and placing it carefully under Gwen's head. 'We need to get her to the hospital. This is a nasty wound on her head and her shoulder's going to need a little work.'

'I think it'll have to be a prison ward,' said Andy's familiar voice from the front door. 'I can't believe I'm saying this, but I need to arrest Gwen.'

28

While Andy radioed for an ambulance, Rhys called Mary and told her what had happened to Gwen, giving as few details as possible.

While they waited, Jack sat at Gwen's side and Rhys paced the floor with Anwen drowsy on his shoulder.

'You could put Anwen in her cot,' said Jack. 'I'm not going anywhere. I'm sure Gwen's going to be OK.'

'I'm not leaving you alone with my wife! You might shoot her again.'

'Hey, don't forget it was you she was trying to kill, not me.'

'Gwen's been acting really strange for a few days now,' said Rhys. 'I don't know what's got into her.'

'It not just Gwen,' said Andy.

'What do you mean?' said Jack, already working through possible scenarios in his own mind for what might have driven Gwen to such violence. As the sirens grew louder, Jack saw yellow dots bounce in his peripheral vision.

Andy filled them in on what he'd learned at the station, why he had to arrest Gwen and the strange pattern he'd uncovered of other women in the area losing their marbles. 'And it's not just that they've gone a bit balmy,' added Andy.

'They also hurt themselves in pretty disgusting ways.'

The arrival of an ambulance and two panda cars interrupted him. 'I'll ride with you and Gwen to the hospital,' Andy said to Rhys, 'and then we'll see where to go from there. But it makes you wonder, doesn't it?'

'Wonder what?' asked Rhys.

'Well, if maybe there's something in the water that's making women, you know, bonkers.'

Jack hid a wince at Andy's expression. 'How many other women did you say have lost their senses and mutilated themselves?' he asked carefully.

'Since yesterday,' said Andy, 'three more round here and at least three or four further north. Could be more by now.'

'I'm pretty sure,' said Jack, checking Gwen's pulse again, then packing a second clean tea towel against the wound on her shoulder, 'that whatever's going on, it's not in the water. But when you get back to the station, Andy, you might want to alert everyone to a possible increase in domestic violence.' He paused, grinning at Rhys. 'I'm guessing Gwen might not be the only wife who wants to shoot her husband.'

'Very funny,' said Rhys. 'Since you're so smart, what do you think's happening?'

Before Jack could answer, Gwen moaned and slowly opened her eyes. Jack tasted peaches. He loved peaches, but he hadn't been thinking about them at all. He wasn't even hungry.

Gwen stared up at Jack, gasped, panicked, tried to sit up, but couldn't. 'What happened?' She whimpered, her memory flooding back, her eyes widening. She cried out, touching her hand to the wound on her shoulder, grimacing at the sopping towel.

Rhys crouched next to her. 'I'm here, love. So's Anwen, and we're both OK. Really.'

Gwen burst into tears, looking first at Rhys, then at Anwen, and finally back at Jack. Outside, two medics were dashing towards the front door, a police constable jogging behind them.

'Who shot me?'

'I did,' nodded Jack, sweeping her damp fringe off her face.

'I guess it was my turn,' said Gwen, taking Jack's hand and squeezing it. Then her eyes fluttered closed and she drifted once again to unconsciousness.

As Jack released Gwen's hand, he noticed her forearm was bleeding. 'What happened here?' He rolled up her sleeve, staring at a recent wound sliced into her arm.

'Christ,' said Rhys, his face draining of colour. 'That must have been what she was doing in the bathroom. She was cutting herself.'

Jack slid his phone from his pocket and before the medics insisted he get out of their way, he clicked a picture of the three overlapping circles Gwen had razored into her flesh.

Later, Jack sat in the house waiting for Mary to arrive. He struggled to remember where he'd seen that shape tattooed on Gwen's arm before. On his phone, he looked more closely at the design, puzzled.

With Anwen playing at his feet, Jack sketched the shape on a sheet of paper, over and over again. He stared at it intently, ran his fingers over it, feeling a familiarity with its overlapping lines and its strange ancient aesthetic, but whenever he thought he had a sense of where he'd seen it before and what it meant, whenever he tried to concentrate, to get his mind to snag the memory, it was useless. Whatever this image was, it kept collapsing under his scrutiny.

The Ice Maiden

29

North Atlantic, same day as the supermarket incident
A fierce storm was buffeting the *Ice Maiden*, a survey ship trawling in the North Sea near the cusp of the Skaggerak Strait. Henry 'Cash' Collins, a brick-house Scotsman – handsome, solid, dependable – stood in the wheelhouse, tucking his flannel shirt into his unzipped jeans, an unlit cigar clamped between his teeth. He checked the radar one more time to be sure. This one was going to be bad. He could feel it in his arthritic knees. Pressing a button on the control panel, he gave the orders to lock the ship down.

The *Ice Maiden* was a beam trawler, equipped to navigate the violent northern seas. Years earlier, Cash and his father had dragged for blue-mouthed redfish in between survey trips for British Petroleum and Exxon – plus more than a few covert drilling operations around the globe for organisations only one or two folks knew about. When his father died, Cash changed the ship's name, retrofitted it with air cannons, state-of-the-art sonar trawls, acoustic sensors and a full deck of mostly illegal electronic equipment, chartering the *Ice Maiden*'s services out to oceanic and geology departments of universities and scientific institutes. Only on the rare instances when he needed money would Cash prostitute the trawler's services to a government or an agency that wanted a mission run under the radar.

This was one of those times.

Cash's principles had nothing to do with his politics, which were situational, and everything to do with his intense-to-the point-of-obsessive curiosity about the world's oceans. Henry 'Cash' Collins had never met an authority figure he could stomach for more than ten minutes, including, if truth be told, his own father.

Before the storm hit, Cash had been losing a game of strip poker to his second-in command, and current ex-wife, Dana, the daughter of a Swedish shipping magnate. Dana was tall and athletic with short blonde hair. She had once worked with MI5 on a mission using the *Ice Maiden*. She now considered the ship her home, loving it as much as, if not a wee bit more than, she loved Cash.

Clipped to a safety harness out on the aft deck in full storm gear – a hooded slicker, thigh-high black wellingtons and skintight black rubber trousers – Dana looked like a lanky teenager dressed as a Storm Trooper as she punched through the driving wind and sheets of rain to reach the main sonar winch. Cash was watching her from the wheelhouse, realising, and not for the first time, that he'd really screwed up when he'd, well, really screwed up.

Cash had already secured the computer gear in the wheelhouse with two of the trawler's crew, Nick Finley and Byron Austin. Both had been dishonourably discharged from the US Navy for dealing in contraband prescription drugs.

Finn was a wiry Irish-American, whose nickname was not only a natural result of his surname, but also because he'd spent most of his young adult life negotiating the treacherous waters of the Baltimore docks, where only sharks survived. Using a brick-sized remote control, Finn was now locking down and securing the satellite dish.

His colleague Byron was an African-American from Chicago, whose grandfather had served with Cash's father in the Second World War. He was double-checking their munitions hold. Given the increase in piracy in many of the oceans in which the *Ice Maiden* had sailed recently, their weapons were as important as any of their sophisticated sonar and computer equipment.

Below deck, the ship's cook, a dangerous-looking ex-shrimp boater from New Orleans named Hollis, and the head engineer, a lithe Canadian named Sam, were ignoring the boat's increasingly rolling gait. They were watching a football match on the flat screen bolted to the wall. When Finn shut down the satellite dish, a wave of static rippled across the television and the picture went black.

'Well, Jesus, marry my mother and have a cow,' said Hollis, his southern accent at its thickest when he was pissed. He pushed away from the table and walked to the door, his legs steady despite the ship's rocking movement. He looked both ways down the empty passageway, then lifted the com unit from the wall and depressed the button. He listened for a few seconds.

'No one in the wheel house,' he said, returning to his beer and to Sam, who was shuffling a deck of cards.

'A storm,' said Sam, who'd been raised in a commune outside San Francisco, cultivating hemp and sixteen varieties of tomatoes. Sam had a chip on his shoulder the size of Mount Rushmore and hated any conversations that required he talk about his hippy family or his mixed racial ethnicity. He was the perfect recruit for this crew, a man with no real ties to a country and a conscience easily adapted to the needs of a situation. 'I heard the whistle in the boiler room. Could be a long cold night.'

'So what'll it be, then?' asked Sam, arching his eyebrows.

'Poker, a movie or what?'

Hollis grinned at him, a smile that could sink ships. 'Oh, ah'm thinking the "or what".'

'Or what, nothing,' said Dana, stepping into the room, stripping off her wet gear until she stood in front of them in damp long-johns, her short hair plastered to her head. 'Cash and I haven't eaten since breakfast and this storm's already on us. We need all hands on deck, boys, not on each other.'

'Dana, darlin',' said Hollis, stepping around Sam but not without giving him a light slap on his cheek. 'Your meal's right here, hon, hot and delicious,' he turned and winked at Sam, 'like me.' He slid two lidded plates from the galley's top oven. 'Anyway, Cash always thinks the worst of any storm.'

Sam began shuffling the cards as Cash stepped into the mess, handed Dana a thick towel and accepted his plate from Hollis.

'Poker, it is,' said Sam.

While at sea, the *Ice Maiden* flew under the research flag of the United Nations, a banner that afforded her a certain camouflaged mobility, but when they docked for supplies they displayed either the New Zealand stars or the Canadian maple leaf, both about the most friendly non-combative symbols and nations' flags under which you could fly.

With the exception of Cash, and, so everyone in the crew assumed, Dana too, the rest of the group did not know what (or who) was funding this latest enterprise. Since the mission began, the crew's wages had been deposited into their accounts from an organisation called the International Institute of Geological Defense with an IP address and a PO Box that suggested headquarters in the Faroe Islands and Puerto Rico. The benefits were generous, and although the ship's shell and hull had seen better days, the deposit from this current mission had meant Cash could afford a long overdue upgrade to his crew's quarters, the facilities in the kitchen, and one or two pieces of sophisticated (and once again illegal) trawling equipment he'd been eyeing for a long time.

For this mission, the crew of the *Ice Maiden* had been tasked to monitor the earth's oceans like a newborn, checking her temperatures from every possible geological angle, observing the slightest changes in wind currents, charting weather patterns and tidal changes, migration shifts and marine population fluctuations. In the past months the crew had sunk so many devices deep into the oceans and recorded so many sonograms from the Indian Ocean to the South Pacific from the Antarctic to the North Atlantic that the *Ice Maiden* had gathered an overwhelming mass of data. Cash had been transmitting their findings to the Institute for Geological Defense, but he doubted that anyone, even there, could possibly be making any sense of it.

Cash was convinced that, although the world had shifted out of crisis mode, countries and their governments had slid back into neutral, cruising along as before, trusting that everything and everyone had returned to normal, turning a blind eye to anything that might suggest trouble was once again looming.

He hoped that all the data they were gathering was suggesting nothing too far out of the ordinary, but he doubted that.

He was right, and he was terribly wrong.

Gwen

30

Gwen's shoulder had been cleaned and dressed. Seeing her flailing like a maniac on a hospital bed, her wrists strapped to the bed's safety bars, her hair matted and oily and her arms bruised and bandaged – it was all more than Rhys could stand. He went into the corridor to wait for Jack.

Thankfully, the detectives from CID investigating the other incidents of violence and disorderly conduct had gone. They had decided that Gwen, like the other affected women, should be restrained and sedated until the doctors could figure out what had caused their mental breakdowns and their severe self-mutilations.

Stepping out of the lift onto the psychiatric care floor, Jack was immediately assaulted by Gwen's anger. He felt it in his knees, a shooting pain, and he tasted it in his mouth – like onions. Gwen's shouts of profanity and her screaming insults were being directed at someone named 'Suzie'.

Rhys was crouched against the wall opposite the Plexiglas screens of the secure ward, the guard at the enclosed desk near the lift watching his every move. Rhys's head was buried in his hands, but when he saw Jack he slowly stood up.

'How is she?' asked Jack looking into the ward, a headache beginning behind his eyes. Gwen was in the first of four beds, writhing against the ministrations of two nurses and a burly male orderly while the doctor, a petite woman in a white lab coat, keyed notes into a tablet. Jack noticed that the other three beds were each occupied with seriously injured women, all sedated, their IV drips standing at attention next to their beds like thin alien sentinels.

'She's bad, Jack,' said Rhys, his voice catching in his throat. 'Because of her concussion, the doctor didn't want to put her completely under, but they may have no choice. Her anger is out of control. She's a danger to herself. To everyone.'

The doctor swiped her ID card at the panel inside the room. She came out and stepped over to them. Jack figured her to be in her early forties, her caramel-coloured skin flawless. She was short, attractive and professional in a pale green blouse and a navy pencil skirt that showed enough of her legs to make Jack and Rhys notice. The badge on her white lab coat identified her as Dr Olivia Steele.

'Mr Williams, I'm Dr Steele. May I have a word?' She proffered her arm, guiding Rhys down the hall for privacy.

Rhys nodded his head towards Jack. 'He's family... brother-in-law. He can hear whatever you have to say.'

Jack smiled warmly at Rhys, despite the worsening headache, and the intensity of the sour taste in his mouth.

Dr Steele nodded. 'Very well, but to be honest, I don't have much to tell you, Mr Williams. Your wife is experiencing a kind of hysterical neurosis and it may be a while before we understand what triggered it.' She looked from Rhys to Jack. 'Is there any history of mental illness in your family?'

'Not that I know of,' answered Jack before Rhys could process the question. 'And if there is or was, I'd know...'

'There's none,' said Rhys, emphatically, glaring at Jack who rolled his eyes and shrugged. 'But what did you mean, it may take a while? How long is a while exactly?'

Dr Steele gently touched Rhys's forearm. 'With the right combination of drugs, a few days if we're lucky, and that will allow us to talk with Gwen and examine her without such acute physical symptoms. Her real treatment will depend on how severe the roots of her neurosis are.' The doctor continued talking to Rhys, but her eyes were following Jack as he shifted to stand at the security glass, staring into the busy ward, his jaw clenched, his hands deep in his pockets.

'If your wife has experienced some kind of trauma that has led to this breakdown,' she went on, turning back to Rhys, 'then that will have to be addressed, too, and that may take years.'

'What about these other women?' interrupted Jack. 'Are they also suffering from some kind of hysterical neurosis?'

The doctor walked over next to Jack and followed his gaze into the room. 'I'm afraid I can't discuss my other patients with you.'

'Even if they may all be suffering from a similar hysteria? Could this be related to… you know, them all being female?' asked Jack, looking directly at Dr Steele.

The doctor looked at Jack, anger flashed in her eyes. 'This is not the nineteenth century, Mr…?'

'Harkness. Captain Jack Harkness.'

'Captain Harkness, your sister isn't a character in a Brontë novel. She's suffering from a very real mental illness that has affected an organ in her body and not, quite frankly, her uterus. The kind of female hysteria you're implying was nothing more than the patriarchal repressive sexual fantasies of the Victorian medical establishment. Your sister's brain, like these other women, is suffering from something quite real. The fact that it's her mind we're dealing with makes it more complicated and more frightening, but I'm more than equipped to help her.'

'So you're convinced there's no pattern to be determined,'

continued Jack, folding his arms, noting the doctor's mouth twitch slightly. 'That there's no related causes in the fact that four females from the same immediate area have experienced a similar hysteria?'

'Oh, for God's sake,' continued the doctor, her rant picking up steam. 'Freud might have believed that Gwen was suffering from some uncontrollable emotional tantrum and just because of timing and one or two similarities among these women,' she swept her hand along the window, 'that they're somehow sharing in that suffering. But, Captain Harkness, let me tell you that, despite what you may have read in the media about what happened to these women and to Gwen, mental illness is not contagious and your sister and these other women are not simply hysterical women.'

Jack nodded and tried to look appropriately contrite.

'If you'll excuse me.' She turned back to Rhys. 'Mr Williams, I'll keep you posted on your wife's condition. For now, I'd suggest you get some rest, the days and months ahead could be long ones for you and your family.'

The door opened again, this time to let one of the nurses out. Gwen's screams were muted, but Jack could still hear her calling for what now sounded like 'Schoozie'.

'May I speak to my sister?'

'If you must,' said the doctor, as she headed towards the elevator, 'but make it brief. I need her to rest. The medication will help her sleep, but I also need to see her blood pressure and her adrenalin levels come down to much safer levels.'

When the elevator closed on the doctor, Jack pulled his mobile from the inside of his coat pocket.

The guard at the desk glared at him. 'Hey, you can't use a mobile in here. Give that over.'

Jack ignored him.

Rhys was staring sadly through the security glass at Gwen, who was slowly becoming less agitated. 'Who're you calling?' he asked.

'Dr Steele is wrong, Rhys. There's a pattern to all this. These woman are not just some kind of statistical anomaly. The doctor confirmed that all these woman are suffering from similar delusions, from similar mental breakdowns, to say nothing of the fact that all of them mutilated themselves in some way.'

Both men looked more closely at each of the women in the ward, this time paying more attention to their other injuries. The woman in the bed closest to Gwen had her head bandaged, the dressing covering the entire left side of her face. Opposite her, a woman in her late twenties had her arm in a cast, only three fingers visible. The third, a heavy middle-aged woman with untidy curls of hair had a thick white patch dressed on her left eye, raw pink welts and lines of scratches covering her cheeks.

Gwen's right shoulder was bound in bandages, soft leather straps fastened across her chest and restraints on her legs to keep her frenetic movements restricted. She looked small and frail, and as he looked at her Jack's heart cracked a little more.

'Something wrong?' asked Rhys. 'I need to get home to Anwen so Mary can come see Gwen. I can't be taking care of you too, mate.'

'Go,' said Jack, his knees aching terribly. 'I'll sit with Gwen until Mary gets here.'

'Sure?'

'More than.'

When Rhys had gone, Jack tapped a number into his mobile. The guard banged on his window.

'Is this line secure?' asked Jack. 'Good. I need you to do something for me.' Jack laughed at something the caller said after Jack explained his request.

'Of course, you should do it Torchwood style.'

The Ice Maiden

31

In the communications room opposite the newly refurbished mess, the *Ice Maiden*'s two analysts sat in front of a bank of computers. Like Sam and Hollis, they were also ignoring the increasingly violent rise and fall of the ship as she sailed into the storm. Vlad Lidenbrok had his feet up on the desk, reading a Steampunk novel balanced on his lap while his computer was plotting a geologic map, its waves of reds, blues and yellows washing across his screen.

Eva Giles was perched on the edge of her chair, leaning over what looked like an old-fashioned printer. It was, in fact, a sophisticated piece of sonar-recording equipment, its shuttle flying across the scrolling paper, while also sending its results to Vlad's hard drive.

'How many is that we've discovered now?' asked Vlad, shouting to be heard over the thunderous waves battering the side of the ship.

'Counting this one forming off the coast of Wales?' asked Eva. She wore over-sized black-framed glasses and kept her long brown hair pulled off her face. Eva was the crew's science officer who Cash had recruited, at Dana's request, from the doctoral program in Earth Sciences at the University of Vancouver. As the crew's youngest and newest recruit, she desperately wanted to be taken seriously.

'Four significant disturbances,' she finally replied. 'That's a lot in such a short time. Should we be worried?'

'You're not?' replied Vlad, pulling up two other sonar maps to his screen. One was from a hundred miles off the coast of Vietnam, the other from the ocean south of New Zealand. Vlad quickly scrolled through a series of windows until he settled on an oceanic map of the world. Tapping the screen on the key places where they'd recorded the other deep-water disturbances, he then dragged the key bits of data and embedded them in each flagged point.

Grabbing the arm of her chair before it rolled against the door, Eva watched Vlad work, knowing some morsel of data, a detail of code, had snagged his mind as he'd been scrolling and he was puzzling over what he was seeing. She watched quietly as he began rubbing his fingers across his short beard, his green eyes narrowed as he stared intently at the screen. Every few seconds, he scribbled a note on a sheet of paper, adding to the scraps and piles that already carpeted his desk. Then he'd twirl his pencil, once, twice, come to a conclusion and then, using the eraser, double-tap each flag on the screen. In one swift gesture across his screen, he made the images and the data fly to a massive electronic map that covered the room's only open wall, each spot on the map pinging bright within seconds of Vlad's touch on his screen.

'Eva,' said Vlad, nudging her. 'Did you hear anything I just said?'

'No, sorry. What?' Eva could feel herself blush. She'd been thinking about Vlad's touch. She couldn't help it. He had the most beautiful hands she'd ever seen in a man. His fingers were long, his nails short, the skin not soft but not rough either.

'Eva!' Vlad shook his head, using two fingers to wipe

data over to the wall map.

'It's the storm,' she said, quickly. 'I'm a bit... nervous. I've never been in a bad one before.'

Vlad softened his tone. 'Well, don't be. It's not going to be that bad. Cash has a tendency towards the drama of a storm, usually so he can comfort whatever grad students we have on board.' Vlad smiled, squeezing Eva's shoulder. Heat shot up from her toes to her tummy. Vlad leaned back on his chair, rubbing his fingers over his lips, concentrating on the data streaming across his screen.

Then he turned, gripped the arms of Eva's chair and dragged her to face him. Leaning into her, Vlad kissed her, his lips soft on her mouth, his tongue parting them gently. She returned the kiss, her own mouth hungry for his. She tilted her head back, exposing the pale skin of her neck, letting Vlad's mouth trace a line of soft kisses from her lips to her neck, his warm lips, his long fingers, moving across her bare shoulders, under her sweater to her hardening nipples. Without shifting him, Eva reached up and loosened her hair, then grabbing a handful of his, she guided him to her lap.

'Jesus, look out!' said Vlad, lunging over Eva to catch a heavy nautical compass tipping from the shelf before the storm crashed it on top of her.

'Are you OK?' he asked, still leaning over her.

Eva was most definitely not OK. Vlad's scent was intoxicating. 'I'm fine. Really.'

She wanted to grab his shoulders and jump his bones, no, not jump him, nail him, screw him, fuck him right here on the cold, hard floor. Eva squeezed her nails into her palms, shocked at her thoughts. She shoved Vlad out of her way and stood up. Forgetting to brace herself against the ship's angry rolls, her chair slammed against the back of her legs and she toppled into Vlad's arms.

155

'Do you need me to strap you down?' he laughed.

Oh, God, yes, she thought.

'I'm sorry. Sorry,' she said, stepping out of his way. 'Still developing my sea legs.'

'Well, make it fast,' he said, sliding her chair back to her desk and setting the compass inside one of the metal storage lockers in the room. 'Because I need you—'

A soft moan burst from Eva's lips. Vlad looked at her, quizzically. 'Are you sure you're OK? You look flushed.'

'I do feel hot,' she said, then quickly added, 'I mean warm... warm.'

'OK,' said Vlad, thinking that this was why he preferred working alone. Vlad had raised a force field around his heart years ago. He was personable, polite and participated in the crew's card games and movie watching, but he perceived his fellow shipmates as nothing more than sophisticated computers, hard-wired to behave in certain ways. They were necessary to the job at hand but immaterial to his personal development.

Vlad had accepted the position as analyst on the *Ice Maiden* after much of the funding for his research on deep-water morphic fields had dried up when his mentor at the University of Prague had disappeared with most of the funding. Vlad's passion for the oceans and his insane knowledge of computers were currently running in second and third place to the growing resentment towards the man who'd stripped him of his future.

'If you think you can stay focused long enough,' said Vlad, standing in front of the wall map and reading some of the information he'd just posted, 'can you run a cross-check of the data from the Paracel Islands with this recent deep-water event off the coast of Wales?'

'Why?' said Eva, trying not to stare at his ass or at the way his faded jeans sat on the muscular curve of his hips, a thin scar set in the hollow above his pelvic bone. Or how his hair curled over the frayed top of his Ziggy Stardust T-shirt.

'Have you got something?' she asked. Oh, you do, she thought, you really do and I want it. Good grief, what was happening to her? Horny didn't begin to describe these feelings.

She turned back to her computer, the pulsing plot points on the map mimicking her racing heartbeat. Eva knew when she had signed up for this job that spending months at sea would mean giving up certain things she enjoyed – a lot. Shopping for cheap couture, eating fresh fruit, running outside on solid ground with unsalted air in her hair, and regular pleasurable sex with one or two of her on-again off-again boyfriends. But until this moment in the middle of the coldest waters she'd travelled, she'd never felt such desire, such intense sexual hunger coursing through her veins, racing to every organ at warp speed.

'Eva, really,' interrupted Vlad, his patience wearing thin. 'Focus. I think we have a serious problem.'

'What?' said Eva, using all her willpower to not look at Vlad below the neck.

'How quickly is the disturbance in Wales growing?' Vlad asked, standing over her to get a closer look at the echogram.

Vlad smelled of Ivory soap and the scent set off a peculiar but not unpleasant ringing in her ears. When he reached across to highlight a point on the graph, her body tingled all over, every muscle vibrating like a million hands on her at once. She crossed her legs and leaned forward, her pulse quickening again, the ringing clanging in her head. Suddenly she could taste a burst of peppermint on her tongue.

She sighed. Christ, she felt really good.

'That was weird,' said Eva, grinning up at Vlad. 'I mean it's weird... the events... they're weird...' His eyes narrowed. She charged on. 'I mean they both displayed signs of a tremor, but neither area is close to any traditional plate boundaries or fault lines. And now there's a deep water geyser forming in each site.'

She pushed away from the desk and Vlad, stepping over to the world map secured on the wall. She needed to see the entire scope of their travels plotted on the map, and she was also afraid of what might happen again if she didn't get some distance between her body and Vlad's.

The peppermint lingered on her lips, tasting pretty sweet.

'OK,' she said, gathering some professional composure, but keeping her back to Vlad to be safe. 'Let's look at what we have. All the waters we've trawled have experienced some kind of seismic disturbance since Tuesday, none of them are on traditional fault lines, and so far, thankfully, none of them have created any major tsunamis or any obvious disturbances on land for that matter. Yet. But who knows what can happen if they continue to strengthen.'

She took off her glasses, and squinted at the map. 'Did you see that?'

'See what?' said Vlad, his eyes still on his computer screen where he'd called up an imaging model of the Norwegian waters they'd just finished trawling. Pushing his hair from his eyes, he watched his projection image rotate on the screen, the same points of Eva's map highlighted on his. He froze the map, and finally turned to Eva. 'Sorry. Say again.'

Eva rubbed her eyes and put her glasses back on. 'It's nothing,' she said, 'I thought I saw the lights on the map flash in an odd way.'

'I think you may need some rest,' said Vlad. 'We've all been working odd hours recently. I can cover if you want to go and lie down.'

And then it happened again.

In her peripheral vision, she could see the lights on the southern hemisphere of the map burst into light at the same time, flashing a regular rhythm, which was odd because each light was recording a different deep sea disturbance. There was no possible geological way that each one of those events, thousands of miles apart, were syncing with each other.

It must be a glitch in their deep-water recorder. Had to be.

32

The storm was sending the ship into barrel rolls, and Cash had hit the lockdown alert for the second time. If that happened a third time, they'd have to strap on their lifejackets, gather the flares and prepare for the worst.

This time walking skilfully against the ship's barrel motion, Eva unlocked a ceiling-high storage locker, took out a camera and a tripod and set them up facing the wall map.

'What's going on?' Vlad asked, watching Eva keying in a series of commands into her iPad to control the camera's time-release.

'Not sure, yet,' she replied, staring again at the pulsing lights on the maps where they'd recorded recent seismic disturbances. 'Going with a hunch. Trying some low-tech recording.'

'OK...' said Vlad, curious about Eva's hunches, but not interested enough to push for an explanation. Instead, he returned to his own screen. 'Not one of these deep-water crevices has ever recorded eruptions of this magnitude before with the exception of this last one we recorded this morning,' he said, zooming in on the ocean off the southern coast of Peru.

Eva was still staring at her wall map, which had red

lights flashing in the same places as Vlad was marking on his computer image: one, their most recent, off the coast of South Wales, one close to the southern tip of New Zealand, one north of Scotland and not far from their current position, and now the latest light off the southern coast of Peru.

'The southern coast of Peru,' added Vlad, 'has had significant destructive quakes and volcanic eruptions that have been getting worse for decades, especially since the 1920s and 1930s.'

Eva stared at Peru on the wall map, twisting her hair in concentration while she spoke. 'I remember when the one in 2007 happened, but the worst quake that area ever had was in 1930.'

While Vlad was listening to Eva, he initiated a statistical program he'd written. When it was loaded, he dumped their data into it.

'I did one of my first field studies on a high archaeological dig in the Peruvian Andes,' continued Eva, glad to have the memories take her mind off Vlad. 'The elders in the local villages still talk about the 1930 eruption. According to their stories, the tremors and eruptions were so powerful that an entire mountain top dropped into the ocean. I can't remember the name, but—'

'We've seen deep-water eruptions and tremors before,' said Vlad, cutting her off. As much as he appreciated Eva's geological skills, he was not quite as impressed with her need to over-explain everything. 'But not like these ones. Look at the way this one in Wales is shifting and spreading.'

'I know. Never this deep and never in these areas.' Eva slid her glasses up on top of her head and rubbed her eyes.

'Eva, we're talking trenches running seven, eight miles deep in the ocean that are emitting sonar waves equal to 7 on the Richter scale. Most of Asia and the west coast of the USA should have been hit by a tsunami by now. It's as if the ocean is not letting that happen. It's keeping these tremors contained for some reason.'

Vlad tilted back on his chair, hooking his leg round the table to stop it from sliding against the wall, while keeping his eyes on his computer as it tracked the statistical program running at full speed. No matter how disparate or how unusual these deep-water events, this program would help the *Ice Maiden* see what was toiling in the darkest depths of the world's oceans.

'I think we should report these findings,' said Vlad.

'But what do we have to report?'

'A pattern of deep water eruptions,' said Vlad, watching Eva stare at the map through the lens of her camera. 'Isn't that what we've been tasked to monitor?'

'True. It's definitely a pattern, but what the pattern means? I've no clue,' replied Eva, making no eye contact at all with Vlad. 'And do we really know what we've been tasked to do? I mean we never get a straight answer from Cash, and if Dana knows, Cash has her so... so smitten, she's not going to tell us anything.'

Laughing, Vlad glanced over at Eva. 'Smitten. Really? Is that the word in Vancouver?'

Eva blushed. Again. 'You know what I mean. If Dana knows anything she's not going to share unless Cash gives her permission.'

'That makes her loyal,' said Vlad. 'Not... smitten. But I get your point.'

Eva went back to her computer and began inputting data streams coming from the echogram. 'Give me a few more days. We can run through all the data with Shelley. Maybe then we'll have something more substantial to share.'

'I still think we should let Cash know we've got something now, no matter how tentative. It may change our course,' said Vlad.

'But we've had so many false alarms recently. I don't think Cash wants the boss, whoever that is, to see us crying wolf again.' Eva tore the printout from the machine. 'I think Cash knows better than any of us what should be reported and what shouldn't. Let's let him decide.'

'Which, as you keep pointing out, isn't saying much,' said Vlad, sliding back across to his station, retrieving his book that had slid off the table to the floor.

Vlad was flipping through the pages to find his place when a massive wave battered the ship, tipping the vessel onto its side and then back upright again in a matter of seconds. The force of the roll sent Vlad and his chair flying into the map wall and Eva and her chair crashing against the open door. Vlad's computer alarm went off at the same time. He scrambled from his upturned chair to check on it.

Cash came across the passageway from the mess, sticking his head into the room. 'Everyone OK in here?'

Vlad stared wide-eyed at his beeping computer. 'Not really. I think you'd better take a look at this.'

Helping Eva up off the floor first, Cash joined Vlad at his computer, anchoring one foot against the desk leg and the other against the cusp of the steel wall. The ship's rocking was getting worse. Vlad's computer alarm continued to wail.

'Can you turn that bloody noise off?' said Cash.

Vlad stopped the alarm, watching in shock as a mass of code rolled across his screen.

'What am I looking at?' asked Cash.

Vlad made a few fast keystrokes, glanced at Eva and then looked up at Cash. 'I think we're under attack.'

'What do you mean "under attack"?' asked Cash. 'We're miles from anything, in the middle of the North Sea.'

'We're being cyber-bombed,' said Vlad.

'We can't be,' said Eva, righting her chair, and wheeling it next to Vlad, fear completely overriding her desire. The *Ice*

Maiden dipped into another massive wave. Water thrashed against the room's two portals, the ship tipping violently on its side again. This time Eva and Vlad crashed against the wall on top of each other.

'But it's impossible,' Eva said, shoving Vlad out of her way and struggling back to her computer. Cash had managed to remain standing, his legs bracing him in place. 'Vlad created an impenetrable system. No way someone's hacking us.'

'I thought so too,' said Vlad, back at his terminal, his fingers flying across the keyboard, 'but someone's definitely in our system. I know my own code and this isn't mine.' He leaned closer. 'It's elegant, but it's not mine.'

'Nothing's a hundred per cent secure,' said Cash, not sure what he was staring at, but trusting Vlad enough to believe his assessment. 'No one in our line of work would expect it ever to be that way.'

For a moment, Eva wanted to ask if someone would please tell her exactly what was their line of work, what they were really looking for in the deepest parts of the world's oceans, but she didn't. Instead, she sat at her desk and started keying almost as fast as Vlad, working her way into the core of the system, trying to catch their hacker before he or she pulled out.

'I've faith in the two of you,' said Cash, turning to leave as the boat dipped and rolled once again. This time they heard a thunderous crash from above as something on the main deck broke loose of its moorings.

'Finn,' yelled Cash. 'What the hell was that?'

A voice from the passageway screamed back. 'I'm on it, boss!'

Dana burst in. 'What's going on?'

Hollis came in behind her – the tight space was suddenly packed with bodies.

'Partaay in here?' asked Hollis.

'We've got a mole crawling around in our system,' said Cash. Turning back to Vlad, he said, 'You'll figure it out. Let me know when you do.'

Cash and Dana were about to leave. Eva grabbed Cash's arm.

'You don't understand, Cash. We can't have a mole. This boat isn't like your house or your office. It isn't cabled to the internet or wired to a server somewhere. We have our own satellite uplink.' She looked over at Vlad, noting the worry that was furrowing his brow. He was chasing code across his screen, the lines scrolling past his eyes at lightning speed.

Cash and the others simply looked confused. They should be worried, Eva thought. Very worried.

'Think of this boat as a massive computer server,' she explained. 'We're only connected to the rest of the internet when the satellite is up. And Finn locked it down when the storm began.'

'Oh,' said Dana, after a beat.

'Shit,' said Cash.

'Well, I must be dumber than a plate of snails,' said Hollis, ''cause I still don't get it.'

'If we're not connected to the internet,' said Sam, who'd been listening from the passageway, 'and we haven't been since this storm began, then how can an outsider be active inside our system right now?'

'Well,' said Hollis, 'maybe he snuck in before the storm.'

'Maybe,' said Vlad. 'But I'm getting paid a healthy amount of money to make sure that doesn't happen and I don't think it did. My traps would have snared it right away. And if it was a Trojan, it wouldn't be trawling live. It would wait until we were wired up before activating and sending its data.'

As if on cue, the alarm on his computer began beeping again. Then a beat later, across the passageway, the television clicked on, the crowd at the football game cheering 'goal', the commentators screaming. The echogram Eva had been monitoring whirred back and forth angrily and the lights on the ship began to flash.

Before anyone could react to the crazy electrical surge, another wave smashed against the ship, flipping it almost 180 degrees. Eva screamed and was thrown into Hollis who crashed against the portal. Cash and Vlad tried to brace themselves against each other and the heavy metal desk. Then one of the equipment storage containers popped its moorings and slammed against the opposite wall, knocking a steel shelf loose above Dana's head. Cash charged her, knocking both of them clear seconds before the shelf stabbed into the chair on which Dana had been kneeling. Cash pulled Dana off the floor, holding her close for a second longer than was necessary.

Hollis helped Eva back to her seat. Each of them with the exception of Eva had survived more than their share of rough seas, but this was getting pretty bad.

At that moment, gripping the sides of the door jamb, Finn stuck his head into the room. 'Cash, everything's secure on deck. We should be able to ride this out. Byron's at the wheel.' He looked at the rest of his shipmates who were pale, shaken and staring back at him. 'What?'

'Is the satellite still down?' asked Vlad, ignoring the storm's violence. Without looking up from his keyboard, despite the broken pieces of equipment that had landed on his desk, he was still chasing their intruder.

Finn looked from Vlad to Cash. 'Yes, sir. First thing we did, and we've not touched it since. If we need to send a... a signal...' Finn was far too superstitious to even think about the possibility of distress never mind saying the word aloud, 'the radios will work from the emergency gen—'

The lights went out.

Everything had shut down – the alarms, the lights, the

television, and, worst of all, the engines.

The *Ice Maiden* was dead in the water.

'What the hell's going on?' demanded Cash, careening off the walls as he and Sam struggled out of the research lab to the passage, which was not wide enough for two men to pass. 'Finn, with Sam and me.'

They stood behind him while he unlocked a storage locker under the ladder with keys hooked on his belt. He lifted out two torches and a gun.

'We may have been hit by a rogue wave,' he said, handing the torches to Finn and Sam. Steadying himself against the sides of the passageway, he snapped a full clip into the gun, adding, 'But we may have been hit by something else.'

'Doesn't really matter what hit us,' said Sam, leading the way to the engine room. 'If we can't get the engines back on… in this storm… we'll all be swimming soon.'

Sam, Finn and Cash cautiously made their way along the tight passage to the engine room, leaving the rest in the dark lab.

Eva was shifting containers to get at a box with emergency lights, which she handed to Hollis who took the lights and strung them across the ceiling. While she was attaching the battery pack, a whirring mechanical noise cut into the screaming wind and the thundering waves pounding into the paralysed trawler.

Eva shifted a steel drawer out of her way. 'It's the teletype. How is that working without electricity?'

The message printed in lower case was an unusual combination of letters and phrases. Eva tore the sheet from the machine when it stopped.

Bracing himself against the door, Hollis looked over Eva's shoulder at the sheet. 'Is that some kind of code?' he asked.

'No, darlin',' Eva said, mimicking Hollis's Cajun accent. 'It's Welsh.'

Gwen

33

Two days after the supermarket incident, most local media outlets were reporting a wave of violent outbursts by women in cinemas, libraries and shops, particularly in rural and secluded parts of the UK. But as the madness appeared to be spreading among small random clusters of woman and no one else – no men and no children – parts of the national press began speculating that these women might be experiencing a kind of mass female hysteria.

One local GP from Cornwall was quoted as saying these women were trying to 'have it all' and, as a result, they were 'cracking under the pressure'. He called it 'Multi-Tasking Madness', encouraged women to stay at home more, to avoid stress and too much over-stimulation.

The backlash was immediate. Soon the media was less interested in the newest cases breaking out in the UK and instead focused on the debate over the feminist and political ramifications of the madness.

Social media muted whatever rising panic was happening among its female followers and responded to the events with black humour and ironic mockery. At the end of day two, the most popular trending topics on Twitter were #realfemmefatales and #nolongerontheverge.

Jack sat at the kitchen table, a laptop open in front of him, scanning reports from the World Health Organization, the International Organization for Women's Wellbeing, Doctors Without Borders and as many international news agencies as he could access.

He scrolled through masses of text, his brain grabbing any repetition of details, slivers of conversations, similarities in descriptions, suggestions and allusions, anything he could discern, no matter how trivial and irrelevant, that might suggest a pattern. Anyone watching him, his body stock still, the occasional shifting of his eyes as lines of text whipped past him, would have thought he was in a trance.

He wasn't sure where his eidetic memory had come from but, for as long as he could remember, Jack had been able to store huge amounts of data in patterns and images.

While he was reading, he noticed that with certain websites, the yellow dots he'd seen earlier in his peripheral vision had returned. He did his best to ignore them, especially when they shifted colour the more quickly he scanned.

On day three, the 'masochistic madness', as a blogger had labelled it, was being reported internationally; the numbers of women experiencing symptoms of violent mental breakdowns were being registered in six or seven secluded regions across the world. From the highlands of Scotland to the island of Rakiura off the southern tip of New Zealand, women living continents apart were committing random acts of violence towards themselves, their families, their neighbours and their communities.

Thousands of women worldwide had descended into a kind of madness that even the most highly trained psychiatrists and experienced neurologists were having difficulty diagnosing. The only thing the medical community knew with any certainty was that this increase in mental illness involved a breakdown of each woman's physical senses, a mangling of what she was feeling, seeing, smelling, and even tasting.

Jack made a few more notes, sent a couple more emails, and made a secure phone call. While Gwen was still in the psychiatric ward, Jack had settled into relative domesticity with Mary, Rhys and Anwen. He knew it couldn't last, but as long as he was trying to make sense of what had happened to Gwen and these other women, Wales was as good a place as any from which to investigate the phenomenon.

Mary had taken Anwen for a walk in town. The house was quiet. Jack scanned the reports he'd hacked into from the World Health Organization, which had become a clearing house of data from the various medical communities dealing with these afflicted women.

According to the recent reports, no two women reacted the same way when the madness descended upon them: some collapsed from an overwhelming sense of smell; others felt as if the volume in their surroundings had been cranked too high; a few tasted emotions so strongly they were physically ill; even more reported that they hallucinated realities they could never have experienced and heard imagined music and disembodied voices.

After three hours of reading, Jack closed the laptop, got up from the table and, lifting his coat and binoculars from behind the kitchen door, went out to stretch his legs and to think. Outside, he could smell the coming rain... and something else – wood smoke, sulphur and the stink of hot tar. It was mid-afternoon on a cold, dreary Wednesday. He was alone in the street.

He could sense a strange tang in the air. The vaguely ruddy scent of blood and rust drifted towards him, leading him south, towards the seafront. By the time he reached the Marina, the rain was falling in heavy, lashing drops and the smell was stronger, as pungent as perfume. It felt ominous. He turned up his collar and hooked his binoculars over his shoulder. While he walked, he became aware of the silence around him. He could hear the rush of the sea, the rain dripping from his upturned coat collar down onto his neck, but that was all.

Jack lifted his binoculars to the horizon, scanning the five or six miles of beach to his right. He held his gaze for one, two, three beats, and then he shifted his focus to the Maritime Quarter behind him.

No cormorants. No sandpipers. No gulls. No magpies. No birds of any species anywhere. Jack was not a suspicious man, but he couldn't help thinking that this was not a good sign.

As Jack was walking across the soft sand, he felt the beach shift beneath him, throwing him off-balance. He recovered his footing and turned back the way he had come, the tremor worsening.

Suddenly, car sirens blasted from the street beyond the promenade, and he saw a small explosion from a passing car, an exhaust pipe popping. As the ground shook, the car shot off the road, somehow soaring over the low promenade wall, diving nose-first into the sand below.

The tremor stopped. But Jack was still reeling, his nostrils full of the stench of burning tyres and hot macadam. He took a couple of strides towards the car, knowing he should help, but the smell clogged his sinuses, and he retched, unable to clear it. He staggered back, breaking into a run, the smell clashing with a nightmarishly amplified ringing of alarms. For Jack Harkness, a man who had leapt into burning buildings and in front of alien war machines, it was all suddenly too much.

Jack ran away.

*

Breathless, bewildered and furious with himself, Jack took off his boots and hung his coat to dry in the kitchen. He put the kettle on, then went to the bathroom and found a towel to dry his hair, which was longer than it had ever been. For some reason, he had very little desire to cut it. He looked at himself in the bathroom mirror, aware, again, of that peripheral vision of yellow dots.

As he stared into the mirror, the dots slowly moved front and centre and began to coalesce. The face of a young woman appeared, floating in front of his own. She had black eyes and thick dark hair flooding over her shoulders.

Jack pressed his hand on the mirror, touching her image. He breathed out slowly.

What the hell was that?

Who the hell was that?

34

Minutes later, Jack stood in the kitchen, waiting for the kettle to boil and staring at a hurried drawing he'd made of the woman's image.

He had no idea who she was. Not a clue. This ignorance, this lack of knowing, this gap in his understanding was as unsettling to Jack as any of the extraordinary and alien experiences he'd ever had. She'd felt real to him, not a hallucination. Setting the pad down on the table, he stared out into the eerily empty street, watching two local constables cycling down the road, presumably checking for casualties from the minor quake.

Flipping open his laptop, Jack checked the weather channel. The earthquake had been recorded at 3.4 on the Richter scale. BBC Wales was reporting most of the damage had been to the sea ports and villages on the south-eastern coast.

Jack noted the data scrolling across his computer and the pages and pages of information about the deranged women spread out across the table. He sighed, lamenting how much he missed his team, missed Owen and Tosh, missed the Hub and its battery of computers.

The kettle whistled on the counter behind him. He didn't

move, letting it build up its steam, missing Ianto most of all.

'I hate doing this shit by myself.'

Coffee in hand, Jack sat down and carried on.

So far, Jack had found nothing of significance, other than the fact that the affected were all women. He was certain this was a critical point, but still couldn't see an angle to pursue that might suggest a solution to diminish or stop the outbreaks, never mind understanding the cause.

Jack sat back in the kitchen chair, sipping his coffee. Ianto would have brought him a biscuit or two.

In his head, Jack flipped through the files of the local women who'd been affected at the same time as Gwen. These women were a good sample of all those who'd been struck. If he could understand the cause – because there was a cause, he thought. This was not random. This was not some kind of mass female hysteria. Jack had lived through far too much to believe for one second there wasn't something or someone behind what was happening.

It wasn't until day five that Jack witnessed something that was the breakthrough for which he'd been searching, the understanding that might help him bring Gwen home.

Jack was stretched across the couch in the living room reading to Anwen. Rhys had gone to fetch Mary from the hospital and bring her home for tea. Gwen and the other women remained sedated and mostly incoherent, their families taking turns sitting watch all day at their bedsides, vigils that were occurring all over the world where clusters of women had been afflicted.

'No,' said Anwen as Jack opened the colourful new alphabet book he'd bought for her. She turned to the bright red apple on the first page with a speckled worm crawling through its core carrying a bag of books.

'A is for Apple,' said Jack.

'No,' said Anwen, slapping the picture of the apple.

'Oh, I'm pretty sure that A is for Apple,' laughed Jack, 'at least in this universe.'

Anwen grabbed the book from Jack and began to flip through the pages until she reached L where there was a picture of a large luscious lemon with striped straws sticking out all over it. She poked her finger at the lemon and said, 'Apple.'

No matter how insistent Jack was, Anwen was unyielding.

He carried her into the kitchen and showed her the fruit bowl. 'Anwen, show Uncle Jack the apple.'

He held her forward and she picked up the only apple left in the bowl. He peeled it and cut it into slices, and they shared the snack, while he thought things through.

Later at dinner, he told Rhys and Mary what had happened.

'She recognises the shapes,' he told them. 'So what was confusing her? Do you think she might be colour blind?'

Mary was clearing the table, stacking the dishes in the sink. 'I don't think she is. She has no problem pointing out colours in her rainbow book.'

'That's what I thought,' said Jack, filling the sink with water and suds to wash the dishes. 'No worries. Maybe she was just mixed up.'

When the house was quiet and everyone asleep, Jack tiptoed downstairs and sat at the dining room table. In the pale moonlight beaming through the windows, he sorted all the information he had gathered, including the image of the women in the mirror, into a narrative of sorts.

By the time the sun came up, Jack believed he had hit on something, and it unsettled him.

35

The security guard on duty outside the locked ward had been eyeing Jack suspiciously since coming on duty at the shift change. He instinctively deferred to a senior officer, but this man's uniform looked oddly old-fashioned – as if he'd stepped out of a vintage comic book. 'You're the kind of man me mam warned me of,' the guard muttered to himself.

Now the man was violating the locked ward's protocols. Looked like he was going to break into the ward with all those nutty women. Before the guard could call for assistance, Jack returned to the desk and handed over his belongings, including his coat, a leather wrist-strap, his passport, and his phone all of which the guard looked at quizzically before dropping into a Ziploc bag. Once Jack had signed the visitors' log, the guard buzzed him into the ward.

'Keep your voice low, your head high and your hands where I can see them at all times. D'ya hear?'

Jack saluted. 'Loud and clear.'

Pausing at the door, Jack was overwhelmed with the sharp pine scent of antiseptic, the metallic odour of blood, the heavy breathing and the quiet moaning of the patients invading his senses at once. His fingertips began tingling.

He stared down at his hands. He opened and closed his fists, but this served only to spread the stinging to his knuckles where he felt a dull throb.

When he looked up, three fiery interlocking red rings shimmered before his eyes. Jack stared over at Gwen quietly moaning in bed below a high barred window. The rings were identical to the image she'd carved on her arm. Jack exhaled slowly. The rings floated in front of his field of vision, bouncing like an animated 3D image on an invisible screen inches from his face. He glanced from Gwen to each of the other women in the ward. The rings followed his line of sight.

Jack took a deep breath, reaching his hand up to touch one of them. The image danced in front of his hand. No matter what Jack did, the rings remained between him and whatever he was looking at.

'Oi. What's going on in there?' asked the guard, his voice crackling through the intercom.

Jack turned and waved at the guard. The rings disappeared.

Jack raked his hands through his hair, knowing that he had been lying to himself and he had been for weeks. Exhaustion, loneliness, blood-letting, the effects of nearly dying, all those were the lies he'd been using as excuses for this deepening emotional fragility he was experiencing, for it was a wave of fear, a tug of intensity and a strange email that had brought him back to Wales in time to stop Gwen hurting her family.

Jack couldn't explain how his need to help her had been triggered by a scent on a distant world, the smell lingering from a dream he'd had or a memory that was seeping back into his consciousness from an age ago. Jack knew he could no longer ignore the rock-hard bad feeling lodged in his gut that something troubling was happening on Earth, and that

Gwen and all these mad women were somehow part of it.

The only other visitor in the psychiatric ward was a stocky man in his thirties, leaning over the woman with one side of her face bandaged. He was gently brushing a section of his wife's hair, an act so intimate and tender that Jack averted his eyes for a beat, but the man caught Jack's stare.

'At night when we watch the telly,' he said, his voice heavy with sadness, 'I always give 'er hair a brush, like. She says it makes her 'ave good dreams. Don't know what else to do to make her be still.' Every few beats his wife would jump, her arms and legs spasming against the blankets.

'Name's Phil Newman,' he said when the spasm subsided. 'This is my wife, Lizzie... Elizabeth.'

'My sister,' Jack said, nodding towards Gwen, who was mumbling in her partially conscious state, and still fighting against her restraints. 'I'm hoping the sedative settles her soon. I'm afraid I don't have her hairbrush with me.'

'Well,' the other man said, 'she's quietened down from when she first came in a few days ago.' He set the brush on the bedside table. 'Did your sister hurt herself too? My Lizzie tore off her own ear. Can you believe that?'

He slumped into the chair next to his wife's bed, looking up at Jack with his eyes swollen and sad. 'How does someone do that to themselves? What must be goin' on in her head?'

Jack came over and stood at the bottom of Lizzie's bed. 'I'm sure the doctors here will figure out what happened to your wife and to these other women. This hospital has one of the best neurological and psychiatric teams in the British Isles.'

'That's grand,' said the husband mournfully, 'but they can't heal her ear, can they?'

'Do you mind if I ask you a couple of questions?' asked Jack. 'I'm trying to figure out what happened to my sister and I think it may be the same thing that happened to your wife.'

'Really?' said Phil, sceptically. 'The doctor told me that whatever had happened to make her hurt herself had come from inside Lizzie's head and the doctor said it weren't contagious.'

'I know, and she is the doctor, but I'm curious anyway.'

Across the room one of the other women began spasming. No sooner had she started than Gwen's body began to jerk and then Lizzie's, their legs and arms twitching beneath the blankets. As if their movements had been choreographed, each of the women were spasming in unison.

Lizzie's husband jumped up and began to brush her hair again, believing his touch was making all the difference when his wife settled after a few strokes.

Jack held his hands on Gwen's feet, keeping her movements limited. He was not so sure his touch or Phil's had anything to do with what he was suddenly witnessing, as each of the women came out of the spasms at the same.

The rock-hard bad feeling yawned in Jack's gut.

'Did your wife have a history of taking drugs, Phil?' asked Jack, coming back to Lizzie's bedside while keeping his eye on Gwen. 'Even if it was only at college or in her younger days?'

Phil stopped brushing for a second. 'Nah. Lizzie was always the straight one, hardly even took a drink, did she. She was always the one who took the car keys when we were out with our friends. Always the mum of the group, making sure the rest of us were right as rain.'

'What about an emotional trauma in childhood?'

Phil shook his head.

'An accident of some kind?'

'The doctor wondered 'bout that too. But my wife's as healthy as an ox. Only time she's ever been in hospital before now was to have the kids. When she's feeling out of sorts, she goes for a night out wi' her pals, shakes it off, like. She just got our youngest toilet trained and she were so happy not to be doin' nappies any more.'

Phil's voice caught in his throat. Jack poured him a glass of water from the pitcher on the bedside table. 'Don't know what I'm goin' to tell the kids 'bout this.'

'You'll think of something, Phil,' Jack handed him the water. 'Do you know when her breakdown started exactly?'

'Was right after lunch four days ago. I'm sure of it. My 9-year-old called me at work and said mum had run out of the house. By the time I got home, police were already there and said she was in emergency. Said that she'd had some kind of a fit in the shop.'

Across the room, Gwen let out a high-pitched moan. 'Shewvee, Shewvee, Shewvee.'

Jack wanted to ask Phil more questions before the doctor returned and before Mary relieved him, but Gwen was becoming extremely agitated again.

Suddenly all the women were.

Jack wished Phil the best of luck and pulled a chair up to the right side of Gwen's bed. He took her hand. The leather restraint on her wrist was lined with cotton, but because Gwen had been fighting against it, her skin underneath the strap's edge was rubbed raw.

Jack dug around in Gwen's bedside locker and found some Vaseline. Scooping some out with a finger, he massaged the ointment into her wounds.

Slowly, she turned her head at his touch. Jack smiled and leaned closer. Gwen was crying.

'Jack?'

He smiled, fighting back his own tears. 'How are you feeling?'

'Jack?'

'Yes. It's me.'

183

She strained to lift herself up, but she couldn't. Too much pain, too many monitors, too little strength, too tight restraints.

Jack put his hands on her shoulders, settling her gently against the pillows.

'Shewvee,' she slurred, adamantly.

'Gwen, I'm so sorry. I don't understand what you're trying to tell me.'

'Esh,' she said, her eyes blazing, her determination fighting against the deepening sedative.

'S?' asked Jack, taking her hand again. She squeezed.

'Shoe. Shoe.'

'U?' Gwen squeezed his hand again, but her grip was weakening. The sedative pulling her under.

'Gwen, that's great. The letters S and U.'

'Wee… wee,' she whimpered, and then her eyes drooped closed, her mouth slackened, her grip on Jack's hand loosened and Gwen was silent and still for the first time in days.

Jack finally understood what she'd been struggling to tell him. Kissing her lightly on the lips, he whispered, 'Come back, Gwen. Please come back.'

36

Jack stood in the hallway of the house, deep in thought. Gwen had spelled out 'SUV', but she had drifted into sleep before telling him where she had hidden the keys, never mind the vehicle itself.

She wouldn't have been sloppy in her hiding place because she wouldn't want Rhys to find them, to know that she had a way to get in touch with him. Hiding them in plain sight would not be an option. Besides all the household's keys were on hooks in the kitchen, an extra set would be easily noticed.

Since returning to the house, Jack had already rifled through drawers, cupboards and Gwen's empty gun locker, the firearms confiscated by the police when she'd attacked Rhys.

He had gone down into the basement and rummaged through boxes of Christmas decorations, old Halloween costumes, discarded wedding gifts and old bikes. He'd taken apart toilet cisterns, lifted floorboards, and cut into walls. He still had not found the key fob. Jack knew he didn't have much time to keep looking, expecting that Rhys would be home with Anwen soon after taking Mary to the hospital.

Jack scanned the papered walls in the hallway, thinking

that perhaps he'd missed a safe hidden underneath one of the pictures, but he doubted it. Then he spotted a splash of colour under the bed in Gwen and Rhys's room. Reaching underneath, Jack retrieved a book: *The Day of the Triffids*. Jack skimmed the back cover, reading that the book was a post-apocalyptic novel (not Jack's favourite genre, but clearly Gwen's or Rhys's), where a catastrophic event has left a few surviving humans blind while giant man-eating plants with poisonous stingers walk the earth. Jack knew all about *them* – a nasty species.

The book was old, its faded yellow cover stained and smelling faintly of cigarettes. Jack opened it, discovering its pages hollowed out and Gwen's dad's watch and wedding ring inside. Jack began tossing books from the shelves next to the window. Ten minutes later he found the Torchwood SUV's key fob hidden in a hardback copy of *Brave New World*. After another twenty minutes, he'd discovered the wrecked vehicle hidden in the nearby lock-up.

Clicking twice on the key, Jack opened the vehicle's hatch and the wave of images and smells that assaulted his senses took him to his knees. Oranges and lilies and musk. He could see the team clambering into the vehicle and racing out to the Brecon Beacons, or speeding through the narrow backstreets of Cardiff. Tosh in the backseat, working on her laptop, Owen mocking her mercilessly, Gwen mocking Owen, and Ianto, dear sweet Ianto, taking care of them all. Jack leaned back on his heels and closed his eyes. Ianto touched his cheek, put his lips on Jack's, his hands moving under Jack's shirt.

Jack let out a sob, and opened his eyes.

A flock of starlings swooped over a nearby roof, panicking at something, darting higher up into the sky. Jack was aware of a rustling sound, close to the lock-up. He walked back out to the street, peering into the darkness.

A dark sleek puma padded across his line of vision. It stopped, turned its head and stared directly at him, its black eyes twinkling in the moonlight.

Ginger flooded Jack's mouth. He inhaled slowly, every instinct telling him to get away, to flee, to run, but he couldn't get his feet to move. Jack felt as if he was being held in place, as if hands were pressing down on his shoulders. His knees buckled again. The puma pounced. Jack ducked, shielding his head with his arms, a draft of cold air hitting his face.

When he looked up, the animal was gone. Nauseated, Jack leaned against a wall, calming his breathing, forcing his mind to clear. A car alarm went off in the distance. His stomach ached at the sound.

Jack slid to the ground against the wall, struggling to control his mounting anxiety, his head between his knees. He was falling through the sky. The ground rushed up to meet him, the air cutting through his skin. Jack tried desperately to tuck into a ball, but his arms and legs wouldn't respond, he squeezed his eyes closed and felt the rough stone of the wall behind his back.

For the first time in his long life, Jack felt sheer terror beyond anything he'd experienced when confronting Daleks, or Cybermen, or – No, this kind of terror was making his bones ache, making his heart feel as if someone was squeezing and twisting it, making him doubt his sanity.

Jack crawled inside the SUV. The scent of the memory replaced with the stench of rust and mould and the stink of shit and rotting leaves.

What the hell is happening to me?

What, he wondered as he sat in the corner, his knees against his chest, what if the Doctor and all his theories about his mortality were wrong. What if this was how Captain Jack Harkness was going to end his existence. His body always able to heal itself, reanimate each cell, restructure every muscle, over and over and over again. Life always winning out within him. Perhaps the price of regaining his immortality after the Miracle had been the loss of his memories, his intelligence, his sanity?

Jack knew he could face death. He had faced death. But how could he face life on those terms?

Jack sat in the shell of the Torchwood SUV and sobbed, letting hopelessness burrow deeper into his psyche, letting emotions he'd never experienced in years course through his veins, letting the enemy inside.

Outside the SUV, the puma stalked the perimeter, its head lifted towards Jack. Then it paused, scratched at the ground around the SUV before fading into the darkness, leaving the smell of eucalyptus lingering in its wake.

Jack felt the tremor in his hands, an uncontrollable itch on each tip of his fingers. He clawed his hands across the carpet of the SUV, trying for relief. The itch spread to his elbows like a million mosquitoes biting him at once. He scrambled out of the vehicle, rubbing his arms against the wall, scraping and tearing the skin. Then he felt the ground roll beneath him. The garage walls surrounding the SUV began to shake, the corrugated iron door buckling as dust and dirt rained down on him.

In the distance he heard a chorus of car alarms start as a tremor ran up the street, ripping up the pavement like paper and scattering trees. One toppled towards the garage, and Jack threw himself out of its way, his momentum carrying him on into the road. Except there was no road any more – the tarmac was fracturing beneath him.

Jack scrabbled to find his footing, but the ground shook around him, ancient pipes and cable snaking and jumping as the earth buckled. Above him, the little row of lock-ups was collapsing, their walls bulging and splitting as the water mains burst through them. Jack fought his way onto a patch of road, and clung to it, a tiny island in a gushing torrent of water. He looked up, trying to see a way to get to the SUV before it was too late, but all he could see was the ground yawning further open, a vast, muddy canyon gulping down cars, wheelie bins and benches, bobbing around in a mundane flotilla. He could hear the cries of other people, could see them running as the crevice zigzagged further up the street.

Then, with a sudden rollercoaster jolt, Jack's little island slipped forward, tipping him into the churning morass, the blocks of concrete landing on his back, pinning him to the bottom.

Blood pounding in his ears, he tried pushing the blocks off him, but the weight was too much. Choking and flailing, Jack began to drown.

Then a great boom travelled through the water, and the surging pool around Jack became a sudden rushing current, dragging and tugging at his clothes. The ground had split still further, pulling the plug out of the basin and sucking the water, cars, stonework and flotsam down deep into the ground.

Jack was suddenly grateful for the masonry holding him in place. It was the only thing keeping him from being carried away. As the last of the water vanished, the blocks on top of him started to shift, and Jack pulled himself coughing to his feet. All around him was mud, sobbing and devastation. Jack was standing on the lip of a great chasm. Echoing up from it was the gurgle of water and the absurd echo of dozens of car alarms.

He tried to get his bearings and groaned. The street was a ruin. Houses crumpled like they were made of Lego. The lock-ups had gone. And there was no sign of the car.

The SUV had gone, taking with it whatever Gwen had wanted him to find.

37

Mary Cooper was putting on a brave show, handing out strong tea and coffee in plastic cups, pretending that helping serve refreshments to those cleaning up the streets was distracting her from worrying about Gwen locked up in that horrible psychiatric ward.

Her husband's fate had left Mary wary of the authorities and the hospitals. She was simultaneously terrified of having her daughter in a hospital and anxious that she wasn't getting the care she needed. The ward was noisy and sterile, cold and unwelcoming. All Gwen really needed was rest, a chance to recover from everything that she'd been through, flying back and forth across the Atlantic, trying to save her dad and anyone else that she could, and all so soon after the birth of a baby. It wasn't surprising that Gwen's mind had cracked; any normal woman's would have, and way before now.

'Thanks for doing all this, Mary,' said one of the area's local councillors. 'No matter what anyone thinks, there's still nothing like a good strong cuppa to make the job go smoothly.'

Especially, thought Mary, when all you've done all morning is parade up and down the streets giving orders, you useless twit.

'Biscuit?' she said to him.

'Don't mind if I do.'

The havoc was not confined to the streets. Out in the middle of the channel, a vast black geyser was shooting steam into the air, creating a grey mist around it that was keeping the coastguard at a careful distance. When the tremor had struck last night, the geyser had burst through the water's surface. Now the sky above was filled with helicopters and the surrounding beaches and cliffs lined with tourists watching the towering fountain.

The wave the geyser had created had hit the corner of the southern coast of Wales like a freight train, water slamming into the cliffs with enough force to crumble a hefty chunk of coastline, littering the shore with debris and stabbing the sand with trees hurled from the cliffs during the quakes.

The Marina was swarming with men and women dressed in yellow emergency vests, gripping black bin bags in gloved hands like an army of giant bees. A squad of local firefighters was tagging the bigger pieces of debris that were safe to have local lads on three wheelers haul to a central dumping site and from there on to the city waste yard.

Local schools had been closed for the rest of the week. There had been injuries, but no deaths, and most of the community was embracing the hard work ahead of them with a sense of humour and grace.

Most of them, that is, except Andy Davidson, who was trying to weave his police car in and out of the tides of people flowing up and down the ravaged Swansea streets. When Andy eventually pulled up outside the Coopers' house, he was jittery and on edge and not looking forward to sharing his news.

'Hey,' he called to Jack and Rhys. The two of them were

busy doing makeshift repairs to the fence. Jack was holding a plank in place while Rhys hammered it with his good arm. They glanced up as Andy approached. Jack noticed the blanched look on Andy's face, and made a quick attempt to get Mary out of the way.

'I could use a cup of that coffee, Mary,' he said.

Gwen's mother remained immune to his charm. 'Well, Mister Captain Jack Harkness, you know where the pot is, because if this is about Gwen I'm hearing it same as you both.' She folded her arms, pursed her lips and waited.

Andy looked from Jack to Rhys and then to Mary. He could hear Bonnie in his head: 'Look them in the eye and serve them the news. How they take it isn't up to you to control.'

'Gwen's gone,' Andy blurted out.

'What?' said Rhys.

'Gone where?' said Mary, not quite grasping what she was hearing.

'What happened?' said Jack, grabbing the hammer from Rhys before he put it through a window or Andy.

'It's standard procedure when the emergency alert system goes off that all restrained patients have their restraints loosened – you know, in case they need to escape to a safe environment.'

'So they just let her walk out of the bloody ward?' asked Rhys.

'Let him finish, Rhys,' said Jack.

'All the women in that ward were sedated when their restraints were removed. The doctor checked. The guards were changing shifts. They assumed because the women were asleep that they didn't have to watch them so carefully. They claim they turned away for only a few minutes, when they checked the ward, the nurse was knocked out and Gwen was gone. The guard says it looked like she had pulled out her IV and must have been faking that she was getting her sedation.'

'Did you check the CCTV footage?' asked Jack.

'We tracked her to the car park, and then nothing. She must have left during the tremors,' said Andy. 'I've got everyone on the lookout. We'll find her.'

Jack and Rhys knew Gwen better than anyone in the world. In unison they said, 'I doubt it.'

Mary whirled round to face Jack. 'I wish she'd never bloody met you!' she yelled.

She dashed inside the house, leaving Jack staring down at Anwen bumping his leg with her plastic trike.

38

The media clamour had been growing for almost a week. By the time Dr Trimba Ormond of King's College, London called an official WHO press conference about the increasingly frequent cases of female 'insanity', it was already too late.

A few physicians and a smattering of politicians and diplomats representing various global health institutes and NGOs gathered at the WHO's London headquarters. They were talking anxiously among themselves, and generally avoiding any acknowledgement that they might once again be facing a global crisis. A few journalists were there, too, but most had decamped to South Wales in search of super geysers.

Two floors above the lecture hall, Dr Ormond sat in her bright but cramped office behind an overflowing desk, touching up her make-up while she finished a call.

'I suppose the good thing is that there has been a learning curve of sorts,' she said, powdering her thin nose. 'We are certainly much better equipped to share resources and information among each other than we were a year ago.'

'That may be the case,' said the Health Secretary on the other end of the line. 'These women might simply be experiencing a reaction to something they've come into contact with, or even some medication they've all shared. And, to be perfectly clear, I'm not dismissing the notion that this is simply mass hysteria among like-minded women. Let's be honest, Dr Ormond, we're not talking about a real health crisis, are we?'

Dr Ormond smarted at the minister's remark and angrily snapped her powder case closed. As far as she was concerned, too many of her colleagues had been slow to respond to this crisis because it was happening only to women, and, worse, it was happening inside women's heads. A far too scary place to inhabit if you listened to some of these men.

'As you are well aware from my report, sir,' she said, 'we've so far found nothing in common among these females except that there's never only one woman affected. Almost every cluster has at least five or six women in it. We have yet to trace only one woman in an area suffering from this mental illness alone.'

'So perhaps that might suggest each cluster has something in common.'

Dr Ormond looked up at her assistant who had entered the office and was tapping his watch face. Three minutes until the press conference.

'As you will also note in our report,' said Dr Ormond impatiently, gathering the notes for her speech from her desk and sliding them into her leather portfolio, 'each woman in each cluster that we've been able to identify has been thoroughly investigated and we have found no correlation in their symptoms and nothing at all in common in their backgrounds. We've tested their ground water and their major food supply, their oxygen levels and their blood types. We have nothing.'

'But you will continue to investigate?'

'Of course! But—'

Before she could finish her sentence, before she could

present him with her plan to continue the investigation, the Health Secretary interrupted her and excused himself. From the speaker, Dr Ormond could hear a mumbled conversation, raised voices and then she heard chairs scraping. A new deeper, softer male voice came on the line. 'Trimba, this is Alan Pride. May we speak frankly?'

She looked up at her assistant, who shrugged and rolled his eyes. Alan Pride was the PM's right-hand man, his amanuensis, his conscience (such as it was) and, when necessary, his fall guy. Alan Pride was in his fifties, and a man of one or two intriguing contradictions. Born to a coalmining family in the north of England, Pride had earned a scholarship to the London School of Economics, where he and the PM had become close friends. A Harvard MBA had been followed by rapid progress to the board of an international bank. When the market crashed, Pride stepped down. Admitting his own bank had been complicit in making bad loans, he testified in front of Parliament and the US Congress against many of his fellow bankers who, he believed, had shamed themselves and their profession. Selling his mansion in Connecticut, his pied-a-terre in Paris and his house in Kensington, he disappeared from the public eye for a few months. His appointment in Downing Street had caused a minor uproar in predictable sections of the press but, as usual, that hadn't been enough to outweigh the support of the Party.

Was Pride a changed man or simply a man who'd changed his approach to power? Trimba Ormond hadn't made up her mind. 'What is it you'd like to ask, Mr Pride?'

'Do you have a plan for what our local hospitals should do with these women who are... suffering? Because you know as well as I do that our mental health facilities are already stretched to capacity. Before you take any of this report to the public, I'd like to talk to you about some ideas

I have on the matter.'

Dr Ormond sat back down at her desk. 'With all due respect, Mr Pride, I have a press conference about to start. I think we need to share what we've discovered right now. Before things get worse.'

'That's not your call to make, Trimba. I'll see you in my office tomorrow at 9 a.m.'

Dr Ormond slammed her portfolio onto the speaker, disconnecting the call. She instructed her assistant to cancel the press conference, but gave no indication if she was going to reschedule. The press would not be happy, and neither would her colleagues. She made a few edits on the press release, then handed it to her assistant.

'How does that sound?' she asked.

Her assistant read the release aloud. 'While we, in collaboration with other national and regional organisations, have not yet uncovered the cause of this widespread outbreak of mental illness in women, we have determined that the number of cases has not increased dramatically. We must, however, remind all care-givers of suffering women that, although it seems not to be contagious, it can be life-threatening to its sufferers and to their loved ones. Therefore, until we can find a way to eliminate, or at the very least reduce the symptoms for these afflicted women, we and our health partners across the world are recommending that health professionals keep their patients sedated and under close supervision.'

'Appropriately informative and necessarily vague,' he said when he'd finished.

'Perfect.'

39

Rhys was slumped at the Coopers' kitchen table, a half-finished beer next to him. His wrist was in a cast, his eyes red-rimmed, his left one circled in purples and yellows. Panic and worry were the only things keeping him from collapsing from exhaustion.

Gwen's attack on Rhys, her subsequent arrest and now her escape from the hospital had made the national news – 'Madwoman on the Loose' – including the drive-time phone-in show on Red Dragon radio that had been debating her plight with a variety of mostly uninformed sources. One of the callers claimed to have a contact in the Welsh police department who revealed that 'This Cooper girl is a violent nutter that should have been sent straight to jail' and that 'the police should be taking a much tougher stance on these attacks, but they aren't because they were women what was doing them.' Within hours, this supposed leak had scratched and clawed its way up to Andy's superiors, who wanted to know what the hell was being done to find Gwen.

Andy had returned to Swansea after his afternoon shift with more information for Jack about the other women who'd experienced public breakdowns around the same time as Gwen's. He had promised more help that night, but since the 'leak' he'd been reassigned to set up a phone bank, taking tips on sightings of Gwen. The news that these breakdowns were now worldwide was sinking in and had also resulted in a deluge of calls from men and women in the area wanting to report their own family members for being 'off their effing rockers'.

Jack poured Rhys another beer, setting it next to a frozen dinner he had zapped in the microwave. 'Andy has squads monitoring the motorway, Cardiff airport, the train stations and all the ports. If Gwen tries to leave Wales, he'll find her. The press are all over Gwen's story, and he thinks that will help.'

'He's wrong,' said Rhys.

'I know. Gwen isn't going to leave you or Anwen. I think she just wants to come home.'

'Andy will have some of his boys watching the house, too, then,' said Rhys. 'He's turning into a smart lad.'

Jack nodded. 'I spotted one on the street, doing a pretty good job of standing casually outside the bookie's having a smoke. If you see him, congratulate him on his choice of tracksuit. Showed off his bottom magnificently.'

For a while the two men sat in silence, listening to Anwen chatter to herself, telling stories about angry giants as she built a tower for her dolls and then crashed her truck into it.

'What about all the other women?' asked Rhys. 'Did they hurt themselves too?'

Jack opened the files that Andy had left that afternoon. 'The most violent clusters in the UK so far are women in the Scottish highlands, one cluster on the west coast and one near John O'Groats. Each of the women severely mutilated themselves, then attacked a close family member. In two cases, the woman murdered a loved one. Andy says the total as of this afternoon is 264 women across the UK. More internationally.'

'Bloody hell,' said Rhys, his wrist throbbing, his dinner congealing on the plate in front of him. He looked about as pathetic and troubled as Jack had ever seen him look. 'What the hell's going on, Jack?'

'Wish I knew, Rhys.' Rolling up his shirt sleeves, Jack lifted Anwen up and set her in her high chair, tucked a bib under her chin, and sliced bananas and toast onto her tray, most of which she tossed back at him, giggling.

'You're good with her, you know,' said Rhys, popping open another beer, quickly heading from numb to useless in any research tasks Jack had in mind for him that night.

'She's a good baby,' said Jack, handing her a triangle of toast slathered in Marmite.

'It's bloody Torchwood again, isn't it?' said Rhys, who had spent most of the past few nights at the hospital, returning in the morning only to check on Anwen, shower and change his clothes and pick up some clean ones for Gwen. Jack was afraid that he might lose himself in his drinking if they didn't figure something out soon.

'Well, I'm fine,' said Jack, wiping Anwen's face which was smeared in Marmite. At least she was eating, thought Jack, forcing down a corner of her toast, the taste repulsing him.

'You don't count,' snapped Rhys. 'And if you did you're not exactly proof that Torchwood isn't at fault considering that you're the only one still standing.'

'Hey, you're still standing,' said Jack. 'And you're doing fine, too.'

He walked over to his laptop and pulled up the TV news. Water traffic in the channel had been restricted. A parade of international scientists and geologists were trying to get close enough to the geyser to examine it. The geyser was slowly turning silver.

'Look at that,' whistled Jack. 'It's actually quite a

magnificent sight.'

The geyser looked like an explosion of silver fireworks against the setting sun. Jack stared at the jet's pulsing spray, letting the images and the noises in his head rise to a deafening roar, knowing that the answer to what was causing this madness and this geological anomaly were locked inside his mind.

40

Flipping open the notes he had made earlier in the day and the file that Andy had given him, Jack went back to the original three police reports and spread them out across the table. The three woman whose files Andy had homed in on were of different ages and ethnicities – the university librarian was white and middle-aged; the second woman was black and in her thirties; the third, Lizzie, was the madwoman from the supermarket. Jack lined up their photographs next to each other.

'All of these women are, according to their families and their friends, peaceful and law abiding,' said Jack, 'and yet in all three cases, like Gwen, they behaved in a bizarre manner and in the process of their... their madness, they physically harmed themselves.'

Jack picked up the photograph of the librarian, handing it to Rhys. 'Ginny Davies plucked out her eyeball with no mind to how painful it must have been. She told the student who sat on her until the medics arrived that,' Jack picked up the notes in the file and read, 'that she "couldn't look at the world that way any more."'

'That's horrible,' said Rhys, looking sadly at the attractive woman who had partially blinded and seriously disfigured herself. 'Do the police have any idea what she meant?'

'The police have no clue, but I think she may've been seeing things, hallucinating perhaps, and whatever she was seeing broke her mind.' Jack stopped and stared at Rhys.

'What is it?'

'Nothing... nothing,' said Jack, going to the sink and pouring himself some water. When he'd thought of the second woman's mind breaking, he felt as if the memory he'd been trying to snag last night in the SUV had for a fleeting second flashed fully formed across his mind. Then it was gone, leaving a thin trail behind, a lingering bad taste in his mouth.

Jack gulped the water before returning to the table.

'This is Moira Firth, 24, a waitress. She'd just served dessert to her family of four when she headed into the kitchen and confronted her husband, the chef, with a long rant about his adultery and then she picked up a butcher's knife and tried to cut out his heart.'

'Jesus,' said Rhys, taking the photo of Moira from Jack.

'Think yourself lucky that I showed up when I did,' said Jack, 'and that it was only your face Gwen was sick of.'

'I've never seen these women in my life before, and I'm pretty sure Gwen hadn't either. But here's the thing, Jack. Gwen was raging at me, but she was really angry at herself too, at not being able to be the action woman she used to be, at how she was a terrible mother. It was like she'd let out all the frustrations she'd always kept inside about being a mum and a wife and the sacrifices she made for Anwen and me.' Rhys wiped his sleeve across his eyes. 'But I made sacrifices too, you know, Jack. I've always supported what she wanted to do, and I've protected her the best way I know how.'

Jack turned quickly. 'What did you just say?'

Rhys cowed a bit under Jack's stare. 'Well, maybe my job wasn't always all about saving the world from aliens or anything but it was still important to me.'

'Rhys, don't be such a— Not that part. The Gwen part. Say again what she was yelling at you about.'

'Mostly about how she was a bad mum, and a bad wife and how she didn't want to be one any more,' Rhys choked back a sob. 'I can't believe that was my Gwen saying all those awful things.'

'That's just it,' said Jack. 'I don't think it was the Gwen who loves you and Anwen. I think it might've been the part of Gwen that's always been locked in her subconscious that somehow took over and wanted to hurt you.' Rhys looked appalled at Jack's train of thought. 'Perhaps that part of her doesn't want to be a wife any more.'

'I don't believe that's how Gwen feels. Not deep down,' said Rhys. As he spoke, he slumped further over his beer and the photographs lined up in front of him.

'This is going to get much worse before any of these women get better,' said Jack, 'but it will get better. And you will get Gwen back.'

'Do you reckon there's something in the drinking water?'

Jack shook his head. 'There's definitely something connecting what's happening to all these women here and abroad, but it has nothing to do with the water. I think something alien is attacking these women.'

'I don't get it,' said Rhys, slurring his words, exhaustion and lager finally breaking him.

Jack turned back to his laptop, staring at the image of the geyser, believing that he finally did. The lip of the sun was kissing the horizon. Jack's fingers tingled at the sight, the geyser like a stiletto stabbing the centre of the sun.

41

After dinner, Jack drove to the university library. The hunch that had gripped him when he was looking at the sunset still held him in its sway.

A librarian accosted him as he stood staring at the shelf on the History of Religions in the Reference room. The woman was in her mid-sixties, short white hair, dressed in grey slacks, a crisp white blouse with a string of pearls at her neck. A pair of pink plastic reading glasses were perched on the end of her thin nose.

'Sir, may I help you? You look lost.'

'More than you'll ever know.'

She smiled at him as if she knew exactly what he meant, even though Jack was no longer sure that even he did.

'You do know we're closing in thirty minutes.'

'I know,' said Jack, following the woman over to her desk. 'I'd like some information.'

'I can sign you on to one of our computers, but you'll have to finish your search in fifteen minutes, I'm afraid.'

'Actually, I'd like the help from you, if that's possible.'

'From me?' she said, putting her hand on her chest and exclaiming as if he'd offered her a bouquet of roses and a box of chocolates.

'Yes,' he said, smiling, offering her his hand. 'Captain Jack Harkness.'

'Bernie Sanger.' She shook Jack's hand.

'Honestly,' said Jack. 'I'd rather have you help me instead.'

'Are you serious?' she said, offering him a seat in front of her desk. 'Is this one of those reality shows, and I'm going to be viral on YouTube tomorrow?'

'Of course not,' laughed Jack. 'That would be a mean thing to do.'

She rolled her eyes. 'Of course it would, but that hardly seems to matter much nowadays. We like watching bad things happen to people. We've become a mean-spirited society. Look at the way everyone's treating the families of those poor women, as if they're lepers. You'd think we'd travelled back in time and hadn't learned a thing about psychology.'

'I couldn't agree more,' said Jack, taking out a sheet of paper with a picture of the design Gwen had carved on her arm.

Jack believed that, in a fleeting moment of lucidity before she had attacked Rhys, for some reason Gwen had wanted to remember the image. Jack knew Gwen well enough to believe that the image was a message of some kind for him. This image was somehow vital to saving Gwen and the other women.

'It's just that I never get asked for help much here any more,' continued the librarian. 'I've become nothing more than a glorified room monitor or a polite guide to the nearest toilet. I don't even have to re-shelf books much, so few are checked out.'

'Sad, isn't it,' said Jack. He looked round the impressive room, its wood-panelled walls, wide windows, and rows of books looking the same as it had in the nineteenth century, when he had first been there. There was something comforting in being surrounded by books all day every day, thought Jack, even for someone like him who was finding comfort in so few things now.

One or two tired-looking scholars and a handful of eager students were hunched over the long rectangular tables. All of the patrons had laptops open next to them; only one had a stack of books. The room was quiet except for the occasional cough or throat-clearing, the low burring of an incoming text message, and the tap-tapping of fingers on keyboards. But in Jack's head the noises were ever present, the flashes of faces and fragments of memory bordering his vision every minute.

Since that afternoon, the image of the beautiful woman from the mirror had haunted Jack's peripheral vision, reinforcing for him that his visions, especially the woman's face, and the sighting of the puma, were related to whatever was happening to female synaesthetes around the world, and he had a strong feeling that all of these things were preludes to something much worse, something he needed to get ahead of before it was too late.

'They mostly come in here for the free Wi-Fi,' said the librarian.

'Or a nap,' said Jack, nodding towards one of the scholars, whose chin was resting comfortably on his chest.

The strange woman's face lingered faintly in Jack's peripheral vision.

'Bernie, I need some research done on a few items, including some information on an Inca tribe called the Cuari,' said Jack, slipping two sheets of paper across her desk. 'I'd be happy to compensate you for the work if it cuts into your day.'

She scanned the two pages. 'That won't be necessary. For a few days, let them find the toilet on their own.'

'Oh,' said Jack, standing to leave, 'and I'd appreciate it if you kept this between us.'

'Captain, I may not be as fast as the internet, but I can keep a secret.' She folded the paper and slipped it into her desk. 'How may I reach you with the results?'

'I'm leaving the country soon,' said Jack. 'If you could email the information to me, that would be great.'

42

Dr Olivia Steele lived in a whitewashed Georgian mansion off the St Andrew's Road, west of Dinas Powys Common. The house was tucked in the woods, its closest neighbour barely visible in the deepening dusk, except as jags of orange light bursting through the trees.

Jack stopped in front of the iron gates at the entrance to the driveway. The only evidence that he had found the right place was a small brass plaque beneath an intercom on the gates that read, 'Steele Manor', which Jack thought appropriate for a doctor who healed people's heads or a confused superhero. Jack had called ahead to make an appointment. When he pressed the bell to announce his arrival, the gates swung open immediately.

The winding canopied approach was long and narrow. The road eventually opened onto a large circular driveway fronting the house. Dr Steele was waiting for Jack at the front door. She led him into a marbled foyer where another woman, dressed in a black jersey dress, revealing ample hips and a perfect décolletage, took Jack's coat while Jack tried his best not to stare.

'My assistant, Win.'

Win smiled, accepting Jack's coat while asking if he'd

like tea or coffee. Jack said coffee, then followed the doctor to a sitting room off to the left of a wide, carpeted staircase.

The room was comfortable and warm, expensive without being excessive. A fire burned in a marble hearth, an original Mary Cassatt hanging above it. Jack smiled. He had met Mary in Paris once or twice during the War. She would have appreciated the irony that one of her paintings hung in a psychiatrist's sitting room in the twenty-first century.

Jack settled in a high-backed leather chair. Dr Steele sat opposite him on a matching leather couch. In white linen pants and a loose yellow shirt, her skin soft and pale, she looked, Jack thought, ten years younger than he remembered.

She folded her hands on her lap, crossing her legs at her ankles. 'Captain Harkness, I must say your phone call intrigued me, especially since currently I have a full ward of women experiencing breakdowns similar to your –' she arched her brows – 'sister's. And, according to many of my colleagues around the country, mine is not the only psychiatric floor full of female patients.'

Her assistant carried a silver tray into the room with a decanter and two crystal glasses on it. Setting it down on the table between them, she said, 'I thought you both might prefer a cocktail instead of coffee.' She rested her hand on the doctor's shoulder in a way that suggested she was more than just an assistant.

'What would I do without you?' The doctor placed her hand on her partner's.

'A great many things, I'm sure, but none of them with drinks served on time.'

'Whisky, Captain?'

Jack nodded.

Leaning forward, keeping her ankles crossed, she uncorked the decanter. 'Win's family own a distillery in the highlands. This is one of their best single malts.'

Jack relaxed into the chair. 'Dr Steele, I want to apologise for getting off on the wrong foot with you.'

'Olivia, I insist.'

'Then it's Jack.'

'And there's no need to apologise. It's forgotten.'

'Friends?' asked Jack.

'Friends,' said Olivia pouring him a healthy dram.

He tilted the glass before lifting it to his nose. He inhaled its smoky peaty warmth, and as soon as he did he heard a distinctive chime of music that sent a jolt of pleasure through him. He gasped. Recovering from the sensation quickly, he answered, 'Wonderful. Truly.'

'It is, isn't it,' said Olivia, sitting back on the couch. She took a sip from her glass. 'Of course, I realised when I got in the lift what you were doing, that you incited my rant so I'd unwittingly reveal patient information. I should probably have had you removed from Ms Cooper's visiting list.' She smiled. 'Although that's moot now, isn't it. An unforgivable error on security's part.' She sipped a little more. 'Have you heard anything about where she might be?'

Jack shook his head. 'Not yet. Her husband is worried she may hurt herself again. Or, worse, someone else.'

'Yes,' said Olivia, 'that's seems to be the worst symptom of this strange illness, doesn't it? But Ms Cooper was given her anti-psychotic medication before she escaped, so I hope she'll be less inclined to hurt anyone and will be back in custody before she needs another dose.'

Putting the glass to his lips, Jack took a sip, this time prepared for his body's startling response. He held the whiskey in his mouth for a beat, then another, letting the warmth of it caress his tongue, the sweet flavours electrifying his entire mouth, every taste bud alive and tingling and then he swallowed, the liquid like velvet on his throat. He shivered.

'You do look like you're enjoying the whiskey,' smiled Olivia. 'Win will be pleased.'

Not as pleased as I feel, thought Jack, shifting slightly in his seat. The intense sexual feelings were wonderful, but not entirely welcomed. Jack was aware that his body was reacting to stimuli in heightened ways recently, and given what had happened during the earthquake, the sighting of the puma, and his emotional breakdown, he was beginning to worry. He tried to focus.

Olivia balanced her glass on the arm of the couch. 'I believe you said you had a theory you'd like to share with me about why all these women around the world are falling prey to this so-called masochistic madness.'

'We know a number of things already,' said Jack, reluctantly setting his glass on a mahogany table next to his chair. 'Obviously, it's happening only to women and each one is self-mutilating in some way during her psychotic incidents. From the reports I've studied, the most common thing they're doing is damaging their eyes, ears or tongues.'

Except Gwen, he thought, who's carved a strange symbol on her forearm.

'Suggesting,' added Olivia, 'that their neurosis is tied to their senses in some way. Yes. I think that's a reasonable assumption.'

'Exactly,' said Jack, reaching to sip more whiskey but thinking better of it, for now anyway. What he had to say was too important. 'I think all of these women are synaesthetes, Olivia, and whatever is affecting them has made their synaesthesia acute and extreme, overwhelming their senses.'

And mine, too, thought Jack. He glanced at the whiskey glass, catching a whiff of its palate and experiencing another kick of desire that went right to the growing ache of pleasure in his groin.

'Fascinating, Jack!' Olivia finished her whiskey and refilled her glass. She held the decanter up to Jack who shook his head, more aggressively than he intended. 'I wrote a paper on synaesthesia in my third year at Cambridge. My professor at the time was one of the first neuroscientists to study the phenomenon seriously, and he made some quite startling discoveries about it.'

'I know,' said Jack. 'I read your work and his earlier this evening.'

Olivia looked into her glass for a few beats. 'You know, you may be on to something, Jack. Synaesthesia operates on a spectrum, but unlike, say, depression or many other mental disorders, synaesthesia is not a mental illness. Far from it, in fact. Many synaesthetes are artists and creative types who believe it's not an affliction but a gift from God, an incredible heightening of their senses that allows them to experience the world from multiple places in their brain at the same time.'

'What do you mean?' asked Jack.

'Are you a synaesthete?'

'I think I am,' said Jack. 'Or… I think I've become one. In the past few weeks, I've started perceiving days of the week and months of the year as colours and shapes, seen time in waves of coloured lines, sometimes even with music.'

What he did not share was that in the past few days, this synaesthesia had been getting stronger, affecting all of his senses in disturbing ways.

'Of course – it *is* the nature of your brain, but it's not the way most people perceive the world. Yours, though, is one of the most common forms of synaesthesia – grapheme to colour.' She stepped over to a set of tightly packed bookshelves and lifted a book from midway up. She handed it to Jack before returning to the couch.

Jack read the title aloud: '*Wednesday Is Indigo Blue.*' He

smiled. 'Mine's golden brown.'

Olivia nodded. 'Most synaesthetes don't know that they are special, that they are experiencing the world through multiple modes of perception. When someone like yourself, say, with a mild form, tastes or smells something he or she will experience the taste as a sound or a colour which heightens perception. Synaesthetes are experiencing all of their senses at the same time.'

'Like our wires are crossed?' asked Jack, thinking of the rush of desire he'd experienced minutes before from the trigger, the taste and smell of the whiskey.

'That's what we used to think, but scientists now believe, thanks to sophisticated brain imaging, that it's not crossed wires, it's more like multiple wires connecting all at once, senses cross-talking instantaneously instead of connecting one to one. I'm simplifying, of course, but in the synaesthetic brain, the connections among the senses are polymodal.'

Jack sat forward in the chair, the smell of peat from the whiskey quickening his pulse again.

'Years ago researchers had a difficult time separating true synaesthetic responses from a person's metaphorical thinking or even separating a synaesthete's response to a sense from a memory triggered by that sense. Olfactory senses in particular evoke memories incredibly powerfully.'

Jack had to stand up, cool his desire, get away from his drink, the whiskey too strong a siren call to his senses. He stood in front of the fire. 'What do you mean, "metaphorical thinking"?'

She paused for a beat, before continuing. 'An artist like Georgia O'Keefe, for example, painted while listening to music, transferring what she heard into her lush images. As far as we know, she was not a synaesthete. Wally Kandinsky, on the other hand, was a synaesthete, and he painted what he heard when he perceived sounds. He painted his perceptions not representations of them.'

'Ah... But if my theory is correct,' said Jack, 'and all these women were mildly synaesthetic before the madness and now something is making it worse... that'll be hard to prove, won't it?'

'Unfortunately, yes, but we can try, and it certainly puts us into a different area of research from what we have been pursuing. It may mean that we have to reduce their sedation in order to stimulate them when we run a brain scan, and, of course, we'll need to talk to their families to be sure they are comfortable with the risks that that may involve. But, Jack – this is a step in the right direction towards healing. Finally.' She finished the last of her drink. 'Unfortunately, for many of these women, they've already damaged themselves beyond repair.'

Jack looked at the Cassatt on the wall, wondering what she had seen when she painted it. 'Synaesthesia is hereditary, isn't it?' he asked, thinking of Anwen and her mismatched fruits, her association of colour with a taste.

'Yes it is,' replied Olivia. 'In my research, I discovered that there is a chromosome marked for synaesthesia, and, although I can't prove it yet, I've always believed that as human beings evolve, a person's synaesthesia evolves too.'

Jack laughed. 'So those of us who are synaesthetes are more evolved than humans who aren't?'

Which, Jack thought, made sense, given that he was from the 51st century. As this thought flashed across his consciousness, it brought with it the face of the beautiful young woman from the mirror, floating in front of his eyes. Jack tried to keep her there for as long as he could, but Olivia was continuing and he couldn't hold the image.

She was laughing at his assertion. 'That's one way to describe it.' Without warning, she clapped her hands excitedly, jumping up from the couch. 'That's it!'

'That's what?'

'No two people experience synaesthesia in the same way,' said Olivia, excitement charging her pitch, 'but some studies have shown that it is experienced more by women than men, present company excepted.'

The clock on the sideboard chimed. A dog barked somewhere deep in the house.

'I'm sorry... Could you say that again?'

'Are you OK, Captain... Jack? You've gone a bit pale.'

'Sorry. I'm fine. Just trying to put some of this together.'

'I was saying that the studies have shown that more women than men experience synaesthesia.' Olivia walked smartly across the room. 'I realise that their gender alone doesn't explain why these particular women are suffering.' The excitement had drained from her voice. 'Especially given that not all women everywhere who are synaesthetes are experiencing a heightening of their senses. And this knowledge certainly doesn't help us explain any possible triggers.'

'Ah, but it's a start,' said Jack. 'It's a start.'

Olivia opened the sitting room door and called for Win to get Jack's coat. While they waited in the foyer, Olivia added, 'At its most extreme, synaesthesia can mean having shapes in your field of vision at all times. It can scramble the senses in terribly debilitating and, as we've witnessed, dangerous ways. Think about how you'd feel if you had an extreme form of auditory synaesthesia which resulted in your ability to taste every single sound that you hear. Loud thunder is rotten chicken, a baby crying is curdled milk. Imagine what Piccadilly Circus would be like for you on a Saturday night, never mind a simple dinner at home with the children.'

'Vomit-inducing,' said Jack. 'Worse.'

'Indeed.'

43

Jack stood with his back to the television, looking out of the living room windows, staring at his own reflection in the darkness, his blue shirt cuffed at his elbows, braces loose at his hips. Hair needs a cut, he thought, running his fingers through it. Maybe a closer shave too.

It was after 10 p.m., and he knew he was leaving Wales the next day. Once he'd returned to the Coopers' house, he'd spent a couple of hours thinking about the narrative he'd created that day from all the data he'd absorbed from his and Andy's research. Add that to the information Olivia had given him, and the hypothesis that had been forming in his mind since he'd seen the image tattooed on Gwen's forearm was all but confirmed.

He knew he needed more information and a different approach from the one he'd been taking, one that needed more than someone, him, who was emotionally connected to the key victim and being influenced just as strongly as she was by some psychic force. Jack wasn't thinking about passing the buck, but spreading the responsibility would help.

Jack was a loner, but he was not anti-social.

With the Hub destroyed, Jack had only one place

where he could go to find some of the answers, to have the equipment and the intellectual power he needed if the worst of what he was thinking was true. So he sent a message.

Jack could feel in his bones that time was running out. He just didn't know whose.

Behind him, the television newscasters were babbling about the cancelled WHO press conference and how the lack of information coming from the government about this strange mental illness was becoming as startling as the disease itself. Every news and social media outlet was circulating Dr Ormond's press release.

Jack turned, aimed the remote at the television as if it were his Webley and silenced the news.

'Hey! I was listening to that,' said Rhys, sitting with his computer at the dining room table, lager in hand.

'It's not helpful,' said Jack, slouching onto the couch, landing on a squeaky toy caught in the cushions. 'Now every Tom and Dick is going to sedate their wives with whatever they can get their hands on as soon as she asks them to play with the kids instead of going round to the pub. There's going to be a run on tranquillisers.' He tossed the toy into the playpen on the other side of the room. 'This whole thing is going to give a new meaning to domestic violence.'

Rhys sipped from his can. 'You have a very dim view of your fellow man.'

'I've a very dim view of all kinds of creatures,' said Jack.

'At least some folks are trying to figure out what's going on. You haven't come up with any brilliant answers, Captain Jack. My Gwen's been mad for a week and now she's out there somewhere doing God knows what.'

Jack understood why Rhys was so upset, but he couldn't tell him what he was working out. He owed it to Gwen not to drag Anwen's only parent further into this.

'I'm thinking about it. Ruminating over the situation.

Gathering data.'

'Oh, that's what thinking looks like, is it?' said Rhys.

'No, this is.' Jack put his foot up on the arm of the couch, posing like Rodin's statue. Rhys laughed, snorting lager across the keyboard.

They were both stopped in their laughter when Anwen's cries burst through the baby monitor.

'I'll go up this time,' said Jack. 'You keep searching for something on that image.'

'You know this would go a lot faster if we could run your Torchwood software.'

Jack stopped at the living room door. 'I told you, Rhys. That's not an option right now. We're on our own.'

Later that night, Jack was stretched out on the couch, unable to sleep. He was still dressed in his shirt and trousers. He had always been able to sleep in the tightest confines, believing the reasons he couldn't sleep in the massive beds that everyone in this century owned – no matter how tiny their bedroom – was as much to do with being buried alive as it was that too much open space made him feel disconnected, like he was drifting from his moorings. It was a feeling he'd thought he'd overcome; however, in the aftermath of his recent experiences, Jack had once again found himself drawn to tight spaces.

Jack heard the front door closing quietly. Quickly tugging on his boots, he ran through the hall, into the kitchen. In the middle of the table was Gwen's wedding ring and, propped against the sugar bowl, a handwritten note:

> *When she's old enough, give this to Anwen.*
> *Tell her I'm sorry and I love her.*
>
> *G x*

Jack charged through the door, pausing in the empty street. There wasn't a sign of Gwen. Not even the distant echo of footsteps. But then, Jack had an idea. These last few days, his senses had been turned up to eleven. Why not use that to his advantage? He took a deep breath and held it, savouring it until he could just catch the tiniest, familiar smell of Gwen – expensive shampoo, old-fashioned soap, masked with a recent layer of hospital disinfectant and industrial laundry. Feeling a little like a bloodhound, Jack sprinted off on Gwen's trail.

The pier had been closed for renovations. Renovations that kept being put back and put back, as though the council were waiting for the rusting Victorian structure to have the decency to give up and fall into the sea of its own free will.

Jack trod across the boards, feeling them creak and shift more than he'd hoped. He made his way gently towards the figure at the end of the pier, silhouetted against the low moon. She must know he was there. He just prayed she wouldn't jump now. Because that's all people really came to the pier to do these days – jump off it.

Jack crept forward, wondering when he dared call out her name. If he startled her, maybe she'd turn and fight – which would win him time. But if she jumped into the sea… Jack started to calculate how long it would take him to reach the end of the pier, to dive in after her, to find her in the cold, choppy waters. He wanted to call to her, try to reason with her, to let her know he was going to find out what was happening, that he was going to save her, but he didn't dare risk it, not yet.

Jack edged forward, plank by plank, feeling them shift and buckle under his weight. Was it his imagination, or was the entire structure twisting slightly in the waves? Had the recent tremors done the ironwork damage? At each step,

Jack caught his breath, to see if there was any reaction. Maybe, just maybe, he'd be able to reach out, to grab her, to stop her...

'I know you're there.' Her voice was soft.

'Gwen, stop! Please.'

She turned, recognising Jack's voice but not yet seeing him. 'Jack? Jack?'

It sounded like the old Gwen. Jack moved faster. 'Gwen, let's stop for a minute. I can help you. You know I can.'

'Jack, please, leave me alone,' she yelled. 'I can't be near them – I'm so afraid I'll hurt them. At the moment, my head is clear. I know what to do.'

'No, Gwen,' Jack pleaded, 'It's not. You're not thinking right – your brain chemistry's been scrambled, you've been pumped so full of drugs...'

Gwen smiled, and it was an odd smile that froze Jack to the spot. 'Jack, I'm just doing what I can to protect them.'

She's going to jump, thought Jack, edging another step closer.

'I can protect them. I'm beginning to make progress in figuring out what's happening to you. I think something's been triggered in your DNA,' he said, doing his best to keep her talking. 'Remember Torchwood. We've solved worse. We can figure out what's happening to you.'

'There is no Torchwood!' screamed Gwen, 'Don't you get it? It's gone. Over. They're all gone. Tosh and Owen and Ianto and poor, poor Esther. You couldn't save them, and you can't save me. There's only you, Jack. It's always been only you.'

Jack froze, stung by her words. Gwen's anger wasn't the fury of a madwoman, but cold, rational rage. He felt like he'd lost his last friend in the world. 'No, Gwen. That's not true. It's going to be you and me. Both of us. For a long time.' He risked a pleading smile.

Gwen turned away from Jack and took a step towards the edge. Jack charged at her, badly misjudging how frail she had become in the past week. He grabbed her waist and twisted backwards. Her fists smashed into his face as they rolled onto the creaking planks, tumbling over and over...

And over.

It took Jack a few seconds to realise he and Gwen were falling.

44

Jack and Gwen hit the water still fighting. The force of the water ripped through Jack's nostrils, bursting inside his head. Gwen's legs tightened around Jack's waist, and they plunged into the black sea.

Christ. It was cold. Jack knew that if they didn't start kicking up, they'd both drown. He'd surface eventually, gasping, gagging, but breathing again.

Gwen would not.

Gwen's grip loosened. She knew she had to free herself from Jack's embrace or he would save her, pull her back to the surface to the madness her life had become, to locked doors, straps on her bed, Rhys in a constant state of fear, and Anwen terrified of her own mum. It wasn't right. She would not live that way. She would not let Jack save her. Not this time. Not ever again.

As they continued to sink, Gwen pummelled Jack with her feet, kicking to free herself from his grip. Jack could feel that Gwen was in a rage again, battering his head, gulping water. Jack knew what she was thinking, and he knew his only chance to save Gwen was to save himself, to get them both to the surface. Now.

Forcing air out through his nose, releasing some of the

pressure in his lungs, Jack dolphin-kicked. Hard. Gwen's movements were working against him, keeping him under the crashing waves, trying to climb onto his back and hold him down.

Where was this strength coming from? Jack wrapped an arm under Gwen's shoulder and for a fleeting moment, his Gwen stared back, the Gwen he loved, her eyes horrified, wide and panicked staring directly into Jack's face.

He would not let this woman go. This wasn't about keeping Torchwood alive. It never was. This was about keeping alive the woman he loved more than a sister, a lover, a friend, more than his life now and for ever.

They finally broke through the surface. Jack struggled to breathe. Gwen was coughing and gagging and trying to force herself back under. The waves were pulling them towards the jagged rocks of the beach, then dropping them back under, the current too strong for Jack to swim against and fight Gwen at the same time.

Jack lost his grip on Gwen. Immediately, she kicked away from him. Jack yanked her hair and pulled her back, but Gwen's rage was so powerful that Jack couldn't tell now if she was trying to kill him, kill herself or trying to fight for her own life, all at the same time.

She went under a third time, lunging away from Jack's grip.

Jack swam after her, locking his arms around her neck. Both of them treading hard beneath the surface, waves smacking hard against their heads. Gwen was coughing and sobbing, her fingernails scratching at Jack's neck.

Jack inhaled deeply, smelling Gwen's terror – iron and lilac.

They went under again. This time Jack swallowed too much water and he had to fight the urge to gag until they broke for air again. When they did, Gwen's grip was even tighter on Jack's throat. Her struggles were wearing them both down. Jack knew he couldn't waste any more energy this way or they were both going to drown.

Jack let Gwen hold him under for the last time. Then with all his strength, he forced her head and shoulders above the surface.

'Sorry, Gwen.'

He drew back his fist and punched her. Dazed, her legs loosened their grip and she slipped under the water. Jack grabbed her before the current could pull her away from him. She moaned. He flipped her into a lifesaving hold, keeping her head above the water, treading water until he was able to get their bearings and strike out towards the distant lights of the shore.

A frantic Rhys was waiting for them in the kitchen, running into the street when Jack, drenched and freezing, every muscle screaming, stumbled towards the house with Gwen cradled in his arms.

Later, the two men sat on either side of the bed, watching Gwen sleep, an ice-pack pressed across the bridge of her nose, the swelling puffing out her cheeks.

'How many families do you reckon are having a night like this one?'

'Too many,' said Jack, leaning forward in the chair, taking Gwen's hand. 'Christ, if all these women are going to start taking their own lives whenever they have a brief moment of sanity then the clock is ticking down faster than I thought.'

Rhys stared sadly at Jack, realising that in all the years he'd known him he'd aged only a little. Still handsome, still larger than life, still with that same killer smile and dimpled chin, but changed somehow nonetheless. Jack glanced over at Rhys. For a fleeting moment, Rhys saw such pain in Jack's blue eyes that his breath caught in his throat. One thing Rhys was suddenly certain of, more than ever: whatever Jack wanted to do, his actions would be to protect Gwen and Anwen and, yes, him.

'This situation can't be left to right itself,' said Jack, turning Gwen's wrist over so he could look for the millionth time at the shape she had carved into her arm. 'All these women can't just be left to heal themselves.'

'Too bloody right,' said Rhys. 'So what are we going to do?'

Jack smiled, tracing his finger above the pink wound on Gwen's arm. 'This has to mean something. It seems so familiar to me, but I can't get the memory of it to settle, to fully form in my mind. And that is driving me nuts.'

'Is it alien?' Rhys asked.

'Yes,' said Jack. 'Maybe. I don't know. But I know I've seen it here… on Earth. Somewhere. I know this is going to sound weird, but every time I look at it I get this odd taste in my mouth.'

'Have to say, Jack,' smiled Rhys, 'not the weirdest thing I've heard you say.'

Jack drew the shape in the air above Gwen's arm, not wanting to touch the pink raw wound again. Closing his eyes, he traced and retraced the image, letting it seer itself into his brain. He kept drawing, over and over again. He did this for so long that Rhys thought he'd put himself into some kind of a trance.

Gwen stirred, the ice-pack tipped onto the pillow. Rhys reached across for it. Gwen's hand shot out and she grabbed Rhys's arm.

'Kill me. Please.'

Part Three

'The moon gazed on my midnight labours, while, with unrelaxed and breathless eagerness, I pursued nature to her hiding-places.'
Mary Shelley, *Frankenstein*

45

Whitehall, London, next day

At 9 a.m. sharp, a severely coiffured woman in her twenties ushered Dr Trimba Ormond into Alan Pride's suite of offices in Whitehall, directly between Horse Guards and 10 Downing Street. The London Eye was visible through the window, a perfect metaphor, Ormond thought, for the man's position in government – there he was at the heart of everything, yet somehow maintaining enough distance to avoid having to tilt too far one way or the other.

The madness that was afflicting women worldwide had been bumped down the news agenda. The sporadic tremors and subsequent appearance of the strange geysers rising up from beneath the world's oceans had captured the attention of the press, in Britain and abroad. Dr Ormond, however, was not about to let the issue slip from Pride's radar. Over breakfast with her husband and daughter, she'd practised exactly what she was going to say to Mr Alan Pride.

'I respect the position you're in, Mr Pride, especially in light of this recent oceanic event, but as far as we can tell these formations are benign. That is not, however, the case with this mental illness that's affecting so many women here and around the world. The public should be kept

231

informed, and these women deserve to be treated with the full resources that we can bring to bear. To simply continue to say that these women just need to be sedated is neither a solution nor a palatable stopgap any more. The public has a right to know what we're doing to find a cure, especially given the increase in suicides among these woman and the rise in violent crimes towards their families. Are we simply going to wait until they all kill themselves and then hope that the problem will disappear?'

Her daughter had found her argument convincing, but Ormond wasn't sure a 10-year-old really counted, or even much cared. Problem was, Ormond was becoming convinced that far too few people in positions of power did either. A few mad women was nothing compared to massive rock chimneys popping up across the world's oceans. If even the worst of the papers had bumped the story to an occasional feature, what chance was there of engaging public interest in a few emotionally unbalanced women?

Ormond had wiped jam from her daughter's chin, kissed her husband and let her driver carry her briefcase and her coat to the car.

'Try to stay sane today,' her husband had called as she left. Funny man.

And now she was sitting waiting for a man who could decide on a whim whether those women sank or swam.

'Mr Pride will be with you shortly,' said the assistant. 'He's on an overseas call at the moment. Can I get you a coffee?'

'Thank you. Black. Two sugars.'

Dr Ormond was sipping her second cup when the heavy office doors swung open and Alan Pride stepped out to greet her.

'My apologies for keeping you waiting, Trimba.'

He proffered his hand, his shake strong and purposeful,

placing the other on the small of her back to usher her into his office. His hand on her back felt warm, his fingers strong. Dr Ormond felt a kick of desire low in her abdomen that took her quite by surprise. She let herself be guided to a round table, where she was surprised to see another woman, about her own age, already seated at the table. Ormond felt a flash of anger that she hadn't been the first one to the table and she wasn't going to have Alan Pride to herself.

Gracious, she thought, where on earth were these thoughts coming from? She was happily married...

'Dr Ormond,' said Pride, pulling out a chair for her, 'this is Dr Olivia Steele, Director of Neuroscience at the Cardiff and Vale Health Board. She's also an expert on issues of women's mental health.'

Dr Ormond shook Dr Steele's hand, feeling another jolt of desire shoot from her fingers to her toes.

This morning, she thought, is turning out... interesting.

'I've asked you both to join me,' said Pride, 'because I've received some good news and some disturbing news about the recent wave of mental illness among women in various parts of the world. As you know, Trimba, many of the international health agencies are at a loss for treatment and, honestly, so are we. Olivia, however, has brought me some new information and I thought in light of your position that you should be one of the first to hear it. I must, though, ask for a caveat: I need your signature on an Official Secrets document.'

As if she'd been waiting for her cue, the minister's assistant marched through the double doors and set a sheet of paper in front of Ormond.

'It's standard procedure in such matters,' Pride went on. 'Olivia has also signed one. It simply states that anything you are about to hear about this "Masochistic madness", as the press have labelled it, you may not reveal under any circumstances.'

'And if I did?' asked Ormond, guiltily realising as she spoke that she was only asking the question because she was annoyed that Dr Steele had signed the papers before her. Ormond's desire had quickly turned to jealousy and she hated herself – and Dr Steele – for the shift.

'If you did,' smiled Pride, 'then I'd have to kill you.'

He tapped the bottom clause of the document where it explained she would forfeit all rights as a British citizen, and she would be considered an enemy of the state. Ormond scanned the paragraph, and then signed the document, but she couldn't quite shake the notion that Alan Pride might actually have meant what he had said.

'Thank you.' Accepting the document, he co-signed beneath it and slid it into a folder sitting in front of him.

He tapped his iPad, the office lights dimmed and a photograph of a man came up on the white wall in front of them.

'This is Captain Jack Harkness. The Captain and I have worked together in the past a number of times. He has a theory about what is happening to these clusters of women. If he's correct in his assessment, then we may have a cataclysmic problem on our hands. I know this man's history, and because of that I'm inclined to grant him his request.'

'And what is he requesting?' asked Dr Steele.

'He's asking for our silence and a boat load of sedatives.'

The Ice Maiden

46

Off the coast of Wales, a week or so before Isela's shot
Eva stood on the port side of the *Ice Maiden*, binoculars in her hands. Next to her, Hollis was leaning against the rails of the ship, his face tilted towards the heat of the late-afternoon sun, smoking a cigarette. Eva lifted her binoculars, scanning the distant Welsh coast, the ship anchored miles out to avoid detection from the British coast guard and the naval ships now surrounding the geyser.

'It's beautiful here,' said Eva, 'reminds me of home. This coastline is a bit like the Pacific Northwest.'

'About the only thing in Wales that reminds me of home is the smell of fresh fish.' Hollis flicked his burning cigarette over the side of the ship.

'Hollis!'

He shrugged. 'My bad.'

Turning from the sun, Hollis looked across the channel to the docks of Bridgend. 'They better bring somethin' tasty back with them. I'm getting tired of finding exciting things to make with frozen tuna and packets of scalloped potatoes.'

'And I'm getting tired of eating them. Any idea who this person is?' asked Eva.

'He's a friend of Cash's from way back. I think they

were on a mission together in the 80s. All very secret and scandalous, if I know Cash.'

Eva caught sight of a fishing boat pulling away from a distant dock and heading towards the *Ice Maiden*. 'Is he a spy?'

'Wouldn't surprise me one bit, darlin',' said Hollis, pushing away from the side and heading to the steps down to the kitchen. 'Whoever he is, they'll expect some dinner before we set off.'

Eva watched him climb below deck, and then she shifted back to watch a fishing skiff cutting through the waves towards them. Below her, Dana was preparing the landing deck and the ladder. Looking up, she waved at Eva directly above her.

Eva and Hollis had drawn the short straws and had been left on the ship with Finn. The rest of the crew had gone with Cash to get supplies and to pick up their passengers. Dana had drawn a new assignment that she had refused to share, even with Eva.

Cash's reaction to reading the message in Welsh that had come across the teletype had been strange and completely in character. He laughed, swore profusely and said, 'Nothing like making an entrance.'

He'd turned to Vlad and told him not to worry about who had infiltrated the computers, it was not an enemy and the power would return in a few minutes. It had, and they'd stormed from the North Atlantic south to a port north-west of Cardiff.

'So who exactly is crawling inside my hardware?' asked Vlad, when the storm had abated and things below deck had returned to normal.

'Torchwood,' said Cash.

'Never heard of them,' said Eva.

'I have,' said Vlad. 'Secret agency. Did some important

stuff to get us all dying again. Ties to the CIA, right?'

'Maybe.'

Cash had Finn alter their course and brought them directly to the south coast of Wales. Where they were heading from here was anyone's guess.

'Permission to come aboard,' said Jack, saluting Dana, who stood on the platform next to the ladder, the wind buffeting her against the ship's iron red hull.

'Permission to do whatever the fuck you want to me,' she grinned, throwing herself into Jack's arms, her head barely reaching his chest.

'Such a lovely way with words,' said Jack, swinging her off her feet.

Rhys was standing on the bow of the fishing boat, his face blanched with worry, watching Cash, Byron and Vlad manoeuvre a stretcher with Gwen strapped to it onto the platform, where Dana attached a winch to the stretcher, then tilted Gwen to a standing position, her head flopping onto her chest. From the controls in the wheelhouse, Finn then hauled Gwen up onto the deck. Eva was waiting at the top, and made sure she landed softly, realising immediately it didn't much matter. Whoever this woman was, she was completely out of it, comatose even.

On the platform, Dana turned to Cash and from her tiptoes, she grabbed his head and planted a long deep kiss on his lips. 'Behave yourself. Or when I see you, I'll take even more of your money.'

'Rhys has everything you'll need, Dana, and you can trust him completely,' said Jack, lifting his bags from the fishing boat.

Rhys held out his hand and helped Dana on board the fishing boat. She lifted her bags and carried them down below.

Vlad picked up Jack's bags and Cash took the heavier cases – weapons, assault rifles, he'd guess, if weight was anything to go by. But, who knows? Jack's diverse and unusual weaponry always amazed Cash and he knew better than to question its provenance.

Within fifteen minutes of the fishing boat docking with the *Ice Maiden*, Jack was the last one remaining on the platform. Rhys remained as close to the edge of the fishing boat's bow as he could without tipping into the sea. His rain slicker was soaked and his face was wet with tears. The gulf between him and Jack and Gwen had never seemed so wide as it did at that moment.

'I wish I could come with you. I could help,' said Rhys, his voice choked with emotion.

'I know you could, Rhys, but you need to stay in Wales for Anwen's sake. Mary isn't up to it on her own, you know that, and if I need something done from this end I need to know I have you and Andy here to take care of it.'

Rhys nodded. When Jack had told him about the *Ice Maiden*, its mission and its crew, and how he thought it'd be safer if Gwen was with him on the ship rather than at the house, where she'd have to be under constant watch, Rhys had reluctantly agreed. In the middle of the night, they'd hustled Gwen to a Penarth hotel, not revealing to Mary that her daughter had been found and certainly not telling her she'd tried to commit suicide.

That morning, while they were transporting Gwen to the fishing boat they'd borrowed from one of Rhys's mates, they'd listened to reports on the radio of four women suffering from the same madness as Gwen having taken overdoses and being found by loved ones too late to do anything but bury them.

'Rhys, you have my word, she'll come back to you whole. I promise.' Jack smiled, slowly saluted Rhys, then climbed up the ladder to the deck of the *Ice Maiden*.

Drenched and despairing, Rhys clutched the stern of the bouncing fishing boat all the way back to the dock, watching bleary-eyed as the ship's engines roared to life and the *Ice Maiden* glided across the darkening horizon back out into the Atlantic.

47

Below deck that night the rest of the crew and its passengers – with the exception of Gwen, who remained sedated and strapped to a bunk in Dana's cabin – sat around the table in the mess for a meal of shrimp étouffée, bottles of Jax beer from Hollis's private stash, and, at Eva's request, a fresh fruit salad. The food had kept them in small talk, their taste buds trumping the crew's curiosity about their passengers. The dishes had yet to be cleared, but Cash insisted that Hollis remain at the table with them for a little longer. Finn took charge in the wheelhouse.

'More drinks all round,' said Cash, who, like Jack, was nursing the beer with which he'd begun the meal.

Sliding his chair closer to Jack's, Hollis said, 'don't mind if I do, boss.'

'That was one of the best meals I've eaten in a long time,' admitted Jack. The music in his head from the meal was, thankfully, soft and sultry. Since his conversation with Olivia Steele, and his understanding of what might be happening to him and the world, Jack had been doing his best to embrace his synaesthesia rather than fighting the intensity of his multiple perceptions. He had noted that, since he'd boarded the *Ice Maiden*, the synaesthesia had lessened. He'd also not seen the vision of the woman's face since he'd left the Coopers' house and travelled further from the geyser.

'You could do with a little more flesh on your bones,' said Hollis, who had used his Creole grandmother's recipe for the étouffée in hopes of impressing this mysterious handsome stranger. Hollis hadn't felt this giddy after meeting someone for the first time since he'd seduced the chef at the Mardi Gras ball after only two mouthfuls of his gumbo.

Sam laughed. 'Who're you kidding, Hollis? You'd like your flesh to *be* on his bones.'

'I wouldn't mind that either,' said Eva, who'd been drinking red wine steadily through dinner.

Everyone was suddenly silent. Vlad's eyes widened in astonishment. Jack bit his tongue. Then Hollis snorted, Sam grinned, Cash guffawed and the table erupted in laughter.

Eva blushed bright red. 'Did I say that out loud?'

'Oh, yes,' laughed Vlad, 'very out loud. Maybe you should switch to water if we're going to get any work done at all tonight.'

Jack put his hand on Eva's. 'Your flesh on mine will be a pleasure I'll look forward to.' Then he turned and put his hand on Hollis's arm. 'Yours too.'

'Well, now that we've got all the important stuff out of the way,' said Cash, shaking his head, 'and I can't believe I'm saying this, but can we get down to some business of the non-sexual kind?' He rolled his eyes at Eva, who shrank into her seat.

Jack explained what he'd learned from Dr Steele about synaesthesia and how he thought something was heightening it.

'The medical community's response,' said Jack, 'has so far been to keep these women sedated, like Gwen. The problem is that when they have any moments of lucidity, some of them are aware of what's happening and have already tried to kill themselves. Some of them have succeeded.'

'Synaesthesia is a pretty cool thing,' said Vlad. 'I mean when it's not out of control. I know a few gamers who can see their compositions and their coding in colours and shapes.' He popped the top off another Jax. 'If you think about it, it's almost like their brains are able to construct meaning from downloading multiple codes all at the same time, like a synaesthete's hard drive is way more sophisticated than the rest of us.'

'Are you a synaesthete, Vlad?' asked Jack.

Vlad shook his head, tilting his beer bottle. 'Only shapes and colours dancing in front of my eyes are drug- or alcohol-induced, sorry to say.'

'I am,' said Eva. 'Well, mildly anyway. And I never knew what it was called until I took a psych class in university and my professor was one. It would really disturb her if we came to class wearing too much perfume. She could hear the smells. Created too much noise in her head. She said she couldn't concentrate.'

'Which is part of the problem with whatever's happening to these women,' said Jack, accepting a slice of pecan pie from Hollis. 'The numbers that are being officially tracked could be much lower than the reality. It's difficult to know how many women are simply dismissing their symptoms and trying to carry on as usual.'

'That's really horrible,' said Vlad, pulling another chair over and stretching his legs across it. Jack noticed how intently Eva was watching Vlad. Jack checked Vlad out, approving of what he was seeing but he thought Eva might have to make the moves. Vlad was either oblivious to Eva's longing or he was consciously ignoring her. Jack thought he could smell her desire from across the table.

'To lose control of your mind,' said Sam, 'that's… that's crazy.'

Hollis leaned across the table and slapped Sam upside the head. 'Mr Understatement, thank you.'

'Hell of a thing,' said Cash, 'if your wife comes after you with the cleaver when it's her time of the month.'

Jack stared at Cash for a beat, then grinned and got up from the table. 'Know what, Cash? I think you might have hit on something. I should have thought of that.' Jack went over to the chalk board where Hollis, in an effort to give the ship's meals a little flair, wrote a daily menu. Jack looked at Hollis. 'May I?'

'Course, darlin'.'

Jack wiped his sleeve across the board, erasing most of the menu. He picked up the chalk, addressing all of them. 'I've been assuming that all of these women with heightened synaesthesia are reacting to something in their surroundings, and according to Dr Steele who's treating a number of the cases in Wales, there must be some kind of external trigger.'

Jack wrote Gwen's name at the top. 'Gwen has the chromosome for synaesthesia.' Jack noted this under Gwen's name. 'But what if because she had a baby recently she also has a particular combination of chemicals in her body that have been triggered along with her synaesthesia.'

'If that's true,' said Vlad, 'then it would also explain why not every woman who is a synaesthete is experiencing this heightening, because it's not just the synaesthesia – it's their hormones, too.'

'I think so,' said Jack. 'But there's still a piece missing.'

Jack drew a circle round Gwen's name and the word synaesthesia, then an overlapping circling with the word hormones in the centre. Then he drew a third and put a question mark in it. 'If we're going to help these women, we need to find what's in this third… circle.'

Jack stared at the image he'd drawn on the board, a Venn diagram. He didn't know if it was coincidence or not but it looked weirdly like the symbol Gwen had carved on her forearm.

Eva, who had been silent throughout the conversation, spoke up. 'I think Vlad and I may have discovered the third trigger.'

48

Eva unrolled a thick sheaf of printouts in front of Jack.

Eva unrolled a thick sheaf of printouts in front of Jack.

Cash rolled his eyes. 'Nothing fancy, lass, keep it simple tonight. He can see the numbers and all the data tomorrow.'

Eva gulped her water and stood up. She put on her glasses. 'For the past week, Vlad and I have been monitoring a series of submerged tremors, eruptions in the deepest parts of the ocean floor. None of which have resulted in major tsunamis as you might expect, and none of them have impacted major land masses. They've hit mostly on the edges of shorelines. But they've resulted in underwater geysers like the one that broke through the surface in Wales.'

'Which ones?' asked Jack.

'Coast of Vietnam. Off the far northern coast of Scotland—'

'And,' interrupted Vlad, 'the islands south of New Zealand, and the southern coast of Peru.'

'Peru?' asked Jack.

Vlad nodded. 'Shelley's running a program that'll look for tick points, see what comes up.'

'Shelley?' asked Jack.

'Tick points?' asked Hollis.

'When you're comparing things in a paper chart the

traditional way,' said Jack to Hollis, 'you'd give tick marks or check marks to elements of similar qualities, to situations or variables that overlap. Sort of like the centre of my Venn diagram.'

Vlad nodded. 'If those geographic areas have anything in common, Shelley will find them much faster than any of our brains.' He looked at Jack. 'Shelley's the ship's artificial intelligence. She also keeps the systems on the ship running, but I think you knew that since you gave her the virus that shut us down.'

'I needed your attention.' Jack sipped his beer, and looked across at Eva, who Jack decided was as adept with technology and probably as smart as Vlad, yet she kept deferring to him in the conversation. 'So you named your AI after a Romantic poet?'

Eva shook her head. 'We named it after a Romantic poet's *wife*.'

'Go on, Eva,' said Cash, smiling. 'Finish your report.'

'The final thing I'd add is... well... I haven't really discussed it yet with anyone else,' she paused, taking a sip of her wine and not her water before continuing, 'but, well, I think there may be a way to connect the underwater eruptions with the cases of heightened synaesthesia.'

Jack looked over the map that Eva had created. 'Let me see this on your screen.'

Eva gathered up her files and led Jack and Vlad across the passageway to the communication centre. Cash headed up to the wheelhouse with Sam, leaving Hollis to clean up in the mess.

'I'll check on Gwen,' said Cash, on his way down the corridor.

In the comms centre, things had been settled back in their place since the storm. The computer screens glowed in the dim light and an occasional beep from a monitor punctuated the silence. Vlad perched on the end of his desk, his hands in his pockets, while Eva picked up her iPad. The massive screen on the wall powered up, displaying a map of the world with the epicentre of each of the deep-water events flashing in red. Jack stepped in front of the map, folded his arms and stared at it in silence.

On the flat screen on Eva's desk, a young woman dressed in an off-shoulder black velvet gown, her hair pulled back from an intelligent pretty face appeared. She was sitting at an old-fashioned writing desk, a fountain pen in her hand. At first glance, Jack thought she looked like a woman from the nineteenth century, demure and modest. Looking closer, he noticed a nose piercing, a neck tattoo and more than a delicate amount of skin showing when the dress shifted from her shoulder.

Jack laughed. 'So this is what you think Mary Shelley would look like today?'

'Shelley, meet Captain Jack Harkness,' said Eva.

A sultry woman's voice with an English accent answered. 'The pleasure is all mine, Captain. Welcome aboard the *Ice Maiden*.'

'Thank you,' said Jack.

'I believe I've corrected the glitch in my programs that allowed you to seduce me so spectacularly.' Shelley's voice was youthful and playful.

'My apologies for that, Shelley.'

'Apology accepted. May I ask... were you the creator of the program you used? It appeared so elegant, so graceful, and yet it was quite brutish in its approach. Its power took me quite by surprise.'

'Let's just say it's not from around here,' said Jack.

Vlad and Eva glanced at each other, puzzled and slightly disconcerted by the nature of the exchange. Shelley was a powerful AI, but social conversation was not her strongest program. They'd never needed it to be.

'May I show the others what I've learned?'

'Be my guest,' said Jack, setting a flat disc the size of a hockey puck on top of Vlad's desk.

Jack tapped the top of the disc and in an instant Mary Shelley was standing in front of Vlad's desk, morphed from a talking head on the screen to a fully formed female, a hologram, but an incredibly sophisticated one. Nothing translucent or wavering about her. To the eye, she looked alive, standing before them clad in a body-hugging calf-length black velvet dress that looked like a character from one of Vlad's steampunk stories. On her feet, Shelley was wearing a pair of shiny cowboy boots.

'I must admit to always having had a silly fascination with the Wild West in America,' she giggled, kicking up her heels. Her fountain pen remained firmly gripped in one hand and her black leather journal in the other.

'Wow!' exclaimed Eva, staring wide-eyed at their avatar.

Shelley curtsied towards Eva.

'Well, fuck me,' grinned Vlad.

'That function,' said Shelley, pirouetting in front of Vlad, 'is not yet operational.'

'Well done, Shelley,' said Jack. 'You've adapted the software to your scaffolding quite quickly.'

'Yes, Captain. It feels as if it has been an integral part of me all along. Although I'm still absorbing a few minor details, I predict I'll be fully functioning for your needs in the next few days.'

'I can't wait,' said Vlad, keying commands into his computer and staring in awe at what he was seeing. 'Look at this, Eva. She's synchronised with all the ship's systems, including a mobility function.'

'Yes, Vlad, I can be accessed in this form anywhere on the ship and off via the satellite.'

'Bloody brilliant!'

Jack laughed, pleased that his gift to the *Ice Maiden* was making Eva and Vlad happy. He knew Cash would approve and he certainly owed him a favour, more than one. It was also the least he could do given what he was coming to realise about the submarine tremors, the wide-spread synaesthesia and his own fragmented memories, Jack had a feeling that their pleasure may be short-lived.

Eva leaned over Vlad's shoulder, checked out his screen then stared back at Jack. 'I've never seen anything like it. You've multiplied her functionality, adapted her modalities, increased her scope and intelligence... It's like you've...'

'Made her bigger, better, smarter and sexier?' said Jack, winking at Shelley who winked back.

'All those things,' said Eva. 'But she still looks like our avatar.'

'This design is amazing; I'm impressed. The algorithms are brilliant,' said Vlad staring at the code, and every few beats glancing up at Shelley smiling next to him. 'You've morphed her in a way that I didn't think we – I mean our governments – had the capability to do yet with artificial intelligence.'

Eva had pulled her chair up next to Vlad. 'This is some serious cutting-edge restructuring. I read about this code-layering in a paper once, but it was based on some sophisticated theories, pretty sci-fi level design.'

'Exactly,' said Jack.

They both paused in their analysis of the program. 'Where did you get this? Are we going to have the men in black chasing us?'

Jack shook his head. 'The few people who know of its existence are gone or deeply sedated or no longer care. I needed a secure home for my program and your system, your Shelley, seemed as good a place as any to be that home.

For now, anyway.'

'I'm gratified and honoured, Captain,' said Shelley. 'Torchwood and I are enjoying each other immensely.'

Vlad was taking furious notes, unable to draw his eyes from his computer screens. 'This shit is amazing!'

Jack put his hand on Vlad's shoulder. 'You'll have plenty of time to enjoy Shelley to her fullest later. Right now, I need to have her do a little work.'

49

'Shelley,' said Vlad, 'show us what you've learned about the eruptions and the geysers from your analysis of our deep-water data, including their current activity and the order in which they occurred.'

'It would be my pleasure, Vlad.'

'What do you mean current activity?' asked Cash, as he walked into the comms centre.

'None of the underwater events are on expected plate boundaries, and none runs along traditional fault lines,' explained Vlad. 'But here's the even stranger thing – each one is still active, low level right now, but active nonetheless.'

'According to the data, Captain,' said Shelley, 'these tremors are not the result of earthquakes but of volcanic eruptions causing a number of hydrothermal vents to crack through the ocean floor.' She was tapping her fountain pen on her journal. As she did so, aspects of the map were highlighted on the screen, red pulsing lights representing the epicentres. 'These vents are similar to the one that has already risen through the surface in Wales and one or two other deep water sites'.'

'What exactly is a hydrothermal vent?' asked Vlad.

'Essentially an underwater geyser.'

'And the order of these disturbances?' asked Jack, fitting this data into his own theories.

'Eva has a hunch,' cut in Vlad, 'that these deep water events are synchronised in some way.'

'The geysers beginning to erupt above the surface that the *Ice Maiden's* probes are detecting,' continued Shelley, 'is a primary consequence of these hydrothermal vents. The first was off the coast of southern Peru, followed exactly one minute later by deep-water eruptions off the coast of Wales, Scotland, New Zealand and Indonesia. And, Captain, these hydrothermal vents are not registering on any of our traditional measurement scales. Currently, according to my data, only one other source is monitoring these vents.'

'Who?' asked Jack.

'The information is being downloaded from a UK government satellite to an office in Thames House, London.'

'Christ,' said Vlad, 'that's MI5. I thought you said this software and this mission weren't going to bring the men in black on us.'

'This particular man in black is on our side,' said Jack. 'And although Shelley can monitor what they're doing, they cannot–' Vlad rolled his eyes. 'Trust me. They've no idea what we're doing, and I have my friend's word, that we'll be allowed some freedom. For now, anyway. He's holding Big Brother and Big Sister at bay.'

Eva was only half-listening to Jack and Vlad. She was much more interested in the unusual discovery that the ocean had a number of new hydrothermal vents erupting from deep within the Earth's core. More than she'd tracked yesterday. As a scientist this was thrilling. Right now, it also helped her to suppress the desire for Vlad that was not far beneath her surface. Her desire was not helped one bit by the fact that the Captain, in a more refined and imposing way, was pretty gorgeous too.

Focus, she thought. Focus.

'According to my calculations,' continued Shelley, 'a highly unusual energy field from the first eruption is creating the ongoing tremors. They are not, in fact, the result of any shifting of tectonic plates as Eva and Vlad had originally speculated from the data.'

'Is it morphic resonance?' asked Jack.

'I've been monitoring the morphic fields,' said Vlad. 'It's one of my areas of interest – was, that is, until my funding was stolen. I've not noticed anything unusual.'

Shelley continued. 'The data also suggests that the water around each of the vents has a considerably higher measure of carbon, iron and sulphur than is normal. I'm also detecting traces of something else. I'll need more time for analysis.'

'The ocean floor always has measurable carbonic acid,' said Eva. 'It's part of the carbon cycle and part of the Earth's natural waste disposal system.' She was graphing the data onto another screen as Shelley presented it.

Vlad was watching Shelley, who said, 'I beg your pardon, Eva, but although you're accurate in your assessment that the ocean is part of the carbon cycle, the amounts of carbonic acid I'm detecting surrounding each of the hydrothermal vents is much higher than what is considered normal, and, along with the water temperature, the levels are rising significantly on a daily basis.'

Shelley drew her pen across her leather journal and projected her numbers onto Eva's graph, showing that the carbon levels in the areas around each of the underwater geysers were more than a thousand times greater than other parts of the ocean. 'I'm also detecting many of the vents are forming vent chimneys.'

'We must have a malfunction in our probes,' said Eva, shocked by the data. 'That's not possible in such a short period of time. Vent chimneys take thousands and thousands of years to form.' She looked at Vlad. 'We dropped the probes at all the places where there had been tremors initially, but something must be wrong. That data doesn't make sense. Shelley, can we activate the cameras on the probes that have them?'

'Activating cameras to the screen.'

Vlad stood and walked across the passageway to the mess, returning with four beers, passing one each to Jack, Eva and Cash. Looking across the room at Shelley, he held up his bottle.

'That function is sadly not yet operational either.'

Vlad took a long pull of his beer, as the live feed from three probes miles beneath the ocean appeared on the large screen. 'All of our probes can't be malfunctioning, Eva. I'll run a diagnostic on the others, but for all of them to fail, at the same time? Not gonna happen.'

Eva peered at the video images on the screen. 'I don't believe it. It's like I'm watching a million years of the Earth's evolution in seconds. What's going on?'

'What exactly are we looking at?' asked Jack, standing behind the two analysts.

Eva pointed to one of the vents where a beehive like structure was forming around the underwater geyser. 'These craters or cracks in the ocean's floor vent a complex combination of superheated chemicals and gases. The only thing that keeps them from actually boiling the water is the pressure from the ocean. In all of these cases, what's known as a vent chimney can be seen rising up out of the ocean, surrounding each of the geysers. Shelley, can you bring up a clearer picture of a vent chimney?'

In the space next to Shelley, an image appeared that took Jack's breath away. He leant against Eva's chair, a wave of images crashing through his mind, one after another – a man, a kiss, a plane, a mountain, a fight, then falling, falling, the ground opening up and swallowing him. A beautiful woman kissing him deeply, passionately, longingly, a sleek, lithe, midnight black-eyed puma. The fierce familiarity of the images shook Jack to his core.

He stared again at the picture that Shelley had thrown up, aware that something had shifted in his mind.

'This,' said Eva, 'is a vent chimney, a massive tower of oxidized iron, zinc and rock rising out of the ocean floor.'

The chimney was spewing black smoke.

And suddenly Jack knew where he'd seen the chimney before. Inside a mountain many years ago.

'Jack, are you OK?' asked Vlad, offering Jack his chair. 'You look like you've seen a ghost.'

'Not a ghost... a sliver from my past,' said Jack, sitting down, calming his racing heart. Jack finally understood that, for whatever reason, his brain was rebuilding a gap in his memory, a void that had been there for a long time, putting pieces together that long ago something or someone had split apart, sending its shards boomeranging across his consciousness. And now they were finally returning.

Jack's brain needed more time to process what he was no longer forgetting, time to let his memory fill the blank spaces as if it were rebuilding a damaged track on a hard drive.

50

'Shelley,' said Jack, gulping most of his beer. 'How many hydrothermal chimneys have the *Ice Maiden*'s deep-water probes detected in the past, say, two weeks?'

'Including the one now forming off the coast of Wales, Captain, seven.'

'What!' said Eva. 'That's impossible. It's just impossible. It takes at least a million years for that kind of geologic phenomenon to happen. The Atlantis Massif is at least two million years old.'

'What the hell is the Atlantis Massif? Sounds like a breed of dog,' said Cash, feeling more out of his league every minute of this conversation.

'Shall I explain?' asked Shelley.

'Please,' said Jack, giving Vlad back his chair. Jack stood in front of the screen, watching all the vent chimneys flashing on the map. Crossing his arms, he stared at it, his jaw clenching and unclenching in sync with the pulsing lights.

'The Atlantis Massif, named after the lost city of Atlantis,' explained Shelley, 'is a submarine mountain in the North Atlantic approximately twelve miles under the sea, rising at its peak approximately 14,000 feet. It can be found off the northern coast of Africa and east of the Mid-Atlantic mountain range.' With a wave of her hand Shelley brought up a computerised image of the underwater mountain in the space between her and Jack. 'Eva is correct. This massif is 2.5 million years old.'

'And,' interrupted Eva, 'the two or three other core complexes on the ocean floor like this one that have been discovered are at least that old too. The Earth simply does not respond to change that quickly.'

'So, Shelley,' said Cash, 'let me see if I understand this correctly.'

'I can talk more slowly, Cash, if that will help.' Shelley giggled.

Despite her growing anxiety, Eva laughed too. Jack shrugged as if a sense of humour was exactly what you'd expect from a Torchwood program.

'These tremors are creating hydrothermal vents and they in turn are forming chimneys like this one,' Cash said, ignoring them. He pointed to the growing conical structures they were seeing from their underwater probes.

'That is correct.'

'And these geological phenomena are happening at a speed of evolution that's impossible,' Cash caught Jack's eye, 'at least by the rules as we know them?'

'Also correct.'

'If all that's true,' said Eva, finally regaining some composure. 'Then what's causing the eruptions in the first place?'

For the first time since he and Eva had started monitoring these deep-water events two weeks earlier, Vlad was beginning to worry that something pretty bad was happening underneath the sea.

'Have you ever heard of the Gaia theory?' asked Jack.

'Yeah,' said Eva, 'but it's a theory with only a few

disparate threads to prove it.'

'Oh, there's a few more threads still to be found,' said Jack.

'How do you know?'

'Trust me.'

'Gaia is one of the ancient names given to the goddess of the Earth,' said Shelley. 'The Gaia theory was named after her and it maintains that all living organisms, including the Earth itself, are part of a complex process of self-regulation that strives for balance and sustainability. This stability, this balance, is dependent on three important functions: the salinity in the oceans, the oxygen in the atmosphere and keeping deformation and destruction caused by the human population in balance with both of those things.'

'Otherwise,' asked Vlad, 'what happens?'

'The balance is disrupted,' said Jack, 'and the Earth can no longer sustain life as we know it.'

'And?'

'Listen,' said Jack, 'We know that global warming is out of control, that the Earth's atmosphere is already damaged, maybe beyond repair, and we know that global warming is affecting everything from weather to crops to species extinction. If we now have hydrothermal chimneys suddenly flooding the oceans with metal sulphides, then we're well on the way to desalinating the oceans and completely disrupting the Earth's ability to self-regulate.'

Eva was poring over the data that Shelley had summarised, using a series of calculations and simulations that would have taken her and Vlad months to complete.

'Jack, you need to look at this,' Eva said. 'We now have a comparison of all the dates and times of the deep-water events with the reported synaesthesia incidents in the world.'

The three of them stood next to each other, watching the

map light up as one by one, the dates of the outbreaks of synaesthesia flashed in orange next to the already pulsing red of the deep-water vents.

Vlad looked from one to the other. 'That's not good, right?'

'It's not good at all,' said Jack. 'Shelley, we need to know exactly what these hydrothermal chimneys are spewing into the oceans and quickly.'

'It will take me a little more time to analyse fully, but on a superficial glance I would say that it's iron, sulphur, carbonic acid, hydrogen and something else that I cannot categorise yet from my samples.'

'Run the data as quickly as you can.'

'It would help if I didn't need to use part of my program for projection.'

'Of course.' Jack tapped the disc, and Shelley disappeared.

51

Southern Ocean, a week before Isela's shot

The first hydrothermal chimney erupted from the ocean's surface and became visible a hundred miles off the southern coast of New Zealand, forming a shell around one of the smaller geysers to erupt.

A charter fishing cruiser was the only boat close enough to witness the event, but the passengers on board, a honeymooning couple from California and two retired lawyers had no chance to report it, photograph it, tweet it, or even comment about it among themselves.

Along with their four passengers, the cruiser's first and second mates watched in awe as an uneven rocky shell began to encase the geyser as if the water was shooting out rocks and building a wall around itself.

In 10 minutes and 42 seconds the geyser was encased completely, leaving a massive conical structure visible above sea level, thin veins of pulsing silver flashing across its ribbed uneven surface.

'Jesus Christ! What the hell is that?' said one of the lawyers, digging around under his seat for his camera. He never reached it.

Seconds before the hydrothermal vent was sealed, his

new wife let out a low anguished howl, picked up her fishing spear and stabbed her husband through his back.

'You should have taken me to Rome,' she mumbled.

She whipped round and slashed the throats of the two retirees with her husband's fillet knife before they knew what was happening.

'I hate the stink of fish.'

The first mate saw the young wife charge at his friend with a bloody spear.

'Danny! Look out,' he screamed, pushing his friend away from the control panel as the woman stabbed the harpoon through the back of his chair.

While Danny scrambled across the floor in a desperate attempt to get away from the woman, his mate darted down to the cabin tearing open all the cabinets, pulling everything from drawers in a panicked search for the hand gun that he knew the owner kept hidden for emergencies. He was tossing books from the locker above one of the spare bunks when he heard his friend's dying screams from above.

Then silence.

Dropping to his knees, he dragged the extra fishing gear from a metal storage locker from beneath the lower bunk.

'Please be here. Please be here.'

'It's not,' the woman said, a beat before she shot him.

Blood-splattered and muttering angrily to herself, the new wife climbed up on deck, surveyed her carnage, then with a trembling hand lifted the gun to her own head and fired.

52

Jack pushed open the iron door of Dana's cabin, stepping quietly inside. He stood over Gwen's bunk, brushing a wisp of hair from her forehead, watching the steady rise and fall of her chest, hearing the slow drip of the IV sedative, hanging from the bunk above. Gwen's arms were covered in bruises and she had a purple target around her eye, but the wound on her arm was healing, the image no longer as visible as it had been.

'You are one tough lady,' Jack whispered.

Lifting her hand, Jack checked her pulse. Normal. He'd been checking every couple of hours, not only afraid of a reaction to the IV sedative but also afraid she might break through the sedation and hurt herself again.

Jack kissed her forehead, tucked her arm under the blankets and backed out into the passageway where he bumped into Hollis.

'Bon ami, perfect timing,' said Hollis, following close behind Jack as he navigated the tight passage to his cabin.

'What can I do for you?' asked Jack when he got to his door.

'I wanted to offer you dessert,' said Hollis.

'I appreciate that, Hollis, but I don't think I could eat

another slice of your grandmother's pecan pie no matter how delicious it was.'

Hollis stepped directly in front of Jack, placing his hand flat on Jack's chest. 'Ah wasn't offerin' pie.'

Jack grinned. 'In that case, you'd better come inside.'

A ship at dawn is never a quiet place. Every space is small, every sound big, every voice amplified.

Cash thumped on Jack's cabin door at 6.15 the next morning.

'Hollis Jefferson Albert the third,' called Cash, thumping again, 'this is your captain speaking. The one you work for not the one you're screwing. If you don't get your worn-out ass into the kitchen and feed me, you'll be sorry you ever set foot on my ship.'

Hollis rolled away from Jack, grabbed his clothes and headed for the door. 'Later, mon cher. He's just cranky because Dana's not here and he had to sleep alone.' Hollis blew Jack a kiss and darted down the passageway naked, his clothes bundled in his arms.

'I can see where you've been, you know,' yelled Sam, sticking his head out of his cabin.

'I'm willing to share,' laughed Hollis.

Jack was climbing off his bunk when Eva pushed into his cabin. She sounded breathless and looked exhausted.

Jack grabbed the sheet, wrapping it around his waist.

'Oh, sorry,' she said. 'I saw Hollis head to the showers. I figured you were free.' She shrugged. 'It's a small ship.'

Jack took two quick strides towards her. She backed into the door. Jack leaned closer, his hip brushing against hers, his hand trailing along her bare arm, lifting her head to his. She exhaled, but she didn't move.

'What can I do for you?' Jack whispered.

'Not that.' She blushed, but didn't duck out of his way.

Jack grinned and backed off, sitting on the edge of the bunk. 'Are you always this easy to embarrass?'

'Not usually,' she admitted, looking away from Jack's piercing stare.

'Been a while, has it? Vlad not fast on the uptake?'

This time even her ears burned. 'Vlad might be if I looked like Shelley.'

'Hmm. Don't confuse Vlad's fantasy with what he really wants; otherwise, it wouldn't be a fantasy.' Jack pulled on his trousers, letting his braces hang loose. 'What brought you charging along here so early this morning?'

'Shelley did.'

Eva set the Torchwood disc on the cabin's small desk and tapped it. Shelley appeared in front of Jack.

'Good morning, Captain. You slept well, I hope?'

'I did.'

For a fleeting moment Jack wondered if Shelley had been in his cabin during the night. He'd left his laptop on in case Rhys or Andy had tried to get in touch and some of Shelley's intelligence was from an alien program, after all.

Nah, he thought. She'd not been sentient long enough to think fully for herself. Had she?

Jack decided he'd need to monitor her evolution. He knew that when you lived in a world with so many powerful machines wired together eventually a consciousness develops. He'd have to keep an eye on Shelley.

'Captain, I wanted to inform you of the results of my analysis from the water that has been surging from the hydrothermal vents.'

'Which,' added Eva, leaning on the door jamb, 'have increased significantly in number.'

'How many more?' asked Jack.

'At least seven additional ones in the clusters we're monitoring, and they're growing as quickly as the others.'

'That's not good news,' said Jack, sitting back on the bed. 'Is my friend still monitoring them, too?'

'Yes, Captain.'

'We may have to do something about that, Shelley.'

'Yes, Captain.'

'Tell him what you've learned, Shelley,' said Eva, wary of hearing too many covert details from this man; after a thorough web search, she'd found only two significant things about him: he'd disappeared after the funeral of a CIA agent and he liked to read.

'Three critical points, Captain,' said Shelley. 'First, I've pinpointed the elements that were proving difficult to detect last night. The first is an ecto-hormone with a high density of androstenal, and the second element is carnosine.'

'Carnosine is a toxic hormone that affects the nervous system,' said Eva. 'It can create birth defects if you're not born with the genetic inhibiter, which has to come from both parents. Geologists will have a field day with this. Who knew it was percolating beneath the ocean? We've never found anything like carnosine in the Earth's crust before.'

'Not so fast, Eva. You can't share any of this until we can stop what's happening. If the world learns the oceans are filling with a toxic hormone we'll have global panic, and we don't behave so well towards each other when that happens.'

'But you can't ignore it, Jack! People are dying. More will. At the rate those chimneys are forming, they'll be spewing toxins into the air in...?' Eva turned and looked at Shelley.

'In exactly four days and forty-seven minutes,' said Shelley.

Jack flipped his braces over his shirt and ran his hands through his bed hair. 'It's enough time.'

'For what?'

'My plan.'

'Oh good. You have a plan.'

Jack put his hands on Eva's shoulders. 'You really need to get laid. You're very tense.'

She shrugged Jack away. 'I'm not sure it matters, but what exactly is androstenal?'

'It explains a lot,' Jack grabbed a towel. 'The heightened synaesthesia among women, the extreme physical responses to their loved ones and the increase in desire to those,' he looked at Eva, 'who are in need of sexual release.'

'I agree,' said Shelley, throwing a graph up displaying the amounts per unit of both elements in the water. 'The quantities are significant and they are building.'

'Would one of you please tell me what androstenal is?'

'Androstenal,' said Jack, 'is not just an ecto-hormone, Eva, it's a female pheromone.'

53

When he'd finished eating breakfast, Cash set the ship's course for the day with Sam, then came back below deck, joining Jack, Vlad and Eva in the communication room. Cash was glad he'd eaten a hearty breakfast to shore up against what was coming because he knew that the information Jack planned to share with the crew wasn't going to be easy to hear.

In the comms room, Jack was watching a CNN feed of the black geyser off the coast of Wales whose chimney was now visible above the surface of the water. Since it was the first geyser to appear and had remained the one closest to a populated area, it had garnered the most attention from the media, the scientific community and the public.

The geyser was almost fifty metres in diameter, and was spewing black steam 15 metres into the air, its rock chimney already constructing itself at sea level. From above, the chimney looked like a clay pot spinning on a potter's wheel, a tower of water surging from its centre.

Although the Royal Navy and the coastguard had set a five-mile no-sail no-fly zone around the Welsh geyser, the sea traffic on the Bristol channel had never been heavier and so many helicopters were now swarming in the sky, it looked like an invasion force of massive buzzing insects was hovering above Wales and the south-west of England.

Cash joined Jack. 'The media are reporting almost all of the country's psychiatric hospitals are full,' he told him. 'Most women are being sent home with prescriptions for sedatives. The numbers in the other parts of the world where the geysers have erupted and chimneys are forming are stabilising. I think the Welsh chimney is worse because of the geyser's proximity to a population mass.'

'And then there's that reaction,' said Jack, watching as the news camera zoomed in on a coastguard cruiser off the coast of Weston-super-Mare, escorting a yacht out of the no-sail zone, its naked female passengers romping to loud music, thoroughly enjoying each other's company.

Cash stepped closer to the screen, grinning broadly. 'I'm liking that reaction to the geyser much more than what happened off the coast of New Zealand.'

'So are they,' smiled Jack.

'Any idea what makes the difference in the way a woman responds to the pheromones the geysers are releasing?' asked Vlad.

'If I may,' replied Shelley, looking at Eva for permission. Despite being a creation of hers and Vlad's, Jack noticed that Shelley deferred to Eva more than Vlad.

'Of course,' said Eva, whose sexual desire had diminished the further south in the Atlantic the *Ice Maiden* sailed, a fact that she had to admit annoyed her a little, even though she knew she was reacting to the pheromones as much as she was reacting to Vlad.

'Scientists generally type pheromones in multiple categories,' said Shelley, 'the most common are obviously sex pheromones, then receptor, trail and signal pheromones, each one triggering a response through a behaviour change or a mood change in one or both members of the species affected. The pheromone that I detected in the hydrothermal vents is an ecto-hormone, a combination of two or three categories which is why it's triggering changes in mood and behaviour in women, particularly fertile women, and the changes seem tied to internal hormonal conflicts the women are already experiencing.'

'Which would explain why some women are responding with orgasms and others with violence,' said Vlad.

'According to my analysis of the patient data, Vlad,' added Shelley, 'currently the other point that explains why some women are responding with violence and some with lust is tied to their synaesthesia. Most of the initial clusters of women, the synaesthetes, tended to respond with violence, but I believe that had more to do with the intensity of their heightened synaesthesia coupled with their emotional stability and how both outweighed their sexual desire.'

Jack thought about Gwen's response – how her frustrations over the sudden changes in her professional and personal lives after the suspension of Torchwood, how this emotional instability combined with the pheromones had shaped a violent response in her. Yet, Jack thought, there was an aspect of Gwen's madness that continued to niggle at him. Why had she carved the glyph on her arm when so far Jack and Shelley's research had not uncovered anyone else who had seen or carved the same mark, other than Jack himself, that is.

Why was Gwen's response so different?

Vlad and Eva began checking the overnight data from the hydrothermal vents, monitoring all seven that had erupted, two of which were smaller in diameter and had already sealed like the one in New Zealand. Shelley shifted next to Vlad's computer, wiping data to the air between them when Eva asked. If not for a slight shimmer around the folds of Shelley's dress that was most obvious when standing close to her, she could easily be taken for another member of the crew.

Jack watched the avatar interact with Vlad and Eva, impressed with how well Vlad's original program had married the Torchwood software with only minor glitches.

'How bad are the numbers?' he asked Vlad.

'Bad,' said Vlad. 'The PH is off in almost every sample. Schools of fish are beginning to wash onto beaches all over the Eastern seaboard and the west coast of Africa.'

'What's happening doesn't make any scientific sense,' said Eva, chewing the arm of her glasses distractedly. She stood and walked over to the screen that Jack had switched from the news feed to the map. Once again, Eva stood and stared at the pulsing lights.

'What are you seeing?' asked Jack, standing next to her.

'Before you came on board I thought I could detect a pattern in the vents,' said Eva, watching the lights. 'But I couldn't figure it out.'

'Shelley,' said Jack, 'can you download the file I gave you from Gwen's phone?'

Shelley appeared next to Eva and she threw the file from Gwen's phone up between them.

'It's the image on Gwen's arm,' said Eva.

'Where's the file from?' asked Vlad.

'Gwen downloaded it to her phone from a computer the night before she tried to kill her husband. At first I thought the message was for me, but given everything that's happening to female synaesthetes, I'm beginning to think that it was intended for Gwen all along.' Jack paused for a beat, then asked Shelley to superimpose the glyph image onto the map and drop out the background details.

Shelley did, leaving only the flashing lights and the outline of the continents.

Jack cleared his throat, and looked at each of them

directly, aware that what he was about to say would change everything, would make this less a scientific mission and more a suicide one.

'Every single one of these flashing lights is a hydrothermal chimney that's already forming above the surface of the ocean, and we can assume when they seal over they're going to force all that pressure, all that heat, all those combustible chemicals back to the centre of the planet.'

'Which,' added Cash, 'will essentially turn the Earth into a bloody big hydrogen bomb.'

'Holy shit,' said Vlad. 'Game over.'

54

Eva was speechless. She slumped across her desk. Her emotions were already in such a jumbled mess that she was having a difficult time separating and categorising exactly what she was feeling. From the moment yesterday when they had discovered how quickly the vent chimneys were evolving, Eva had felt as if she was caught in a bizarre training simulation and at any moment someone would step onto the ship and tell them all they'd performed well on this mission and now they could go home.

If what Jack, Cash and Shelley were suggesting was true, in a couple of days she might not have a home to return to. No one would.

'Shelley,' said Jack, 'let's see this model of the Earth from above.'

Shelley flipped the animation and zoomed out, the glyph linking all the chimneys with the top one, the geyser in Wales.

'Fuck me,' said Vlad.

'That program is not yet operational,' said Shelley.

'When all the chimneys are linked together like this, it's Gwen's design,' said Cash. 'And the map to a bloody big bang.'

'If that is what's occurring,' said Shelley, 'then we must assume that these hydrothermal vents are connected deep inside the Earth. Like this.'

Shelley reconfigured the image, stripping the top layers from the earth, slicing the earth in two, and showing what the linking of the hydrothermal vents might look like from beneath the Earth's crust: three overlapping, smouldering tunnels of fire stretching across the world.

'What does this all mean?' asked Eva, her voice high pitched with fear, the colour draining from her face the longer she looked at Shelley's model of the core of the Earth.

'I think it means,' said Jack, 'that the Earth is self-destructing.'

'That's ridiculous,' said Eva. She looked from Jack to Vlad to Cash to Shelley and back to Jack.

'Is it so hard to imagine, lass?' asked Cash. 'Think about it. We've worn this planet out. It's over-populated, terribly polluted and the oceans' temperatures are rising fast. The old girl might just have decided she's had enough.'

'Look,' said Eva, standing and pacing across the tiny space, her fear tightening in her chest. 'I can believe that the Earth is a series of complex organic systems. I can even believe the Gaia theory that the planet's constantly changing and evolving on a massive scale to stay in balance, to sustain life, but the Earth is not a sentient being.'

'But what if she is?' interrupted Jack.

'O puhleeze,' said Eva. 'The Earth's not thinking, she's not processing all that's happening to her and keeping score. Oh, too many people now. Check. Too much global warming. Check.' Eva was ticking off on her fingers as she spoke. 'Oceans are losing salinity. Check. Until one day the sun rises in a smoggy haze and the Earth says to herself, screw it, had enough, time to blow myself up and start life somewhere else in the universe.'

'Snark all you want, Eva, but I think Jack's right and that's essentially what's happening,' said Cash.

'And we need to stop it,' said Jack.

'Eva,' cut in Vlad, 'in that entire rant why did you keep calling the Earth a she?'

'Because everyone does... you know... Mother Earth,' Eva spluttered, throwing herself onto her chair with such force she almost tipped it over.

'Eva,' said Jack. 'Do you have any other explanation for what's happening?'

'If I may interject,' said Shelley, who appeared behind Eva's desk. 'Every culture from the ancient Greeks to the Egyptians, the Native Americans, African tribes, the Chinese, the Norse, and the Celts have a creation story and many of those creation stories have humanity being birthed from the Earth in some manner. The Earth is the mother to humanity. One sustains the life of the other. Even Judeo-Christianity gave us the garden of Eden, a paradise on Earth and—'

'Shelley, stop! I get it,' Eva yelled. Cash scowled at her. Vlad put his hand on her arm to try to calm her. She pushed him away. Everyone was looking at her, except Jack who was using the pad to zoom in on the map of South America.

She stared at him for a beat, an awful realisation dawning. 'You bastard! You knew this was happening,' hissed Eva. 'You knew before you even boarded our ship.'

'What do you mean?' asked Vlad, sensing he had missed something important.

Eva pointed at Jack, who stood and faced her. 'He was the one who sent us to monitor those hot spots in the ocean. He knew the Earth's crust was cracking, that these fissures were forming. He's the one who's paying for the *Ice Maiden*'s mission. He's the one responsible for all this incredible equipment.' She looked for confirmation to Cash. 'Isn't he?'

'Aye,' said Cash.

'How could you possibly know this was going to happen?' Eva shouted at Jack, her yelling drawing Hollis out of the mess to the passageway where he hovered, listening.

Eva stood up, her fear and anger morphing to a dangerous mix. 'Tell us how you knew this was going to happen! Tell us! Because if we're sailing to the end of the world we deserve to know everything.'

Jack glanced over at Cash, who nodded. Jack moved away from the flat screen. Cash shot him.

55

Jack gasped, once, twice then sat bolt upright, a bleeding hole in his forehead slowly healing.

'Fuck me,' said Vlad.

'Still not operational,' said Shelley.

'I need a shot,' said Hollis.

'Bring the bottle,' said Jack.

'I thought your head would be less of a mess than your chest,' said Cash, helping Jack to his feet and returning his Webley to him.

'I appreciate that. My head's taken more bullets than I care to think about. Takes me out instantly and the pain on the recovery is more tolerable. A bullet to the chest hurts like hell before it kills me.'

Hollis set the tequila bottle and glasses on Vlad's desk, poured each of them a shot, refilled his glass twice, made sure Eva, whose face was frozen in horror, drank hers before he grabbed a chair from the mess and dragged it into the comms room.

'I knew you had better recovery abilities than most,' he said, grinning and handing Jack a glass, 'but that's friggin' ridiculous.'

Despite the pounding headache, Jack laughed, knocking

back the tequila.

Then everyone began talking at once, the craziness, the ridiculousness, the amazement over what they'd witnessed filling the room. Finally, Jack whistled and brought some semblance of order to their curiosity.

'So you're like immortal, darlin'?' asked Hollis.

'Not really. I can die, and, believe me, it hurts to die, but I heal, so technically I'm able to resurrect, which, I guess, if you stretch the definition a little, does make me immortal.'

'But how is that possible?' said Eva. 'Is it because of what happened with the Miracle? Did you not get cured after that happened?'

'No, Eva, I've been unable to stay dead for a very, very long time. My cell structure was altered, oh, a couple of thousand years ago in my timeline.'

'And Cash knew?'

'Cash's grandfather was a colleague with Torchwood in Scotland.'

Cash nodded. 'The auld bugger was full of secrets, but a few of the important ones he left with me.'

'So I'm guessing,' said Hollis, 'with that kind of power you've seen some things we haven't. Am I right?'

'Oh, you're right.'

Jack pushed his hair from his eyes, rubbing the closing wound as he did. 'And it's from my longevity, my experiences, that I think I can explain what's triggering these changes in the Earth.'

Eva took another shot of tequila.

'A long time ago,' said Jack, 'a dear friend and a brave woman told me a story about energy forces called the Helix Intelligences.' Jack shoved his hands into his pockets. 'Sarah Jane said it was possible that when our solar system was forming one of the helixes was trapped in the centre of the Earth.'

Eva held her glass out to Hollis who refilled it. Again.

'My first inkling,' continued Jack, 'of what might be happening under the sea and to me, and to all these women, including Gwen, was a hunch, a response to the fragment of a memory, and the urgency of a thin voice in my head reminding me of Sarah Jane's story.'

'Great!' snorted Eva, recovering from the shock of what she'd witnessed, the tequila helping too. 'We're supposed to trust you because of a voice in your head.'

Jack shrugged. 'Listen. I know this is difficult to get your head around—'

'You think?' said Eva.

'But I think given how quickly these chimneys are forming we don't have much time to act.'

Eva exhaled a long exasperated sigh. She sat at her desk, close to tears. Vlad put his hand on her arm. This time she let it stay.

Hollis passed her another drink. 'It'll cure what's ailing you, darlin'.'

She shot back two.

Jack refused another, but Cash joined Eva and shot back two. 'Can't have the lass drinking alone.'

'I know about the Helix Intelligences,' said Vlad. 'There was a cadre of physicists in the 1960s – some said they were a cult and spent too much time experimenting with LSD. Anyway, they posited a theory that a powerful sentient astral force was caught in the Big Bang and part of the astral force broke off and was later fused into the centre of the planet. The energy force gives the Earth its organic nature and it's from this sentient force that life evolved and is protected.'

Eva looked at Vlad. 'Do you really believe that? It sounds like another creation myth, only one that involves aliens of a sort.'

'And that's the strangest thing you've heard today?'

'The Helix Intelligences are not aliens per se,' said Jack, 'but sentient astral forces. The Greeks called them Titans, the gods of the gods.'

'How do you know?'

'The friend I was telling you about, she witnessed the Helix splitting.'

Eva looked at Jack, then Cash and finally Vlad. 'You're not seriously believing this, are you?'

'Eva,' said Vlad, 'Shelley has data to prove that Earth functions that should be taking two million years to develop are suddenly happening overnight. Thousands of women across the world are being driven mad from an ecto-hormone, a sophisticated pheromone that's slowly seeping into the atmosphere. Jack's explanation is the best one I've heard, and,' he held his hand up to stop Eva who was about to interrupt him. 'And in 2009 a virus infected the net. It was a fragment of a Helix Intelligence. I was one of the techs tasked to study it.'

Eva put her head down on the desk. Hollis pulled his chair next to hers, and gently stroked her back.

'Hollis, what about you?' asked Jack. 'Are you buying my theory?'

'Jack, I'm buying anything you're selling, darlin'. I'm from N'Orleans. I've seen plenty of weird shit in my day too.'

56

Five miles off the coast of Wales, HMS *Churchill* reached its cruising depth at 300 feet below the surface of the Atlantic.

'Torpedoes at the ready.'

'Ready, sir.'

'Position confirmed.

'Confirmed, sir.'

'Release torpedoes.

'Fire!'

Inside the brightly lit sonar room, three officers of the Royal Navy and two visiting commanders from the US Navy watched the screens as the torpedoes shot through the water to the ribbed trunk of the hydrothermal chimney. Both torpedoes hit the structure at the same time, detonating against the surface of the rock, sending a screaming sound wave bouncing back to the submarine. The waves spiralled around the entire ship, shorting every piece of electrical equipment inside, and flipping the submarine a full 360 degrees in the water.

The emergency generators switched on immediately. Only a handful of men and women sustained injuries. When the engine crew adjusted the ballasts and the submarine steadied itself in the water, the officers, shaken but remaining steady on their feet, took a closer look at the damage the missiles had inflicted on the hydrothermal vent.

'Let General Laine at HQ know that the chimney has sustained no damage from our attack,' said the British commander. 'We are awaiting further orders.'

57

'For months,' said Jack, 'fragments of a memory have been haunting me, flashes of something that until recently I thought was part of a dream, or perhaps some kind of genetic memory. But when Cash sent me your data and I reviewed your discoveries about these eruptions, I knew my blood had triggered something deep in the Earth's core, and that I had started a countdown to the planet's self-destruction. Again.'

'Again?' asked Vlad. 'This has happened before?'

'My blood,' Jack told him, 'along with global warming, over-population, the extinction of certain species, all the things Eva was mocking, started decades ago, in 1930 to be exact, but a friend saved me and unwittingly saved all of us. I think the helix, the astral energy force trapped at the centre of the Earth, has been searching for me ever since. It needs my genetic code, my 51st-century DNA, to free itself. This sentient mass at the centre of the Earth has a limited time span.'

'It's like the Earth has a planned obsolescence,' said Cash.

Jack nodded. 'Sort of.'

'Aliens were here,' said Vlad, 'and they slapped a Best

Before date on us, and now humanity's reaching its expiry date.'

'That's one way to put it,' said Jack, smiling. 'But the timing is wrong. If global warming and those other elements continued then the trigger should have been in the 51st century. Not now. Not today. But my DNA in the morphic field messed up the geologic time scale and stimulated the archetypal memory of the helix.'

'What's the geologic time scale?' asked Hollis.

'Shelley, explain please?' asked Jack, his exhaustion making his bones ache. The closer the *Ice Maiden* got to the Panama Canal, the worse his synaesthesia.

Hollis slid the chair he'd been sitting on across to Jack, who straddled it. Hollis parked himself on the edge of Eva's desk, his weight nudging her. She lifted her head and looked into Hollis's dark eyes. 'You're awful sexy.'

Hollis winked at her.

'Geologists,' explained Shelley, appearing next to Jack, 'and other scientists use what's called a geologic time scale to map the history of the Earth. The time scale describes the relationships among critical biological and geologic events, using strata studied in volcanic rock formations, fossil analysis, population growth as well as climate and oceanic changes.' Shelley tapped her pen to her leather journal, opening a chronological spiral above Jack's head, spinning the conch shape only slowing it down at critical points as she spoke. 'There have been numerous cataclysmic events that are marked on the geologic timeline. The breaking up of land masses, the freezing of the polar ice caps, the mass extinction of dinosaurs and other plant life, to even a minor ice age in the northern hemisphere. All of which suggests the Earth adjusting and shifting to balance her systems.'

Jack leaned over the back of the chair, looking directly at Eva. 'So, yes, Eva, the *Ice Maiden* has been monitoring the oceans for me, but I was hoping that you'd not find anything out of the ordinary. But then when the behaviours of certain women started to be affected, especially Gwen's, and when I discovered that Gwen had carved a message to me on her arm, then I knew there was a connection between the two events. First tremors and changes in the body of the Earth and then tremors and changes in the bodies and minds of women, especially a woman I'm close to. Not a coincidence.'

'So what's the connection?' asked Vlad.

'When Shelley confirmed what was spewing from the hydrothermal vents then I understood that women who were synaesthetes were being affected for a reason, but not the one I initially thought.'

Eva pushed away from her desk. 'I can't get my head around this. I need some fresh air.'

She wobbled to her feet, and all the tequila shots had their effect, toppling her into Vlad's arms.

She smiled up at him. 'You're very sexy too.'

Vlad rolled his eyes and sat Eva back down at her desk.

'Go on,' she said, resting her head on her desk. 'I'm listening, Captain Harkness, sir. Mister bossy spaceman. I'm listening.'

Jack pointed to the seven vents that as of today were all visible above the surface of the oceans. 'Each one of these vents triggered synaesthesia in clusters of women living close to them. I think their heightened synaesthesia was simply a by-product of these deep-water vents. I think the Helix Intelligence, the sentient force at the centre of the Earth, was looking for me.'

'But,' interrupted Hollis, 'and I say this from quite convincing experience, you're pretty much all male. How come you've been affected by this female hormone.'

Jack smiled at Hollis. 'Thank you, but my DNA, my cell structure, is much more complex than yours and much less a dichotomy between male and female chromosomes and if I'm right about my dream, about some of the... the hallucinations I've been experiencing then, because I've connected with the force at the centre of the Earth before... it wants my DNA to free itself.'

'It's as if Jack's the helix's exodus code. It's way to escape back to the universe,' said Cash.

'The Helix Intelligences are sentient astral forces,' Jack explained. 'They've existed everywhere in the galaxies before any life forms. They may in fact have been responsible for the first life forms. They are neutral, impassive energy forces. But I think after this helix was trapped in the Earth's core, over the eons it has absorbed many of our human passions, especially the ones that make us dangerous to each other – anger, hatred, revenge. Think about how much blood has spilled on this planet since the beginning of time, never mind in the last seventy-plus years. I think it needs my life force to break free.'

Cash started to laugh, a loud deep infectious one.

'What's so funny?' slurred Eva. 'The world's facing annihilation and you're laughing.'

'My Calvinist father was right all along,' chuckled Cash. 'The world is in the hands of a spiteful, vengeful God. He must be rolling in his grave.'

'So what are we going to do?' asked Vlad. 'Other than call our families and say goodbye.'

'I'm going to convince the Helix Intelligence that it's made a mistake – that it needs to stop its self-destruct.'

'How the hell are you going to do that? If the Helix Intelligence is at the centre of the Earth, you'll need to go there to stop it.'

'That's the plan.'

'That's the plan?' asked Eva.

'Well, sort of,' said Jack. 'But we do have one or two

obstacles to overcome before we get there.'

    'We?' repeated Eva and Hollis in unison.

    'One or two obstacles,' said Vlad.

    'Maybe three.'

58

An hour later, the comms room was taking on the look and the feel of a Hub. The tequila had been put away and maps, graphs, notes and calculations spread across Vlad and Eva's desk. Shelley was running diagnostics with Vlad's help and Jack's supervision. Jack smiled to himself, glad to be part of a team again, and then he remembered that if his hunches were wrong, if his plan didn't work, they'd all be dead in four days.

All. Everyone. The entire human race. No reset. Nothing. The End.

Except what would the complete destruction of the world do to him?

Best not to find out.

'Can I help?' said a slurred voice from the passageway. Jack jumped from behind the desk as Gwen stepped into the room. 'You didn't think I'd let you save the world without me. We're a team, remember.'

Jack took Gwen's arm and helped her over to chair. 'How are you not comatose?'

'Oh, you know.' Gwen managed an easy shrug. 'If a Welsh girl can shake off six pints and four jaegerbombs and then order a flaming Sambuca, don't expect the strongest

tranquillisers known to man to keep her down for long.'
She smiled wearily. 'Although I could murder a bacon
sandwich.'

'Me too,' said Vlad.

Cash was taking apart a computer drive in the back
corner of the room. Without taking his eyes off the task, he
raised his hand. 'Me three.'

'Coming right up.' Hollis headed off to the galley.

Jack brought Gwen up to speed on his plan, the others
passing her notes and graphs when she needed them for
clarification. By the time Hollis returned with a platter of
sandiwches, Shelley was playing them the video of the
vents building under the oceans.

The footage ended on the feed of the chimney rising
higher off the coast of Wales. Gwen stood at the screen with
Jack, watching the rocks around the geyser get taller.

'Are Anwen and Rhys OK?'

'They are, and so is your mum.'

'Do you think Rhys will ever forgive me for what I tried
to do?'

'Of course. It's Rhys. He loves you unconditionally.' Jack
pulled his handkerchief and dried her tears. And so do I, he
thought.

'Are you sure this plan is going to work, Jack?'

'Have I ever been wrong?'

Suddenly everyone stopped what they were doing,
waiting for Gwen's answer.

'Well, there was that time…' She let her voice trail off.

Eva's eyes widened.

'Trust him,' said Gwen. 'He's the world's last best hope.'

Eva put down the notes she was looking at, and said to
Gwen, 'So you don't think we should let someone in power
– I don't know, like the President or the United Nations –
know what's about to happen so they can create some kind

of evacuation plan?'

'And flee to where?' asked Vlad. 'Anyway, even if every country had their own space shuttles, it still wouldn't be enough to save everyone.'

Eva tore into her sandwich, hot sauce dripping down her chin. Vlad reached over and wiped it off with his thumb.

'You don't think anyone else could be monitoring the hydrothermal vents who can hypothesise, as we did,' said Eva, her mouth full, her pulse quickening, 'about what's going to happen when they all seal themselves?'

'The US Navy and the Royal Navy have submarines full of scientists already examining the vents in Wales and off the coast of New Zealand,' said Shelley. 'For the past twenty-four hours, they've been trying unsuccessfully to take a rock sample. Nothing is permeating the structures. They've tried an array of weapons from their arsenal. It will take them longer to trace the ecto-hormones in the atmosphere and the increase of carnosine in the water; most of their technology is not yet equipped for the tests.'

'Unlike ours,' said Eva.

'Unlike ours,' said Jack.

'Because some of our technology is alien,' said Vlad.

Jack scanned the room, making eye contact with each one of them, then he nodded. 'Most of my technology is alien.'

'Fuck me!' He waved his hand at Shelley before she could respond. 'I know. I know. Not operational yet.'

'I predict,' said Shelley, 'that it will be another three days before the world will be fully aware of its predicament, and at the rate of evolution of the hydrothermal chimneys, by then it will be too late.'

'Someone else must realise we're facing an apocalyptic event and know what to do to stop it, right?' asked Eva, the full force of what was happening finally, incontrovertibly sinking in to her consciousness. She began to cry.

Jack and Cash glanced at each other. Jack shook his head.

'That's not fair,' said Eva, tears running down her cheeks. 'Why should we have to be the only ones who know the Earth is a turning into a big, stupid, awful bomb? I never asked for that responsibility. I don't want that responsibility.'

'Hey,' said Jack, 'I'm taking most of the responsibility and I really do have a plan, but—'

'But you need our help,' said Vlad.

'I need your help. All of you. Because there are a few other events at play that need to be handled before I can implement my plan.'

'Are you sure we can't just throw you into the stupid mountain and get it over with?' asked Eva, wiping her face with her sleeve.

'Not going to be that easy,' laughed Jack.

'Of course, it's not.'

'The helix needs my consciousness, my humanity, as one of the pieces to initiate its big bang and to seal the chimneys. I'm going to give her exactly what she wants, but with a slight change in the code.

'You're going to fool Mother Nature?'

'That's the plan.'

'Well,' said Hollis, 'I'm tired of being the chief cook and bottle washer on this ship. I'd like to earn a little respect. Think savin' the world might be the thing to do.'

'If my plan works, Hollis, no one is going to know what you or any of us have done.'

'Trust him,' said Gwen. 'It's better that way.'

Jack tapped the map on the screen until it zoomed in on the southern coastline of Peru. 'This is where it all began. And this is where it will end.'

He smiled at them all. 'One way or another.'

Part Four

'All the earth is a grave and nothing escapes it'
Ancient prayer

59

'How could it get any damn worse?' yelled Rex Matheson, pacing in front of the screen.

'Watch.'

Darren forwarded the tape until he found the image on the screen that had brought him running from his office in the first place. He paused and zoomed.

Staring up at the flat screen, Rex started to laugh. He couldn't help himself because frozen on the screen was a picture-perfect close-up of Captain Jack Harkness sipping an espresso at a table in the piazza in front of the Hacienda Del Castenado in the middle of one of the most important raids of Rex's rising career.

And Jack was smiling at the camera.

'How the hell did he get in there. We've had that hacienda under surveillance for days. Only our guys getting in.'

'Not sure, sir, but there was a bad storm the night before. I'm thinking, maybe then?'

'And how the hell did he get wind of our operation?' asked Rex, impressed with Jack's intelligence capabilities despite being furious that he was interfering with the closest any agency anywhere in the world had come to even a distant cousin of one of the three families.

'I don't know, sir,' said Darren, one of only a small group of agents on Rex's team who knew anything about Jack and Torchwood, and who had been tasked to monitor his movements on a regular basis. 'Must be a leak on the Peruvian end.

'Or else Harkness knows something we don't about what's going on in that village.'

'What's going on in that village is a multi-billion-dollar kidnapping-for-hire business,' said Darren. 'One we got lucky enough to uncover in time to blackmail Donoso's wife into letting us take her husband instead of the kidnappers. Why would Harkness care about any of that?'

'Unless,' said Rex, wiping Jack's image to the corner of the screen and changing the source to CNN where the geysers and the impenetrable rock chimneys forming around them were now getting continuous coverage from every major news outlet, 'unless being in that village in Peru has something to do with these geysers. And given Harkness's history, that wouldn't surprise me one damn bit.'

'Sir, I've had an eye on Harkness off and on for months and he's been nowhere near any of these geysers… Except…' Darren paused, letting his words trail off, realising he may have made a mistake.

'Except what?'

'Well, sir, I'm not sure but I think I remember reading an intel report that Gwen Cooper from Torchwood was one of the victims of that "masochistic madness" that so many women are suffering from. She was institutionalised for trying to shoot her husband. Hang on, let me check.'

Darren opened another page on the screen, bringing up Gwen's file. He double-tapped a small section at the bottom. 'Oh shit.'

'Oh shit, what?' yelled Rex.

'Gwen Cooper escaped from the hospital.' He turned and looked at Rex. 'On the day the vent chimney burst through the surface of the Bristol Channel. That's near Wales, isn't it?'

Rex slammed his hand on his desk. 'Yes, it's near Wales. Doesn't anyone study geography any more? I knew Harkness was involved in all this.'

'But what could Harkness know about the geysers that we don't? The best scientists in the world are trying to figure them out.'

'Just because we have every scientist in the world testing those fountains every way possible doesn't mean a goddamned thing because it hasn't stopped any of those chimneys from growing,' said Rex. 'Harkness knows a lot of things most of us do not. Believe me.'

'So what's he doing in Peru? The closest geyser to that part of South America has already sealed itself, and the authorities are evacuating the locality.'

Rex stared at Jack's image. 'I don't know what he's doing, but I'm going to find out.'

'Sir, I still think it might just be that he's figured out on his own the relationship between Donoso and the three families. Maybe he's going to try to get to Donoso before we can. We should warn our tactical unit to keep him on their radar.'

Rex walked closer to the screen and stared at Jack. 'Does Harkness have any support down there?'

'No. Everyone in the village was marked when our team arrived.'

'If he was bringing in any support, he'd have been smart to arrange for it to arrive after we'd placed our people.'

Darren fast-forwarded the video feed to the dust cloud coming over the horizon on to the meseta, the camera lodged

301

high in the wall of the canyon.

'The minibus,' said Darren. 'If he's got any support, they were going in on that bus with Donoso. There's no other way in and out of the hacienda right now.'

'Still nothing from Carlisle?'

'Nothing, but things went pear-shaped pretty fast down there once the girl crashed the bus.'

'Shit. I hate kids.'

'Sir, keep in mind this is a live feed and this video is only about eight or nine minutes behind. We may still be able to salvage something, including Donoso. Carlisle wasn't alone. We've a full tactical unit in the piazza. Their orders are to wait until Asiro kidnaps Donoso and takes him into the compound, then they'll move in and kidnap him from the kidnappers. It lets us keep his disappearance invisible if he is connected to the families. They won't know we're getting closer.'

'I know what the plan is on paper, agent, I designed it. The problem is when you mix in people things shift pretty quickly, and Harkness is no ordinary person.' Rex shoved his hands into his pockets to stop himself from punching a big hole through the highly polished mahogany walls of his stupid office. I should have gone in with tactical, he thought. What am I doing, delegating from a fancy office?

'Where are we monitoring this from?' he asked Rex, jogging out of his office and into the hallway.

'A warehouse in Cuzco via Tactical Room 14,' said Darren, holding open the door to the stairwell. 'This will be faster, sir.'

Both men sprinted down the stairs, Rex moving faster than his agent. 'I want to see everything that's going on down there,' said Rex, 'and I want a direct line to the unit's commander in the piazza. Yesterday.'

When Rex was in the tactical monitoring room and

the feed from the piazza was running live, Darren finally sheepishly asked him, 'What's your plan, sir?'

'To figure out what the hell Jack Harkness is up to.'

'And?'

'And either stop him or help him.'

Isela

60

Southern Peru, present day, minutes before Isela's shot

Jack finished his coffee on the piazza, taking particular note of the peasant women spreading their glazed pots and fabrics across the steps of the church, their striped ponchos draped loosely around their shoulders. He watched two food vendors wheel their carts close to the high gates of the hacienda, clumsily unlocking the lids of their steaming food trays, their eyes darting on everything and everyone.

In the distance, a cloud of red dust suggested the first tourist bus from Lima was climbing the last leg of the canyon road onto the meseta. The girl in the belfry was an unknown, but Jack decided she was the lookout for the bus and her job must be to alert the hot young man doing the James Dean imitation in the centre of the courtyard.

Jack concentrated on the sounds around him, filtering and marking them in his mind, the only way he knew to track the woman, the Cuari guide he needed to descend into the mountain with him.

Click. Click. Click.

Jack tasted oranges and a hint of ginger.

She was nearby. Did she know he had returned?

Jack tipped back in the seat, the sun warm on his face,

glancing longer at one of the women on the steps as he stretched, Doc Martens peeping out beneath her layers of multicoloured skirts. Touching her hand to her ear, she mumbled something into the collar band of her poncho.

Jack smiled. Gotcha.

Click.

Citrus flooded Jack's mouth. The ginger was fading from his tongue. She was on the move.

Time to die.

Jack stood and threw some coins on the table. Glancing up at the bell tower, he saw the young girl duck quickly out of sight. Jack was aware that he was not going to be able to stop what was about to happen but, if he was lucky, he could minimise the damage, find what he needed and still reach the mountain before nightfall.

According to Shelley's calculations, at the rate the chimneys were evolving and sealing, the Earth had six hours and twenty minutes left.

Jack ducked to the rear of the café and onto the airstrip where he bribed the boys to sell their football. He took it and then dropkicked it over the hangar to the jungle beyond. At least he could keep them away from the fighting for a while.

When the boys had safely cleared the area, Jack sprinted across the airstrip to the rear gates of the hotel, keeping his eyes on the belfry. He tapped the comms unit in his ear.

'The condor is in position.'

'Glad to hear your voice, Condor,' said Cash, from his seat in the rear of the minibus. The driver, Juan, glanced at him curiously in his rear-view mirror. Smiling across the aisle at Vlad and Eva, Cash folded up his laptop and popped a disc into his pocket. Loosening his seatbelt, he manoeuvred down the aisle to the couple two seats in front.

'May I borrow your map, please?'

'Yes, of course,' said Gwen, who was stoned enough to keep her synaesthesia at bay, but alert enough to participate in the mission. Gwen had refused to be left on the ship, even threatening a call to Alan Pride, who Jack had confided to her had helped Dana with her intelligence. If anything happened to them, Pride had promised his help to Anwen and Rhys. He had also made sure that Dr Steele had given Gwen the right balance of drugs to be useful to the team when the time came.

Cash took the map back to his seat, scribbled on it that Jack was inside the compound and so far Dana's intelligence had been accurate. There were other forces at play in the Hacienda, Jack thought CIA, and that might make it more difficult to get what Jack needed.

Cash returned the map to Hollis and Gwen.

On the *Ice Maiden*, before they jumped ship to get to Lima as quickly as possible, Jack had been clear about his intentions and how they could help. Given his memory of how the mountain had affected him when he was last here, he knew he would need their help to make it to the top. The final stage of the plan was the only phase Jack had never explained to any of them.

Once Jack found what he was looking for in the Hacienda del Castenado, what was he going to do when he reached the top of the mountain?

61

At the rear gate of the hotel, Jack signalled to the guard that he'd forgotten his cottage's key.

'I'm a guest of the hacienda,' said Jack pointing through the wrought iron gates. 'Numero seis ocho seis.'

The guard smiled, nodded his head that he understood, but refused to open the rear gates to the actual compound. 'No entrada, señor. Deliveries only. Please follow path back to piazza. Enter there.'

'I really don't have time for that walk,' said Jack, smiling and then reaching through the gate, he grabbed the guard's head, and slammed it against the edge of the wall. The guard dropped to the ground.

Climbing up onto the gate, Jack flipped over to the other side, landing gracefully on his feet directly behind a second guard, who turned immediately at the sound. Jack raised his elbow, slamming it into the guard's nose. Then he pulled the guard's body behind the nearest cabana, where he removed the man's red T-shirt, his assault rifle, a knife, and his radio, which Jack clipped to his belt, slipping his earpiece out and putting the guard's in his ear instead.

Stripping off his coat, his shirt and his braces, Jack pulled on the guard's T-shirt. He walked over to the fountain, splashed water on his hands and slicked back his hair. He needed not to be an easy mark for Rex until he was ready to be.

Jack knew Rex had to be watching this entire raid after he'd made himself obvious in the piazza. Hugging the vine-covered wall, Jack sprinted to the front of the hotel, the speakers above him blaring traditional Aymara music like the tinny soundtrack to an old Western.

Inside the compound, the hotel was made up of six pastel-painted bungalows in a U-shape around the main house that sat at the opening. Each bungalow had an inner courtyard containing a private swimming pool and its own lush tropical garden. After his arrival last night, Jack had discovered that all the bungalows were empty. Given the real function of this hacienda, Jack doubted there ever were very many guests who stayed voluntarily.

The main building housed a massive colonial dining room, the kitchens and the Castenado family's private quarters. Through a locked gate just beyond the main building, tucked under the heavy canopy of the jungle, Jack had discovered the camouflaged barracks for Asiro Castenado's men.

Dana's intelligence had informed them that Castenado was running drugs and a sophisticated kidnapping business. A wealthy businessman goes missing while on vacation, his family, his business, his shareholders are alerted, and no one else; the money changes hands and after the exchange the businessman is found wandering the mountains, dehydrated but unharmed.

Problem was the kidnapping scheme was the smallest obstacle Jack had to overcome to get what he needed in the village if he was going to get to inside the mountain in time.

Six hours left.

When Jack reached the locked gate to the barracks, he

stopped, adjusting the volume on the radio. In his earpiece, he could hear Antonio calling Asiro's guards to their positions.

A voice in Jack's earpiece crackled, 'Acción!'

From the belfry, someone fired off a shot.

Damn! The girl was not just watching. Something else was going on.

Jack sprinted to the wall, climbing quickly and in time to see the minibus's front wheel explode. The bus careened off the sides of the canyon wall like a pinball, once, twice, and then wham, a final ricochet flipped it over, sending it skidding on its roof, coming to a rest against the canyon wall at the edge of the piazza.

The bus was blocking the only road off the meseta.

62

For a few seconds after the minibus hit the canyon wall, Juan didn't move, taking stock of his situation and his injuries. A cut above his left eye was bleeding heavily and he felt as if he'd been in a cage fight. Shoving the deflated airbag off his lap, he listened. Steam hissed from the engine. The bus creaked and moaned as it settled against the canyon wall. He could smell hot rubber. Behind him, the student, Eva, he'd heard her boyfriend call her, moaned and then was silent, her head flopping on her shoulder, blood trickling from the corner of her lips.

Through the shattered windscreen, Juan saw the UN soldier sprawled a few feet from the wreckage. He was breathing, but bleeding from a head wound. Juan couldn't worry about him right now because suddenly a line of armed men were fanning out from the gates of the hotel. As soon as they did, the piazza was ablaze with gunfire.

Unfastening his seatbelt, Juan hit his comms.

Nothing. Static. He decided to stay with the plan despite the chaos outside.

Easing out of his seat, pressing his hands on the floor that was now the roof above his head. He stared at the other couple who had been tossed up to the front of the minibus and were unconscious, an avalanche of luggage piled on top of them.

They were alive, but they were not likely to be making any sudden moves for a while. Juan crawled out through the shattered windscreen and, hugging the side of the van to avoid calling any attention from the gunfight in the piazza, he slipped round to the back of the minibus, and released the emergency exit. Gunfire strafed the top of the van. He pulled open the doors and threw himself into the rear of the bus.

'Señor Donoso,' he called, tossing backpacks and camera bags from his path. 'Señor, you must come with me.'

Suddenly, Juan's earpiece crackled to life. 'Get him out of there now. This is Deputy Director Rex Matheson. We need you to take Donoso straight to the extraction point. Do not, I repeat, do not go near the piazza or the hacienda. Do you copy?'

Juan tapped his earpiece twice. 'Señor Donoso, please come with me. You will not be hurt. Your freedom has all been arranged.'

Donoso shoved his wife off his chest and scrambled up. 'I'm already hurt, you fucking idiot. This was not supposed to happen. Who took out the bus?'

His wife was regaining consciousness, calling his name over and over again.

'Olivares, please, what has happened?' she cried.

'Now, Juan,' said the voice in his earpiece. 'This village is a war zone. Get the mark to the extraction point.'

'Sir,' pleaded Juan, trying to ignore the demanding voice in his earpiece. 'We do not have a lot of time. You must come.' Juan did not speak Portuguese so he spoke in English. The cut above his eye was stinging as sweat dripped from his forehead. The temperature inside the van was stifling.

Donoso scrambled to his knees in the debris, sliding a

gun from his jacket pocket as he did so.

'Sir, please,' said Juan, drawing his.

With no hesitation Donoso shot Juan in the head. His wife screamed, scrambling frantically inside her Louis Vuitton satchel looking for something.

'Is this what you're look for?' With his free hand, Donoso lifted a second gun from under his waistband, holding it up for his wife to see.

Cash began to stir from the backseat, his earpiece screaming static. Donoso pointed his gun at Cash's face.

Cash raised his hands in surrender. 'Stop. Wait. I'm nobody.'

'Everyone's somebody!' Donoso glared at him, cocked the gun, but then after a beat he lowered it. 'Don't move, Mr Nobody.'

Cash slid down in the seat, fiddling with his earpiece. A cut on his leg was bleeding down his calf, wetness seeping into his boot. That can't be good, he thought. Up ahead, Vlad was staring back at Donoso and the executed driver in disbelief.

Donoso pushed Juan's body out of his way, watching his wife crawl frantically to the nearest smashed window, dragging her LV bag behind her.

Cash put his fingers to his lips. Vlad closed his eyes. Cash couldn't see Hollis or Gwen because of debris, but he could see that Hollis's arm was moving, trying to shift a section of the side door that was pinning him on top of Gwen.

The minibus reeked of petrol, the iron odour of blood and Donoso's own perfumed stink. Donoso pulled a cigar from his pocket, inhaling its scent, then he crumbled it in his hand, flaking the tobacco over Juan's limp body. He shoved his wife's gun into the waistband of his trousers then reached across and grabbed his wife's leg before she could make it all the way through the window. She screamed. Shards of broken glass shredded her arms and legs as her husband hauled her back inside the wreckage. She raised her arms to shield her face.

'You stupid bitch,' he spat at her. 'Did you really think your skinny body could buy you more loyalty from Antonio than mine?'

Through the open emergency doors at the rear of the bus, Antonio raised his weapon and shot Donoso's wife. Vlad gasped. Donoso turned and stared at him, then he picked up the LV bag with his ransom money in it, reached his hand out to Antonio and stepped from the rear of the bus.

'You have ten minutes to gather your men,' said Donoso, kissing Antonio on the mouth before heading for the other side of the bus where two armed guards waited next to a hummer. He handed one the LV bag.

'Then we must go. I've business to take care of.'

63

From her position in the tower, Isela couldn't believe what was happening. The entire hacienda was under siege and it was all her fault. She'd watched the bus flip, but that was part of the plan. It always was. Crash the bus. Give the driver time to get the mark out and turn him (almost always a male) over to her father's personal security guards, leaving enough doubt among everyone on the bus as to whether or not the mark survived the accident while his ransom was negotiated.

If the money came through, the mark survived the crash. If not, well it seemed his injuries were more serious than first thought.

Peering over the edge of the belfry, Isela watched in astonishment as one of the old women draped in a colourful embroidered poncho, who moments before had been lounging on the church steps beneath her, tipped over a vendor's cart, dived behind it and began shooting at her father's men, who tipped over tables in front of the restaurant and returned fire. The other women were in fact men, pulling automatic weapons from their baskets, stripping off their shawls and skirts to reveal black special ops uniforms adorned with enough ammunition and grenades to take out

317

the entire piazza, the tower included.

Stunned, Isela watched as the food vendors pulled guns from inside their steamers and began returning fire. The few real villagers who had been in the market were trying to flee for cover, some inside the café and others out across the airstrip to the cover of the jungle.

Without warning, a burst of gunfire sprayed the wall of the belfry. Isela threw herself to the ground, covering her head with her arms. Dust and rock rained down on her. After a few beats, she realized that the shots were collateral from the firestorm erupting in the courtyard. Antonio and her father were the only ones who knew she was in the tower. They'd have no reason to fire at her.

But neither would anyone else. Everyone in the village was in her father's pocket, which made imprisoning the mark as a doped-up patient in the hacienda one of the more manageable aspects of the plan. As for her role, it was stop the bus, create the diversion, climb down unseen as soon as Antonio extracted the mark, and then get back inside the ranch compound and wait for the ransom.

After the chalky dust settled around her, Isela watched in confusion and disbelief as Antonio and the mark, a super-wealthy businessman from Brazil, emerged from the bus, kissed… Kissed? She was stunned.

The pair split up, the mark heading for a car tucked behind the canyon wall. Isela let the scene sink in, pinching herself that she'd really seen what she believed. She slid down the wall. She needed to think. It was bad enough that the bus had flipped more violently than she intended and that she had no idea who the other set of soldiers were in the piazza shooting at her father's men, but Antonio attracted to men. How could she have missed that detail?

Isela lifted her binoculars and focused on the hotel compound, scanning the area surrounding the ranch. The doors to the house were closed, the shutters too. The entire house looked deserted. Behind the ranch, she could make out the staff barracks – they too looked empty. All of her father's men were fighting below her. Where was her father?

Isela tapped her earpiece. 'Antonio, what's going on?'

No reply.

After the initial burst of gunfire, the shooting had stopped for a few minutes but, each time anyone moved, a volley of shots sprayed across the piazza. The scene looked and sounded like a battle from *Call of Duty*, but with one disturbing difference. Isela had no idea who the bad guys were and what the goal of the game had become.

The perimeter of the hotel compound was unprotected although she spotted a couple of bodies lying near the delivery entrance. None of her father's personal security guards were on the roof and the men who'd been shooting from the walls were dead or had fled. She counted three bodies under the wall and at least three on the ground inside the compound.

With all the shooters hunkered down behind their crude barricades, the dust from the courtyard was beginning to settle and the reloading and firing of automatic weapons was replaced with the cries and yells from the tourists left trapped inside the café.

Isela watched as two passengers from the bus crawled through the shattered windscreen, the man tossing backpacks out ahead of him and then helping the woman through. She was cradling her arm and let herself slide down from the smoking, crumpled vehicle. A second man and woman followed them out.

Isela watched the first couple inch across to the soldier and drag him to the rear of the bus. They had no sooner found cover than the shooting began again in the piazza. Isela kept watching the bus, waiting for Juan to crawl out next, but he never did.

In the piazza, no one screamed. No one yelled. No one raised any alarm. Isela had not expected anyone would. Like everyone else in the village, when a kidnapping was in progress they all had a part to play, especially if they wanted to stay on the mountain and be protected.

64

The kidnapping of Señor Olivares Donoso, one of the wealthiest men in South America, a man with links to the three families, was in play and Jack recognised that so far nothing was going according to plan – not his, not the kidnapper's, or, he surmised, the CIA's.

From a corner inside the compound, Jack activated his comms unit.

'Cash, do you read? Cash!'

Nothing. Static.

Jack tasted sage, heavy and distinct. And ginger, stronger than before. And then the voices in his head started, a serenade of low-pitched humming.

Too soon. Too soon to lose my mind, he thought. I need my notebook if this is going to work.

Jack's stomach knotted at the state of the bus, on its roof, steam hissing from its engine, no movement from anyone inside, but he had no time to react let alone get to the wreckage to help Gwen and the *Ice Maiden* crew. Seconds after Isela's shot, Castenado's men swarmed from the barracks, leaving the inside of the hacienda protected only at its distant corners.

This might be Jack's only chance to search for his

notebook. He knew that if either the CIA or Castenado's gunmen won this fight, he'd not be free to roam the mountain and time was ticking away.

Five hours and fifty-eight minutes.

Jack darted into the canopy of the jungle shading the perimeter of the tropical gardens and the terraced courtyards. When the last of Castenado's armed guards charged past heading out into the piazza, Jack slipped his belt from his pants and jogged in line behind the last man. When he was sure he was at the end of the line, Jack snapped his belt against the guard's head, the buckle drawing blood. The guard whipped around. Jack smashed his fist into the guard's throat. He crumpled. Dragging him behind a copse of bougainvillea, in seconds Jack had stripped the guard of his automatic weapon, and the night goggles hooked to his belt.

Before abandoning the body, Jack took the guard's shades too.

Jack silently slipped inside the main house, finding himself in a glittering foyer, its ceilings flecked with gold leaf, its walls covered in Diego Rivera-like murals depicting scenes from the family's dark and chequered history.

Jack figured he had about three minutes to get to Castenado himself before the piazza outside became a bloodbath. Jack wasn't entirely sure what was going on, but a simple kidnapping had become something much more. He thought he had an idea what, but he couldn't take the time to stop and check for sure.

A curving marble staircase dominated the foyer. Jack knew from his earlier reconnaissance that Castenado's private offices sat at the back of the house, looking out at the peak of the mountain.

'Hey, who the hell are you?' A large heavily armed American stepped out on to the corridor, blocking Jack's advance.

Jack had about ten seconds to make his decision. Footsteps pounded down the hallway behind the guard. In seconds, he'd be surrounded.

'I need to talk to Castenado, and I need to do it now.'

Jack was surrounded.

'No one gets past me unless I say so, and I want to know who the hell you are.'

Jack raised his hands into the air. 'Tell your boss that I need to speak to him about Renso Castenado.'

The guard squinted at Jack. 'Are you some kind of nutcase?' He took two steps closer to Jack, his gun pointing at Jack's chest.

'No doubt about it, but you really don't have time to debate the point with me,' said Jack staring down at the gun.

Without warning an explosion from outside shook the building. Jack pivoted, taking out the guard directly behind him, catching his gun in mid air, then rolling across the floor, the second guard's bullets shattering a statue of Inti the Sun God displayed in an alcove.

'Hold your fire!' a man called to the guard about to take another shot at Jack, who was scrambling back to his feet, arms raised, prepared to return fire at the two guards who remained standing.

A tall, olive-skinned man in grey trousers, a loose white tunic, carrying a black case, came out of the room at the end of the hall flanked by two guards carrying heavy black bags.

An explosion of gunfire pelted the house.

'We're under attack, boss,' said a guard, another North American, sprinting in from the courtyard. 'It's what we thought. Antonio's taking most of the men with him. The rest are pinned under fire in the piazza. Americans. Maybe ATF or CIA.' The guard took the bag from Asiro's hand. 'We gotta go, boss.'

Jack heard a voice answer in Spanish in his earpiece that the trucks were loaded and in back.

Asiro stepped up to Jack's face. 'If it is you who has interfered with my business, Señor, you should know I'm not a forgiving man. I will return and I will hunt you down.'

Jack let his weapon drop to his side, and stepped closer to Asiro, a sad smile on his face. 'My God, you are your grandfather's double.'

'You knew my grandfather?'

'Yes. He saved my life a long time ago. And that's why I'm not going to stop you, but your grandfather kept something of mine that I need. I don't care what's going on out in that courtyard. I don't care about your kidnapping scheme, but I need my notebook.'

Asiro nodded to his guards, who dropped their guns, and began carrying luggage and supplies out through the rear of the house.

'Who are you?'

'I'm the man who fell from the sky.'

Asiro's eyes widened. He stared into Jack's face. 'It can't be you… You'd be at least as old as my grandfather.'

'Let's just say,' said Jack, 'I've aged better than he did. But if you want more details, I'd suggest you pull back your men from the piazza and cut your losses with the Brazilian. You're a marked man, Asiro, and I'd like to see you live to be an old one.'

A wounded guard, obviously one of Asiro's commanders, burst through the front doors of the ranch. 'Boss, I don't know what the hell's going on out there, but we're taking fire from all sides out in the piazza.'

Asiro's eyes drilled into Jack's. Jack held his stare, noting Asiro's tense but cut jaw, a look of such concentration in his face that for a beat Jack could see only Renso in his grandson's stare.

'What do you want from my family?'

'I need to find a small leather notebook, one your grandfather probably kept safe, in a place where he kept his secrets.'

The gunfire in the piazza was getting louder and closer.

'Asiro, you're running out of time. Take your wife and your daughter and go.'

'My daughter, Isela, has the diary,' said Asiro, jogging down the stairs to the foyer with Jack following. He paused as a guard handed him a bullet-proof vest. He pulled it on and then turned to leave.

'You may need this sooner than I will,' said Asiro, handing his assault rifle to Jack.

'What about your wife and daughter? You're leaving them here?'

Asiro waved his guards on and stepped over to Jack. 'If you knew my grandfather as well as you say you did, then you know that he married the mountain and neither my daughter nor my mother can leave.'

65

Shouldering Asiro's assault rifle and harnessing his Webley, Jack sprinted from the ranch towards the hotel's gates. From his earpiece, he heard Asiro order his only guard left inside the compound to open the gate and let Jack leave. Jack sprinted quickly to the overturned minibus, sliding to safety behind it as a volley of fire rained after him.

'Is everyone OK?' asked Jack, crouching beside Gwen.

'Minor injuries, thank God,' said Cash. 'Sam got it worst. A concussion, I'm sure.'

Hollis slapped Sam upside the head. 'That's what he gets for missing our flight and then almost missing the bus.'

'The fleet was in town,' said Sam, stretched out against an overhang of rock that the rear of the bus had lodged under when it flipped, an icepack on his head.

'It's Miami,' said Eva. 'Pretty sure there's always a fleet in town.'

'And you didn't even eat Hollis's sandwiches,' said Sam. Hollis slapped him again. 'Ow! I'm in serious pain here.'

'And it could get worse,' said Hollis.

'How are you doing?' Jack asked Gwen.

'I'm OK. I probably shouldn't operate any industrial machinery or drive a tractor, but I'm sure I'll cope.'

'What's going on out there?' asked Vlad, making sure his laptop was functional. 'I thought the hardest part was going to be getting you up the mountain.'

'It still may be,' said Jack. 'The noises in my head are stronger, I'm seeing ribbons of colours in my peripheral vision and I've got a rock in my gut.'

'Wheeee!' giggled Gwen, squeezing Jack's arm.

'I think I know what's going on,' said Cash, tapping his earpiece. 'The soldiers who were undercover are a joint task force of CIA and ATF. The other fighters are split between guards loyal to Asiro and those who've switched allegiances to his stepson, Antonio, who, by the way, was sleeping with Donoso, the mark. After we crashed, Antonio shot Donoso's long-suffering wife, who, you may be interested to know, was the one trying to have her husband kidnapped in the first place, and, who, I may add, was also sleeping with Antonio.'

'Doof, doof, doof, doof, doof, doof, doof-doof-doof!' Gwen sang the theme from *EastEnders* before collapsing in giggles.

Jack glanced at her in concern. 'How do you know all of that?' he asked Cash.

Nodding towards the chapel, Cash tapped his earpiece. 'A lovely young woman told me so.'

Peering round the bus, Jack confirmed what he already knew: Dana had used her powers of persuasion and her covert connections to infiltrate the CIA's unit, and she was one of the women he'd spotted undercover on the chapel steps.

Across the courtyard a handful of Asiro's soldiers had taken cover behind overturned food carts. Jack caught a glimpse of Isela peering over the top of the belfry wall.

Beneath the tower, the peasant women had stripped off their colourful rags to expose their black unmarked tactical uniforms. Jack watched as one of the soldiers was setting up to climb the tower.

'Shit,' said Jack. 'Cash and Hollis, cover me. Eva, Vlad and Gwen get Sam into the house in the compound and wait for me there.'

'Where are you going?' asked Vlad, already helping Sam to his feet.

'I'm going to rescue a princess from her tower.'

Jack dodged bullets across the piazza, diving behind an upturned table outside the café, whose doors were wide open and its windows blown out. Taking fire from Antonio's men, Jack darted to the cover of one of the arches.

On the other side of the courtyard, four CIA 'vendors' had tipped over their souvenir and trinket carts and were using them as barricades. These soldiers were shooting at Jack along with the other guards from the hacienda.

It's the red T-shirt, thought Jack.

Throwing himself to the ground, Jack rolled behind an upturned food cart, its vendor crouched behind the steaming metal bucket.

'Who the hell are you?' the guard snarled, raising his gun at Jack, who whacked him with a steaming container of pinto beans. The man screamed, dropped his weapon, and swiped wildly at his face trying to stop the red-hot beans sticking to his skin.

'None of your business,' said Jack, grabbing his gun.

Flipping its handle, Jack struck the vendor's forehead, knocking him unconscious. Crouching low as he ran towards the tower, Jack pulled on a black Che T-shirt from another cart. A bit tight, but it would do. He yanked two grenades from an injured soldier's belt as he sprinted to the edge of the arched veranda.

Dropping low, Jack ran to the last archway before the

tower. The rapid gunfire flying across the courtyard was not abating. Staring out at the piazza, Jack knew the shooting wasn't going to stop until there was no one left standing. But Jack didn't have that kind of time. He could already feel his mind slipping, his concentration fragmenting, his stomach doing double flips. Glancing at the tower, he could see the soldier beginning to climb up the wall to reach the girl.

Five hours exactly before all seven chimneys were sealed.

Jack needed to stop this gunfight at the Inca corral. So he pulled the pins on the grenades. Keeping his fingers on the triggers, he raised his hands in the air and walked out into the middle of the courtyard. With shots chipping at his feet, Jack tossed the grenades up into the air above his head.

66

As the gunfire worsened beneath Isela, the clanging amplified in her head. She was comfortable with her heightened perceptions so she thought nothing of their intensity.

She couldn't believe her eyes when the *cóndor* leapt from behind the cover of the arched veranda and tossed two grenades high above his head, scuttling Antonio's guards who were nearest to him. The American soldiers threw themselves to the ground behind their barricades. The explosion kicked up a thick cloud of smoke and dust, the *cóndor's* body collapsing in the middle of it.

'Holy shit!' said Isela, her rifle clattering to the stone as the man, the *cóndor*, jolted upright and gasped for breath. A little unsteadily, he stood up, brushed off his trousers, rolled and stretched his neck muscles, then picked up his rifle and walked out of the swirls of dust.

Instantly, the shooting stopped. Her father's guards dropped their weapons and ran towards the airstrip. Antonio's men followed them, firing wildly.

The *cóndor* stopped for a minute under the heavy canopy of the huarango tree, its wide trunk full of divots from centuries worth of armed attacks even before today's stand-off.

When she could stand the noises in her head again after the explosion, Isela lifted her binoculars and stared out at the airstrip. Four heavily armed men were escorting Antonio to a black Hummer. Isela recognised their insignia as that of Donoso's private army.

Hundreds of black and yellow dots floated across Isela's eyes, her anger piling on top of her shame. Why had she listened to Antonio? He'd set her up and he'd betrayed her father. What a dick she'd been.

67

The American soldiers who'd been covering the airstrip fanned in and took control of the piazza. Most of the dead and wounded were draped across the bricks, their blood seeping into the clay, staining the pink in a mockery of its playfulness. The music blared for a few more beats, until one of the soldiers shot out the speakers.

Jack sprinted to Dana who was in full SWAT gear and standing at the bottom of the belfry. 'Have I told you recently how amazing you are?' said Jack.

Dana smiled. 'Never gets old. What's the plan?'

'I need the girl. She has my notebook, which I believe has the code I need to trick Mother Earth.'

A voice yelled in Dana's earpiece; she held her finger up, silencing Jack. 'I need the girl at the extraction point. I want to know everything she does about Donoso. Someone's going to pay for this fiasco.'

'Our friends at the CIA want the girl, Jack.'

'Can't let that happen, Dana.'

Jack figured he could make a run at the tower and, if he was lucky, get inside to the girl before the soldiers.

Suddenly Jack's earpiece let out a high-pitched static squeal. Jack tore it from his ear. His mouth filled with the taste of cucumbers and lemons and ash. His knees buckled, his joints ached so badly that he didn't think they could take his weight.

'Go to the others,' Jack yelled to Dana over the chaos. 'Tell them it's started and be prepared.'

The ground beneath Jack trembled. At first it was just a slight rolling beneath his feet, but then the planks of the veranda began to pop up one at a time all around the piazza. Jack stared in horror as the ground opened underneath the bus, dropping it twenty feet into the ground. Two soldiers were pinned beneath a massive rock crashing off the canyon wall when a long fissure shot out from the meseta along the dirt, across the middle of the piazza, opening a gaping hole in the ground sucking down anything in its path, including the huarango tree.

The fissure shot between the roots of the massive tree, swallowed up the ground beneath it, spitting up its long roots and tossing the tree over the far wall of the hacienda where its tendrils gripped the mountainside like claws as the tree tumbled into the sea below.

The soldiers standing at the bottom of the tower sprinted from the fissure as it snaked directly at them. They never stood a chance, swallowed into the earth as the tear opened wider and wider, taking walls and buildings with it as it snaked across the village towards the tower and Jack.

Jack sprinted parallel with the fissure leaping over crashing adobe walls, ducking to avoid torrents of debris. When he reached the tower, he yanked at one of the lines.

'Get down!'

The soldier bounced against the wall as she pointed her gun down at Jack. 'Sir, this is no time to be a hero, get back to safety with the other tourists. This will be over soon.'

A clap of thunder rolled across the ground. Jack ducked against the wall for cover, thinking someone else had tossed a grenade. Roaring, the fissure snaked up the wall of the tower, crumbling the stones to chalk on either side of her.

'Soldier,' Jack called up to her. 'You need to come down.'

Letting out her line, she rappelled to the ground seconds before the entire side of the wall collapsed, bricks crashing down on her, leaving the bell swinging precariously on the edge of the tower wall.

Jack helped her free herself from the rubble, seconds before the bell crashed down into the rubble where she'd just been buried.

Her radio crackled in her ear. 'What the hell is going on? Do you have the girl or not?'

'Not yet, sir,' answered the soldier. 'We've just had a minor earthquake here. The piazza is destroyed. It's still happening. This needs to be a search and rescue, sir. Our unit's getting the civilians out to the airfield. We'll need a couple of copters, sir.'

'They're on route with units trained in S&R,' said the voice in her ear. 'Your mission has not changed. Get the girl and make the rendezvous. That's an order.'

'Yes, sir.' She cut off her comms unit, and returned her attention to Jack. 'Who are you?'

'Why does everyone keep asking me that?'

He brushed grit from his face and stared up at the tower, which looked as if someone had taken a bite out of it. The fissure had stopped when it had collapsed the side of the tower.

It had nowhere else to go, thought Jack.

Thunder rumbled off the distant mountains, the ground beneath them trembling every few seconds, sounding like a series of tiny explosions under their feet. Jack's vision was clouding with dots once again and he had a powerful desire to jump from the wall and follow the tree into the ocean.

'Hey!' The soldier grabbed his arm. 'Where are you

going? That's not safe.'

Jack ignored her, climbing up onto the rubble as high as he could, but it wasn't enough to see into the belfry and expose Isela's hiding place.

The soldier regained her composure and her weapon, which she shoved into the small of Jack's back. 'Down. Now.'

'Do we have the girl in custody, yet?' hissed her earpiece.

Jack turned and hooked his hands above his head, looking into the soldier's eyes. They were smouldering with anger, but it was the only emotion he could read clearly from her expression. 'I'd be more than happy to cooperate with you, soldier—'

'Captain Anderson.'

'Ah, Captain Anderson.' Jack cocked his head. 'A pleasure to meet you, but right now my priority – yours too – is to get that young girl out of that tower before the next tremor comes. If I'm right about what's happening here, the next one will be worse than the one we just experienced. It makes no difference to me,' he grinned at Captain Anderson, 'but you and the girl may not survive being buried alive.'

Captain Anderson stared at Jack, noting the cocky, self-assured grin, the piercing blue eyes that seemed to suggest that no matter what he decided somehow he was going to get his way.

'What do you want me to do?'

'I want you to put your gun away and let me bring her down.'

She looked over at the other soldiers from her unit who were helping free the injured from the rubble, setting up a triage out in the airstrip. 'OK. You get her down.'

Captain Anderson holstered her weapon, stepped aside, and waved Jack towards the tower.

'Thank you, Captain.'

It would take too long to disengage the pulley and the anchor from the rubble so Jack hung a rope over his shoulder, cuffed his trousers, dug a toehold with his boots, then another with his fingers and began to climb up into the tower. At the halfway mark, he stopped, aware of Isela watching him from above. He didn't think she'd try to stop him until he got closer, but she was trapped and she had to know that she was in serious trouble.

'Isela,' he yelled. 'You need to get out of this tower, and your best chance to get out of this mess is to come with me.'

He continued his ascent, hearing Isela load her gun and scramble to the other corner of the belfry.

After two more steps, he was about to pull himself up and over the crumbling edge and into the belfry when he heard Isela cocking her rifle. He looked up. She was pointing it at his head.

Jack sighed, but kept climbing.

'I'll shoot you!'

'I've no doubt that you could and that you would, Isela, but killing me will only make your situation worse,' Jack said, digging his feet deeper into the crumbling rock, creating a ledge from which to balance for a few seconds. 'That soldier below is from the American government. They have orders to arrest you and hold you while they figure out your role in this mess here this morning.'

On the ground below, Captain Anderson responded to a radio request that two transport units were on their way in from Lima and when she returned her attention to Jack he was shoving the nuzzle of Isela's gun out of his face and hoisting himself up into the belfry.

'This tower survived the last two quakes,' Isela said, backing away from Jack, her rifle still aimed at his head. 'I'll be safer up here.'

'No, Isela. You won't,' Jack anchored the rope to the bell,

tossing the excess over the side of the tower. Isela's voice tasted like vanilla and cinnamon.

'How do you know?' she asked.

'Because that fissure wasn't the result of an earthquake. And I think you know that. I need something you have of mine and I need you to take me to your mother.'

Isela looked at him, deciding whether or not to trust him, keeping her rifle at his head. Captain Anderson climbed up into the belfry next to them both.

'Well isn't this cosy,' said Jack, moving to the other side, away from the still crumbling wall to more solid footing.

'Is. She. In. Your. Custody. Yet!' squawked the voice in the Anderson's earpiece.

'Isela, I'm Captain Anderson,' she yanked the comms unit from her ear. 'I work for the US government—'

'So you have no jurisdiction here,' snapped Isela, backing away from her and a little closer to where Jack was standing.

'I'm part of a joint task force with the Peruvian government—' she continued.

'Even the Peruvian government has no jurisdiction here,' Isela laughed, dropping her rifle and sliding it into its case. She looked up at Captain Anderson. 'Besides I haven't done anything wrong. I was up here shooting at targets on the airstrip. You can't prove I wasn't.'

'Until we can locate your father and your stepbrother, I've orders to take you into my custody.'

'And how exactly are you going to do that?' asked Isela. 'You can't cuff me or neither one of us will get down from here in one piece.'

They both turned to Jack. He shrugged. 'She has a point, Captain.'

'I thought you were on my side?'

'I said I wanted to get the girl down from the tower,' said Jack, stepping closer to Isela, 'but I never said I was on your side.'

Isela looked at the soldier and grinned. She stepped closer to Jack.

'On the other hand, Captain,' said Jack, pulling his belt from his trousers. 'I didn't say I was on her side either.'

In one swift movement, Jack had the belt tight around Isela's shoulders and arms, pinning her like a straightjacket. Responding quickly, Captain Anderson bound plastic cuffs round Isela's ankles. She lost her balance and fell at Jack's feet.

Jack flipped a squirming screaming Isela up and over his shoulder. 'Isela, if you want to survive this climb, I'd suggest being as still as possible. I wouldn't want to drop you.'

Isela mumbled an obscenity into Jack's shoulder. While he tied the rope around his waist, he feigned dropping her.

She screamed.

He said, 'I'm sorry, I didn't hear what you said.'

'Nothing,' she said aloud and under her breath again, 'What a dick.'

68

When the three of them were safely on the ground, Jack set a relatively subdued Isela against the rubble. In the sky behind the hacienda, Jack spotted two Blackhawk helicopters cresting the plateau.

'The girl is secure,' said Anderson into her comms.

'Copy that,' said the voice in her ear. 'Someone will meet you at Cuzco to transport her back to DC.'

'Let's get her to the airstrip.' Anderson crouched, cutting the plastic ties from Isela's ankles. When she did, Isela kicked out at Anderson who saw it coming and grabbed Isela's foot instead. 'Listen, I don't care how you get on that helicopter, but you're going to get on that helicopter.'

Jack's head was pounding, and twice since he'd set the girl down he thought he had stopped breathing. They had to get to Isela's mother soon.

Four hours and ten minutes soon.

Isela glanced at Jack who held her stare for a beat. He saw dots, outlining the girl's face, dancing across her high cheekbones. Picking up Isela's rifle and slinging it over his shoulder, Jack hiked over the debris toward the airstrip.

The piazza looked as if a monster has stepped into the middle, crushing everything in its wake and leaving its footprint. The fissure had split the courtyard in two, cracking through the arched verandas and toppling two of the buildings as well as the tower.

Anderson pulled Isela to her feet. They followed Jack.

Seconds later, Anderson yelled for Jack and Isela to stop, bringing her rifle in front of her. Isela crouched, playing in the rubble.

'What is it?' Jack came over to Anderson, who was staring across at part of the hacienda's wall where the fissure had torn it asunder.

'I saw something,' she replied. 'Over near the wall. Might be someone injured.'

She freed the rope from her shoulder, lassoed it around Isela's waist and handed the end to Jack. 'Get her to the airstrip. Those copters will be on the ground soon. I'm going to check it out.'

'Yes, Captain,' Jack said, smiling.

Jack towed an angry Isela towards the airstrip where Anderson's unit was busy with the triaged wounded, many of whom were propped against the concrete hanger, sharing canteens of water. The dead were covered and lined up on the other side of the airstrip.

The two helicopters were coming in low, like the advanced guard of an alien invasion.

Jack tapped his comms. 'I'm bringing in the girl. May have company on my tail when I do.'

When Jack dragged Isla out to the airstrip, he reached down, threw her over his shoulder again, and ran towards the rear of the hotel.

Anderson rounded the corner. 'Hey! What the—' She lifted her rifle. 'Stop!' She fired a warning shot above Jack's head.

Directly behind Anderson the helicopters began their descent, whipping up a tornado of dust, rocks and brush.

Anderson sprinted towards the hotel.

Jack could hardly see five metres in front any more. His vision was clouded with black and yellow dots, his head clanging with strident chords of tinny music.

Dana pushed open the hotel gates. Jack charged through. Dana fired a series of shots at Anderson, who hurled herself behind a copse of brush.

Jack dropped Isela onto a lounge chair and helped Dana close and bar the gates.

'Now what?' asked Dana, freeing Isela.

'I need you to give me the notebook, Isela. I know you have it,' said Jack, his knees buckling. 'Give me a minute.'

'You can have five,' said Cash, leading the others through the tropical gardens to the cabana where Jack was down, his eyes closed, his heart racing one minute then slowing, almost stopping, the next.

Gwen looked as bad as Jack felt. She was being carried between Eva and Vlad, taking two steps on her own then being dragged and carried for two.

'What happened?' When Jack sat up a wave of nausea pulled his head back against the pillows.

'She punched Hollis,' said Vlad. 'Thought he was her husband, I think.'

Hollis was bringing up the rear of the line with Sam, each had assault rifles criss-crossed over their shoulders. 'On my honour, I did not touch the lady.'

'I upped her dosage,' said Eva.

'Hey everyone! It's Jack,' grinned Gwen. 'I missed you, Jack!'

'Why do you need to see my grandfather's notebook?' asked Isela, sitting on the edge of the lounger next to Jack.

'It's my notebook, Isela. A long time ago, on this mountain, your grandfather saved my life. He held on to the notebook for me.'

'So you are *el cóndor*? From the stories my mother tells?' Isela sucked her upper lip, a movement so childish that Jack received a vivid flash of her sitting cross-legged on a dusty tiled floor, listening wide-eyed to her mother. Isela searched Jack's face suspiciously – trying to reconcile this wild, infuriating stranger with the heroes of her childhood chronicles. Sensing his moment, Jack licked a finger, and traced in the air the pattern of overlapping circles. Recognising the symbol, Isela grinned, and dug around in her garments, pulling the notebook out of a pocket along with a handful of spare ammunition. She handed Jack the notebook.

'Thank you,' said Jack. As he closed his fingers over the book, he heard a deep sonorous boom.

'The *cóndor*,' said Hollis, 'That's a nickname with some cachet.'

'Do you actually know what a condor is?' asked Cash, moving to the gates where Dana stood guard, the drone of the helicopters shaking the hacienda's walls while they loaded the wounded.

'Four under par?'

'It's a bloody vulture, a bird that feeds on the dead,' said Cash.

'It's a sacred bird to the Cuari, to my mother,' said Isela. 'We believe that the *cóndor* comes from the heavens and it can take messages back and forth between the three worlds. It is the key to keeping the universe in balance.'

Jack carefully unfolded the cloth, and was shocked to see that tucked in the back were a series of letters that Renso had written over the years to Jack.

'Were you the friend that my grandfather wrote those letters to all those years ago?'

'I loved your grandfather, Isela.'

'He loved you too,' said Isela. She stood and held out her

hand. 'Come. I'll take you to my mother.'

'Thank you,' said Jack. Before crossing the lush courtyard with Isela, Jack skimmed across the pages, tore out the relevant ones, and handed them to Vlad. 'Do what you need to do.'

Cash sent Hollis and Sam to watch the other gates. 'If the CIA want this girl bad enough, they'll charge in and take her. Jack, we have less than four hours to get you up the mountain.'

69

Leaving Gwen stretched on a lounger singing in Welsh to herself under the watchful eyes of Eva and Vlad, Jack trailed behind Isela inside the main house. His field of vision was contracting. Running ahead of him, Isela looked as if she was moving along a narrow tube. The ache in Jack's joints and the drumming in his head had worsened. He hobbled across the foyer.

'Jack,' said Cash into his earpiece, 'it looks like the helicopters are going to have to make one more run. We're safe from Captain Anderson's unit until then. She's got a guard on the edge of the canyon. She knows we're still in the compound.'

Isela led Jack along a narrow side passageway decorated in blue and white-flecked wallpaper and a plush carpeted floor.

'The walls and the ceiling in this part of the house are all soundproofed and shaded to make it easier on my mother.'

They stopped outside a pair of arched double-doors with the three-circle symbol that Gwen had carved on her forearm displayed in the centre.

'What's wrong with your mother?' asked Jack, even though he already knew.

'The doctors have a long list, but they say the main disease is vitiligo. She can't go out in the sun. She has no... no...' She was struggling for the word in English. '*Color en piel*?'

'Pigment?'

Isela nodded. 'She has no pigment, so she burns up in the sun. Oh, and she's sensitive to sounds and touch and so many other things. It's why I want to get away from this place.'

'Why?'

'Because it is the mountain that's making her sick and one day it will make me sick too. My grandmother said so, and my mother says so. My father refused to name me after my mother and grandmother because he believes the name is cursed.'

'What should you have been named, Isela?'

'My Cuari name is Gaia.'

Jack flipped to the pages with the most writing in his notebook. There it was. Her grandmother's name scribbled across the page, the guide Jack now recalled had taken him into the mountain to sacrifice him to the Helix Intelligence, to the astral force locked inside the Earth's core.

In the line under the name Gaia, Jack had scribbled, *means goddess of the Earth.*

'I will go inside first to prepare her for you.'

When Jack entered the room, the first thing he noticed was the silence. Every noise in his head shut down. Then he realised his knees were no longer aching, his heartbeat had steadied itself, and the rock in his gut had gone.

The walls were dressed in a similar flecked fabric to the hallway but inside, instead of blue and white, the colours were maroon and gold. The carpet was thick, soft and black, and the tall arched windows were made of smoked glass. The view of the mountain and a tiled fountain were visible from the draped four poster bed where Isela's mother was propped in front of layers of soft pillows.

'I've been expecting you,' said Gaia. 'The mountain won't wait much longer.'

'Then you know what's happening? To the world?' asked Jack. He tasted ginger.

'Of course, it has been marked in the mountain since the beginning of time, noted in the beads by my ancestors and written in the scrolls by yours. It's part of the prophecy.'

'But then you also must understand what has to happen.'

She smiled sadly at Jack and then at her daughter. 'I've known my entire existence. It is what a star guide is born to do. There are so few Cuari left. The prophecy must be fulfilled this time.'

Jack walked closer to the bed. Gaia let out a painful ear-piercing wail. Jack quickly backed away.

'Everything about you hurts me,' she sobbed, her breath catching in her throat.

'Sit there,' Isela said, pointing to a long red velvet couch in front of a wall of cloth-bound books. Isela stroked her mother's palm, calming her immediately.

Jack sat on the couch and studied the woman in the bed. She was painfully thin, but her beauty and sensuality were undeniable. Patches of her skin were as white as Jack's and others were as brown as Isela's, the mottled texture and the uneven tones of her skin only enhancing her radiance. Gaia's hair was jet black, easily reaching her waist, but it was her eyes that Jack found so mesmerising, so enchanting. They were deep midnight black. The longer he stared at this woman – this being on the bed whose spirit was ancient and ageless, prehistoric and primal – the more clearly his memories of the mountain and its power fitted into place, and the more he doubted the success of his plan.

Jack had got some of it terribly wrong.

70

Swansea, same day

Rhys leaned over Anwen's cot, tucked her in, settling her stuffed bear close to her side. He kissed his finger and touched it to Anwen's heart, and for a while he stayed in that position staring at the wonder of his daughter until she snuffled, rolled onto her side, and high-kicked her blanket to the bottom of the crib.

Rhys smiled, lifting out the blanket. 'You've definitely got your mum's legs.'

Downstairs, he switched on the TV news, and stared at the footage of the tower of water shooting into the heavens. The scaffolding enveloping it looked as if an oil rig had been constructed around it, lights blazing from the navy ships, making it easy to watch the tower of rock slowly but surely engulfing the entire jet stream. The press, the crazies, and the curious had all stayed bobbing out there in the sea, as they had at the other geysers, despite most governments asking those closest to the chimneys to evacuate further inland.

And somewhere out there, Jack and Gwen were fighting to right the world.

Rhys sat down on the sofa, and prayed that the morning would come.

71

Standing on the wide porch of the hacienda with his gun over his shoulder, smoking a Cuban cigar, Cash wondered how they were ever going to make it up the mountain given Jack's deteriorating condition, never mind what he planned to do when he got there.

Savouring every puff of his cigar, Cash stared out at the Pacific. The late-afternoon sun was lingering over the horizon as if considering whether or not to be swallowed by the coming darkness.

According to Shelley's calculations, they had three hours until the vent chimneys would be sealed.

The climbing procession was organising with little fuss in the foyer when Dana alerted Cash in his earpiece that Captain Anderson's team were preparing to breach the south wall.

'If you're going, love,' she said, 'I'd say now would be good. Sam and I can hold them off until you get out of the compound.'

'Then what?' said Cash.

'Then we'll improvise.'

Cash waved at Dana, then pinched the end of his cigar,

353

setting the rest of it on the edge of the veranda. 'I expect everyone to be there when I return.'

Inside, he told Jack they had to move. Now.

Gaia insisted that the prophesied ritual be followed to the exact glyph. Dressed in a black suede jumpsuit with padded earmuffs secured under her hood, she and Isela would lead them. After some trial and error, she was able to tolerate Eva more comfortably than any of the others, so Eva was positioned in front along with Isela.

Jack refused to wear the traditional Cuari tunic. 'If the world is going to end tonight, I'm going out with my trousers on.' He sent Vlad to retrieve his coat from the rear gates.

Jack was unsteady on his feet and close to incoherent for significant chunks of time, so Cash and Hollis decided they were the best equipped to handle him.

Vlad was travelling with Gwen, who was more than a little wobbly on her feet. All of them, including Isela, carried weapons.

Twenty minutes into their climb, they reached the steep canyon hiking pass, the trail that centuries ago had been used by the great Inca warriors leading their sacrifices up the mountain.

Jack's field of vision looked like a Jackson Pollock painting, dripping with dots and dollops of blinding colours. Snarling voices were screaming in his head and he could hardly walk, his knees crippling him. With Cash and Hollis supporting him on either side, they tramped into the rocky jungle path.

Gunfire erupted from the compound below.

Eva stopped at the sound, but Cash urged her on.

'Dana and Sam know what they're doing. We need to keep moving, Eva.'

Eva was glad she had been put in the lead a good few

metres in front of Vlad because she was afraid that her own heightening sexual desire, which was getting more intense the higher they climbed, would put Vlad in more danger than the soldiers snapping at their heels. Eva was breathing heavily when they entered a clearing at the top of the canyon pass.

The volleys of gunfire echoing from the compound below were almost continuous.

'They must have breached the wall,' yelled Cash. 'Let's go, people. Let's get this done.'

When they finally arrived at the deserted ruin of the Cuari village beneath the mountain's plateau, the darkness had descended like a lid on the basin of the mountain only a few hundred metres above them.

With the descending darkness came a change in Gaia that was startling. Her steps quickened, her breathing became less laboured. She shrugged off Eva and Isela and bounded towards the final leg of the canyon pass. Jack, on the other hand, was being dragged between Cash and Hollis. No one was speaking. Only the bursts of gunfire from the compound below punctuated their progress.

The air in the clearing was rank with sulphur and ash. Jack tasted rotten meat and sour milk and ginger, the taste of the mountain. Then the gunfire ceased.

'Cash!' yelled Dana. 'Anderson's coming.' Then her comms went silent.

'Jack,' said Cash, leaning him against the ruined wall of a brick cairn. 'You're going to have to do your best to go on without us. Hollis and I will hold this clearing for as long as we can.'

Jack nodded, guessing what Cash was saying to him, but the words felt like water on his face, splashes of yellow wrapped in despair. Jack kept brushing his hands over his cheeks, nodding that he understood. When he looked at his hands, he saw that his tears were pink.

Accepting Gaia's offer of support, Jack linked his arm through hers. Then he turned and saluted Cash, who'd taken a position at the mouth of the canyon, tucking himself under the jungle's canopy.

'Remember,' said Jack, choking the words out, 'make their progress difficult, but don't shoot to kill. They're only following orders.' Cash nodded and returned Jack's salute.

Jack winked and blew a kiss to Hollis, who caught it in his fist. With Vlad and Gwen tottering behind, they climbed the final metres to the basin of the sacred mountain.

72

The darkness engulfed the rag-tag gang as soon as they emerged from the canyon pass and onto the plateau. Eva lost her footing and fell, tumbling off the path and into a tangle of trumpet trees bordering the steep ridge. Vlad abandoned Gwen and slithered down the hillside after her.

'Are you OK?'

She smiled, nodded and reluctantly broke free, scrambling to catch up with Jack, who was slumped a body's length from the lip of the massive mountain basin. Eva could barely make out Isela up ahead already marking out their positions with a ceremonial feathered brush, the peak of her markings leading down into the mountain. Like her mother, the higher the motley crew had climbed, the more compliant Isela had become, the mountain's sway over her as strong as it was over her mother. At this altitude, a thin sheen of ice coated the edges of the rocks surrounding the basin itself, the mountain etched in silver.

'Jack, where's Gaia?' asked Eva

Jack struggled to his knees, pulling the night-vision goggles he'd taken from one of the guards from his pocket. 'Give these to Cash,' he said to her. 'He may need them.'

Jack's eyes were red-rimmed, bloodshot and he wanted

nothing more than to have the cacophony of noise in his head be silent if only for one minute, one second, one beat of his pounding heart.

'Jack!' This time Eva screamed. 'Where's Gaia? We can't lose her. Not now.'

'She's right there.'

Eva heard a low growl and in terror dragged Jack from the edge of the basin against an outcropping of rocks as a mountain lion, a sleek black puma, pounced from the jungle landing next to Isela. The puma was bathed in a faint yellow light, transforming the plateau into a movie newsreel, the crew, Gwen and Jack, players on a sacrificial stage.

'Oh my God,' said Eva, backing away from Jack and closer to Vlad and Gwen.

Isela put her hand out and gently stroked the puma's neck. It nuzzled against Isela for a beat and then it turned, darted to the rim of the basin and roared, the sound bouncing off the steep rock walls and waking the mountain.

Seconds later, the ground began to shake violently, throwing Vlad, Eva and Gwen to the rocky ground where they frantically crawled to the massive boulders for something to anchor themselves against. A flaming fissure broke from inside the basin and shot up along the edge of the mountain, circling it once, twice. And then the fissure shot out across the plateau following the area Isela had marked with the ceremonial feathers, creating three interlacing fiery circles, the peak of the third one descending into the flaming rim of the mountain itself.

The puma leapt from the edge and landed in the centre of the top circle. The entire mountain trembled, a thunderous roar bursting from the bowels of the Earth, spewing ash and rock out across the plateau.

Gwen scrambled forward, grabbing Jack by the arms. 'Do you know what you're doing?'

'Each circle represents the three worlds that must be kept in balance for the Earth to survive. The world above, the world below and the world here and now. I was wrong. I thought that the Helix Intelligence – the astral force – was our enemy, that it was trying to break free, but she's not. She needs this sacrifice, needs our genetic and cellular codes to heal herself. If Renso had let her have me all those years ago then we wouldn't be here now.'

Gwen had been here before. She'd seen Jack walk into the shadow of a demon and stare into a void in the heart of the Earth. And always – when anyone else would show fear, panic, or indecision – suddenly, this most heavy-hearted of men would become cold and rational. He'd clench his jaw and square up to the universe.

Jack squeezed her shoulder. 'Gwen Cooper, you know the drill.'

'You bloody idiot,' said Gwen.

'Yup.' Jack nodded, kissing her.

Gwen brushed his hand and stepped away, walking on wobbly legs with as much determination and dignity as she could muster to the boulders where Vlad and Eva were clinging, shaken by the worsening tremors. She dropped behind the safety of the jagged outcropping next to Vlad and Eva. With images of Rhys and Anwen in her mind, Gwen prayed for a tomorrow. She glanced back at Jack, calmly waiting, and then she cleared her throat. 'Come on, kids,' she said. 'Let's get out of here before the world ends.'

Jack was about to step into the circle that was burning next to his feet when Captain Anderson charged out of the canyon pass and fired a volley of shots into the air.

'Hold it!'

The puma leapt from the lip of the mountain, flew across the air and knocked Anderson back against her men. With her massive paws on Anderson's shoulders she roared, opening her mouth as wide as the smouldering circles themselves.

Cash broke through the dense jungle brush and fired at the massive cat that was about to swallow Anderson whole. The shot hit the puma's hind leg. It howled. The ground thundered and shook in response, throwing anyone still standing off their feet. Fissures were shooting out across the plateau from every circle, crumbling and crushing anything and anyone in their path.

'No!' yelled Jack. 'Don't shoot her.'

The puma leapt off Anderson and pounced into the lead circle. Jack turned and watched as Gaia now stood in the centre of the blazing rings, blood dripping from a bullet wound in her thigh.

'I don't know what weirdness is going on here,' said Anderson, scrambling to her feet, 'but give me the girl and you can all go about your private orgy when she and my unit are clear.'

Jack turned and stared in horror as Isela began sinking into the earth, being pulled towards the edge of the basin next to him.

'No, Isela! Not you,' he screamed, his throat raw. 'You don't have to be part of this.'

'But the sacrifice must be three,' choked Isela, the smouldering ash thickening around her. 'Gaia, the puma from the darkness of the underworld, you, the *cóndor* from the heavens, and someone of the Earth, bound intimately to our world. There is no one else. It must be three. That's the prophecy.'

Overwhelmed with the intoxicating fumes, Isela collapsed to the ground, silver veins shooting out of the mountain, darting along the smoking crevices and binding Isela's feet, then her legs in threads of silver light.

Suddenly Jack realised why the hydrothermal vents had

been pulsing out the ecto-hormone; it needed to find the third sacrifice, the female whose connection to the Earth was strong, and who would be a worthy sacrifice.

But not a child. The universe could not take another child. He would not allow it to take a child again.

The pulsing veins of silver were whipping themselves round Jack's ankles, and he felt himself welcome them, the sensation as wonderful as he now remembered it. Renso stepped into the circle with him, wrapped himself in his arms, kissed his lips, then took his hands in his. Jack tasted lemons and felt every fibre of his being ache with longing.

'Get that girl out of there, now!' screamed Anderson, shooting into the sky because she didn't know what else to do.

Jack was being sucked into the ground, being tugged towards the dark abyss of the basin. He turned to the outcropping of rocks where Vlad and Eva were hiding and watched in terror as Gwen shot out from their grasp, sprinted across the clearing, hit a sheet of rock and leapt from it, landing in the circle next to Isela.

'Gwen! No,' screamed Jack. He tried to clamber towards her, but his feet were encased in the earth, wrapped in the tightening silver veins that were dragging him fast towards the rim of the mountain. He threw himself flat on the ground and stretched out his hands towards Gwen.

Behind him, the ground opened and the mountain swallowed Gaia, her descent marked with a thunderous boom that bounced across the mountain peaks.

Anderson dropped her gun. Loosening her rappelling wire from her kit, she dodged the widening crevices on the plateau to get to Gwen, who ripped at the tendrils and veins, freeing Isela from the earth's grip. At the edge of the circle, Anderson shot the hook into the trunk of a smouldering Kapok tree, tossing the other end to Gwen, who hooked it onto Isela's belt. Anderson slammed her palm on the switch and the winch dragged an unconscious Isela from the circle of fire into Anderson's arms.

'Gwen, what are you doing?' screamed Jack, most of the lower half of his body mummified in silver threads, the pain and the pleasure indistinguishable.

'What any good mother would do,' she sobbed, her eyes stinging from the sulphur and the burning chemicals in the rock, 'saving the world for my children.'

A fissure shot from the lip of the mountain into the circle, pulling Gwen to the ground, the silver veins quickly mummifying her. She stretched out her hand towards Jack, their fingers touching for a second, for the briefest moment in time.

'You made my world a better place, Jack.'

The earth shook, the circles tightened around Jack and Gwen like fiery lassos, pulling them over the lip and into the vast gaping abyss.

Rhys woke up suddenly, and stared in horror at the television in front of him.

The news channel showed the picture out at sea, of the chimney of rock growing around the fountain of water appearing to spin out of control, rising higher and higher above the jet and then folding in on itself, falling down like a pile of building blocks, falling in on itself and the sea, sending an enormous wave crashing out towards Swansea.

He was about to turn for the stairs, run to Anwen and carry her down to the basement, when a tower of silver threads, like electrical filaments, shot up from the sea, spiralling around the disintegrating chimney and then exploding like a flowery burst of brilliant fireworks, blasting the remnants of the chimney in a million points of light.

The Ice Maiden

73

Off the coast of Miami, two weeks later

'Permission to come aboard, Captain,' said Jack, climbing off a classy speed boat being driven by an expensively dressed sailor.

'Are you sure that's what you want?' asked Hollis, steadying the boat as Jack climbed out and onto the *Ice Maiden*'s platform.

'Permission granted,' said Cash from the deck above.

Jack laughed and embraced Hollis. 'I'm more than sure. Besides I've been missing your po'boy sandwiches.'

'I could go for one of them too,' said Sam, leaning over the portside next to Dana.

'I'm all about sharing,' laughed Jack.

'It's going to be a long noisy voyage, I can tell,' said Cash, grinning and slapping Jack's back. 'Glad to have Torchwood on board.'

Climbing up the ladder to the *Ice Maiden*'s deck, Jack hesitated. He had a sudden memory of the horrible climb out of the smoking volcano where he'd lain, broken and mummified for days, waiting in agony for the Earth, the mountain and his body to heal, believing then that with Gwen's sacrifice his heart never would.

And then he'd rolled over the lip of the basin into the hazy ash-filled sunlight and he'd seen her, sitting on a deckchair next to Vlad and Eva in the cracked and swollen clearing, waiting for him as they had been every day since the mountain had taken him.

When Jack had walked out of the white haze, Vlad nudged Gwen who scrambled out of the deckchair and raced into his arms.

Suddenly, Shelley morphed at Gwen's side, looking in every way identical to her, including a chromosome sequence that Vlad had coded into the avatar mimicking Gwen's genetic code, using the information in Jack's notebook.

'Fuck – me!' said Gwen, who had very little memory of the previous few weeks.

'That program is now fully functional,' said Shelley.

'Luckily,' said Vlad, leaning over and kissing Eva, 'I don't need it.'

Acknowledgements

To bring Captain Jack and *Torchwood* alive in these pages was a distinct privilege if a bit daunting. We may have an inside track on the Captain, but *Torchwood*'s creator, Russell T Davies, remains the Titan in the *Torchwood* universe and ours. We salute you, sir.

Many thanks to the folks behind the publication of *Exodus Code*, especially to Steve Tribe and James Goss, our terrific editors, who are masters of the *Torchwood* universe, and to Albert DePetrillo and Nicholas Payne at BBC Books. Thanks also to Gary Russell and all at BBC Wales for allowing us to tell this tale in the first place.

A team of talented friends and family toil behind the scenes to make it possible for us to collaborate on our many projects. First, we're sending cake and hearty thanks to Gavin Barker of Gavin Barker and Associates Inc., Georgina Capel of Capel and Land Ltd, and Rhys Livesy.

Without Kevin Casey, Carole would spend all day in her pyjamas, eating only chocolate raisins, and getting in fights with her imaginary friends (there are many).

Without Scott Gill, John would not know the wonder of a bacon buttie on a Sunday morning.

And without Marion, John, Clare (welcome to Team

Barrowman, Casey) and Turner, we would think everything we did was funny and worth sharing.

Finally, the histories of the ancient peoples of Peru are rich ones, but the Cuari tribe in this novel have no relationship to the city in Peru and the people living there, then and now. The Cuari living within these pages are purely fictional.

John & Carole